I0654532

SKY ROBERT

A FATED MATES ALIEN ROMANCE

FROM THE UNIVERSE OF TREASURES OF TRILLUME

Broken Books
Kent, WA 98030

First published in the United States of America by Broken Books LLC, 2024
Her Alien Warrior Copyright © 2024 S.M. McCoy writing as Sky Robert
Version Second Edition: ISBN: 978-1-963669-99-2
Cover Design: Taurus Colosseum Cover Design

Fuck the expectations that others have for you.

Pursue what gives you happiness because when you have joy in your soul, it spreads to those around you!

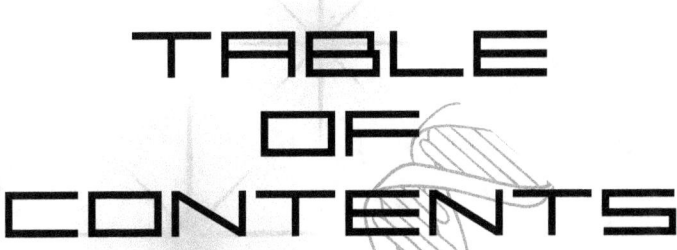

TABLE OF CONTENTS

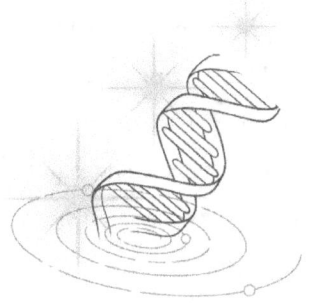

Trillume Universe Glossary

All the books in the Trillume Universe are standalone romances. You can jump right in with any book without reading this glossary, all information about the species and customs are trickled in throughout the book and can be enjoyed without reading section. Every book layers beautifully with each other, start anywhere, from Jewel of the Alien Bandit, Her Alien Prince, or Her Alien Savior, or Her Alien Warrior, but know the more you read the more you'll enjoy the interwoven bits of information that really make this series shine! But if you like to know context before diving in, here you go, or perhaps you want a refresher on things after reading a different book a while ago:

Necia warriors: From the planet Necias Prime, centuries ago the trill from Trillume came to their planet and took control through the tribal laws to conquer their planet through manipulation, it is an unstated understanding that if the necia did not submit to the new rule that many lives would have been lost in a hostile takeover. This species is very open about their sexuality and anything pertaining to what is considered normal biological needs, this includes their species accepting exhibitionist/voyeuristic culture as it is life threatening to not keep their bodies in balance with sharing fluids like blood and sexual release.

There is blood play, primal play, and many honored traditions within the tribe. They have an exoskeleton (epul) under what they call their second skin (the first layer of skin) that protrudes like spikes from their skin, making them a lethal weapon. Their second skin hardens when threatened. Human-like in appearance, though they are larger in stature with their extra bone structure, and two hearts, it's possible this species has had previous contact with Earth as giants from mythology. They have retractable fangs, and their peens have epul nodes (not sharp) that extend and fill, while also being the means that they knot and impart their D.N.A. into their chosen mate. They also have an epul the extends from the base of their shaft like a tuning fork which pushes out as their skin pulls taunt and perfectly reaches a human's clit. Though they are open sexually, once they bond with a mate, they are loyal and dedicated lovers.

Necia/Necias: necia is lowercased similar to human. Necias is capitalized as it references a short phrase for the planet, a proper name.

Necias Prime: the main planet necia are from

Necias Delta Fal: an outlaw planet ruled by King Sylve when he abandoned his home planet.

Cial: the necia language

Epul: the spikes that protrude from the second skin of a necia warrior

Epulknot: what necia call their peen

Epulslip: What necia call female pussy

Ellopul: What necia call come, ello for short

Galactic Trill Authority: a council of diplomats that oversee the rule of the universe, like many overseeing bodies there is corruption as well as decent aliens

Ganpan-fal: world destroyer

Hargom's Cliff: a cliff off the mountains on Necias Prime that spawnlings have used to play a game similar in nature to human chicken to see who withdrawls from the cliffside first and leaves in dishonor or victory.

Human Exchange Trade: H.E.T.

Horv's great vine: Horv a necia warrior that defeated a great thorned creature hidden in the vines deep within the forest against the great mountain.

Lorm: Necias flying beast that preys in the forests

Lorma beast: a bird-like rat beast that lives in the forests of Necias Prime that curls in on itself in death

Pulsunne: a fated mate in necia culture, means heart's song in their tongue

Rak blossoms: sweet blossom from the fresh marshes around the tribe of Necias Prime

Rakture: Ancient battle for mating rights of the necia tribe. Can be referenced to the mating duel itself or dueling a competitor for rights to a mate.

Rakturan: a tradition of honoring a mate that has been mated to another, earning rights to challenge the mate claim of another

Rutting: sex/fucking in necia culture

Rut: a condition with necia warriors where their adrenaline must be balanced by the act of copulation to regulate their body's chemistry.

Sodenmar: a Necias beast known for exposing their genitals to the sun's rays and then throwing their own shit in the sky, only for it to land around them, creating a foul-smelling barrier for them to lounge in? Their name essentially meant shit thrower in the Cias tongue.

Spawnling: name of youth/children of necia warriors.

Torglo beast: from Necias Prime. They were skittish creatures that stayed in a herd to protect themselves, running from threats, and eventually became a popular pet on Necias Prime as they were malleable, and tamed well for companionship.

Unne mark: necia mating mark

Unne: necia's mate

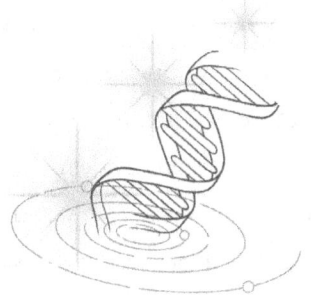

Chapter One
Renee

"I think this is the best fucking decision you've made in the last ten years," my best friend, Holden, said with a smack to my back, jarring my balance.

"You would," I snarked.

But it was my own mom that shook her head at me and dabbed at her eyes like I was about to walk out the airlock of a shuttle before reaching port. "I don't care what you and your husband have said to each other about this. If you do this your marriage is over. Renee, what will the kids think of all this?" She looked over to Holden with disappointment when she said, "I thought you of all people would stop her from going, after what happened with your own relationship."

"Ah, don't be like that Ms. G. It's because of my past that I think she should go for it. It wasn't until after I had a bit of separation that I realized I'd settled and was barely living. If her marriage can't handle this then fuck 'em."

"Language, Holly," my mom chided with a shake of her head, using his nickname that I gave him for always being the one to make me smile and never letting life take that away from him. Always jolly but with an H for Holden. Around Christmas time he used to tell my kids that he met Santa and Holly Jolly Christmas came from him.

They were grown now, capable of handling themselves. My youngest was moving out soon, and that's when it really struck me how alone I was going to be. They were both moving away, and all I had left was my husband, Tyler. I sighed with that same heaviness that set me on this course to the unknown to begin with.

"Renee's situation isn't yours," my mom tutted.

I simply stared at them both bickering back and forth about a decision that was already made. That's why we were here, hanging out at Holden's condo since it was closer to the H.E.T., Human Exchange Trade, offices. It was difficult to get accepted into an exchange program, especially on the planet Trillume, but this was a short-term research study that would give me the clarity I needed to move forward with my life.

Clearing my throat, I got both of their attentions. I took a deep breath to calm the nerves that came with completely uprooting my life as I knew it. I had no excuses anymore. Holden thought I should have done this years ago, and maybe I should have, but my children needed their dad as much as they needed me. It felt like pulling teeth to constantly remind my daughters to give their dad a hug, to spend some time with him, while also reminding him that he needed to make an effort, plan a day with them, don't snap at them for not warming up to him right away. I was the glue that gave them time together, and if I figured my own shit out then it would have been damaging for both of them.

My daughters were grown, they could make their own decisions on how they spend time with their dad or not, and he could make his own decisions on whether he made the effort to be part of their grown-up lives. But, I never kept anything a secret from my husband, including this. I even told my mom long ago about our issues, but stopped telling her that it was still true after realizing that I didn't need my mom's permission to make decisions for my own life. It took having a bit of separation from her when I was younger to finally say, 'no' to her when she tried to plan out my life, though the guilt still ate at me. That's why I was doing this exchange into the cosmos now.

Separating myself from my mother when I married Tyler, was exactly what I needed to gain perspective and take back my life. I was doing the same thing again. Why change what worked? I was running away again for the separation I needed to redis-cover myself, this time I used the exchange to force myself to stay away long enough to know what I wanted.

"Dishonesty is what destroys relationships," I finally said to both of them. "I never lied, but I never did anything about what I was feeling either."

"What are you saying?" my mom's voice trembled.

"I'm saying I need to know that what I'm feeling is all there is, and if this trip confirms things... then I'll make the most of it. But if I find out that I can fuck an alien and feel more than I do with my best friend that I had two beautiful daughters with then I'm the problem. I can't do that to my best friend. I can't live with myself that I took away the chance my husband had at finding a wife that could feel that way for him when I didn't."

"Hey, I'm your best friend," Holden teased, making light of the situation, and that's what I loved about him. Loved... I thought with a pained expression. It was true, I loved Holden just as much as I loved Tyler. That was the problem. Nothing more, and I felt like there should be more.

"But you love him..." my mother insisted, still shaking her head in disbelief. And I did, love Tyler, that's why I had to do this. I loved him more than I love any other stranger or family, not including my daughters that are my world, and yet it was because of my daughters, and because of Holden, that I knew something was wrong with me.

I knew I was broken and would one day have to make this choice to figure my shit out. Being around my daughters, I felt drawn to them. I wanted to be in the same space as them, I wanted to feel them near me. And when I hugged them, I got a high like no other person on Earth. When they made me sad, I felt like my heart was being torn from my ribcage.

I was a coward, even now.

Left with the reality that when my youngest daughter, Laurel, left my home that I would have nothing. An empty, sinking feeling rotted in my gut when I understood that I felt alone with my 'best friend' by my side. The prospect of spending the rest of my days existing with my husband and no one else... haunted me.

"I'm going to the Blue District. I may not end up doing anything, or maybe I fuck an alien and come back home to live out my mundane life. I don't know, but no one looking for a relationship goes to the Blue District, so you can breathe, mom. I'll be back after a month on Trillume."

"You'll be back in an Earth year, it's not really a month, is it? You're leaving your husband for a year. I could die before you come back," my mom whimpered dramatically.

"That's a bit extreme, Ms. G," Holden said while rolling his eyes. "She needs time to figure out her life. Consider it a gap year, and Tyler agreed to it."

"Tyler, that sweet man, would agree to anything she asked for, Holly. That is no way to treat a man that has been by her side, giving her anything she wanted for the past twenty years. She's in her god's damned forties, knocking on fifty, and going to an establishment of sin and debauchery!"

I sighed, feeling my age catch up with me. "I'm no spring chicken, I get it. Men can snag a twenty-something with their salt n' pepper charm at sixty, but women over thirty, God forbid—"

"You aren't over thirty," she snapped, about to remind me that I was forty-six... again.

"Thank you, mother," I strained to keep myself from yelling at her. "I'm aware of my age."

"She's fucking hot," Holden retorted while giving me a nod of encouragement. "She'll have her pick of alien cock wanting a taste of humanity."

My mom's nose wrinkled and I glared at Holden. He knew I didn't want to discuss the details with her. My mom was aware of what was happening, and I didn't need her to have the imagery of me shacking up with an alien in her head. She was still my mother. Saying I was going to fuck one felt less descriptive than talking about alien cock.

"This isn't some breeding kink, is it?" my mom asked carefully. "I've heard rumors about the aliens using humans as brood mares."

"Mom, as you've reminded me already, I'm old and not breed-able."

"Well, you aren't in menopause yet, darling."

I groaned. Conversations with my mother were never easy, and I was glad for Holden being here for this since Tyler had declined to be part of any goodbye plans. He accepted what I was going to do, but I knew as well as my mom did, that if I got on that shuttle, the only way he was taking me back when I got home was if I said I went and failed. If I came back begging for his forgiveness, and admitting I was having some kind of temporary mental break.

Which was a real possibility. And I wasn't certain I'd return to him even if I didn't get the answers I was searching for.

The door of Holden's condo flung open, and footsteps stormed up the stairs before I heard my daughter Laurel huff, "Oh good, you're still here. No one is having a meeting about this without me. Becky, get your ass up here."

My other daughter's footsteps tapped up the stairs slowly and they both took a seat at the dining table, passing by my travel bag that Becky stared at with a sigh before joining.

Laurel plopped down with dramatic flair, like she usually did and smiled at me.

"What are you two doing here?" I asked but added, "Not that I don't enjoy seeing your lovely faces, but you have classes later."

Laurel waved me off. "Every assignment is listed on the syllabus, mom. I've already done all of my assignments in the first two weeks of class."

I looked to Becky, who merely nodded to say she was telling the truth and it all made sense how she could slack off all the time and not worry about studying. She disappeared for weeks in her room and spent that whole time getting ahead. My eyes watered up at how proud I was of her.

"Don't get emotional on me," she warned, but her arms were around me and squeezing before I could say more. "We're here to tell you we support you."

"What exactly are you supporting?" my mom clipped back.

"Mimah," Laurel groaned. "You think we wouldn't find out?"

"You too?" my mom looked to Becky, who was always a little more shy, but much more mature for her age than I ever was at nineteen, blushed and nodded silently.

I didn't tell them why I was going, but I did say I'd be gone for a year. I'd message them whenever I could and I'd be back before they ever had time to miss me, since they'd be busy focusing on their college studies. Laurel would be out of high school soon, and Becky had been accepted into a program for psychology. She swore she didn't want to become a psychiatrist and assured me that there were lots of different types of jobs that required researching why we do what we do. There was apparently some study abroad program she was enrolled in soon. I looked forward to seeing both my daughter's progress and how much they'll have grown in the year I'll be gone. I still couldn't believe I was leaving, and having Laurel's arms around me was making me reconsider leaving Earth at all.

Laurel pulled away and kissed my cheek, hard. "I'll take care of dad while you're gone," she said, and I smiled weakly, unable to voice that her words broke my heart because what I was going to do would destroy what she'd known her whole life. I was ruining our family. For a moment, I worried she actually found out where I was headed to on Trillume.

And then my disillusionment shattered with her next words, "I hope you find a nice alien daddy to fuck, mom!" And she said it with an absolute devious smile on her face as my jaw dropped.

"Language!" my mom stammered, "Laurel Diane Grady, you will take that back this instant!"

"Mimah," Becky prompted quietly wanting to say something.

"Yes, little bean," I interrupted my mom from talking over her, to let her say what she wanted to say.

"Mimah," Becky began again when she had our attention, "We can see that dad and mom don't spend time together, and they haven't for as long as I can remember."

"What are you talking about? They haven't spent a day apart from each other since they dated."

Laurel groaned. "That's what Becky said until I pointed out that being in the same space doesn't mean they are together."

"Where is this all coming from?" I finally asked them both and they looked to each other before answering.

"Mom," she patted my knee like I was a toddler, "You are the most honest person I know. Why can't you be honest with yourself?"

I pressed my lips together, not sure what to say, when my sweet, quiet Becs turned on me too.

"We didn't see it, not right away. Laurel's girlfriend said something that we couldn't get out of our heads."

"And what exactly is that?" I prompted, not sure I wanted to know the answer.

Laurel answered, "She said you had the same look she used to have when she dated her best friend sophomore year. He was everything she should want, but he wasn't me, he wasn't what she needed."

My hand reached out for hers that rested on my knee and squeezed. The tenderness I saw in her eyes, had my daughter already found something special? Someone special? My lip quivered and I couldn't hold back my happiness for her.

"Oh, Laurel Bean, I'm so happy for you," I cooed.

"Mom," Becky said sternly, and I stared at her in shock. She was usually so shy, but there was an assertiveness to her tone, "You're diverting the main topic. This isn't about Jessica and Laurel, this is about you and how this whole trip to Trillume isn't about an adventure. This is about you creating distance so you can find someone who is more than a best friend."

"I love your father," I tried to explain.

"I'm not saying you don't, mom," Becky said quietly, averting her eyes from me.

Laurel jumped in to add, "We're saying go get laid and then find someone that is more than a best friend."

"You have the best kids," Holden sniffled, and then I was covered with limbs from everyone piling in to hug me. I could have died right then of happiness that all of them cared so much, and tomorrow I was getting on a shuttle. Even my mom begrudgingly added her arms around the group of us and patted my head in the only way she would say she supported me too. She certainly wasn't going to voice it with words that she approved of sinfully seeking out alien cock when I was still legally married to a man that met all of her standards. He should have met all of mine too, and this was probably a huge mistake I'd regret for the rest of my life, or the biggest relief I never knew I needed.

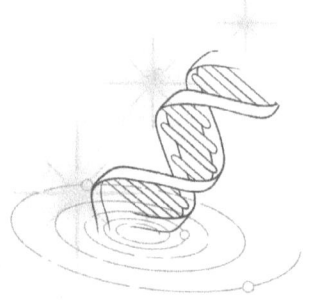

Chapter Two

Renee

B ecky and Holden grabbed my personal items, one suitcase and a backpack that would have to last me a month on Trillume, because I'd be asleep for the rest of the time in stasis, unless I took the opportunity to stay awake for a month on the ship to enjoy the trip before climbing into my pod. It was an option, and I considered giving myself some time to contemplate things before arriving at Trillume for the temporary exchange program. Assignments on Trillume were rare, so the only program I qualified for was exactly the one I needed to be open to for experimenting on human compatibility with the species across the universe.

I didn't have to sleep with any of them, that was the beauty of the program. It wasn't about forcing me to breed like my mom thought, it was about gauging my sexual attraction to various species, including a base line for attraction to humans. I didn't need to be fertile, to birth some alien hybrids, or even actually have sex with any of the offerings. That data had value too. I'd just be another statistic of probability of interspecies compatibility.

Both of my daughters supported me, and even my shy, college-abroad Becs didn't seem upset that I'd be gone for a year. She was always more attached to me than Laurel was, and she never missed mother-daughter date night on Thursdays, even when she could have been hanging out with her friends. I was going to miss them both terribly.

My mother grimaced with her arms folded over her chest in one last attempt to convince me to stay... through guilt. "Renee," she touted with disapproval. "What will you do with yourself when you return? You think your husband will support you after this? You'll be on your own, with what skills, what credit to your name?"

That was the only thing that could give me pause, and she knew it. Like a heat-seeking missile she knew exactly where to strike. What talents did I have? What would I do when I returned? At least some of my concerns were covered and I used that as my armor. "The research program pays its participants, mom. I'll have enough credits to figure something out when I come home."

"What home?" she doubled down with a tremble in her voice. "It certainly won't be the one you left."

This wasn't just about me leaving my husband, I finally realized. This was about me leaving her all those years ago, and again today. "I'm not leaving you. I'm finding my life, my future."

"At fifty!" she said with exasperation. "Is this a mid-life crisis?"

I didn't even have the strength to correct her that I wasn't fifty yet, and even if I were, what did it matter? Did her life end at fifty? It certainly didn't appear so. Finally, Holden came out of the condo with the bags, and broke up the building tension that was going to have me crying before I ever reached the exchange offices.

"Mrs. G," he chided, but kept a playful tone as to not encourage her to dig her heels in and make things worse. "She's been treated at the labs with alien technology to prepare for space travel, and part of being accepted with any exchange program is access to advanced medical technology that will significantly increase her lifespan. She will outlive her own children probably, unless they joined a space program themselves," he added sheepishly and averted his eyes before rushing me towards the car and waving goodbye to my mom.

I wished I could say I had a better send off from my mother, but that was it. Her frown never lifted as we drove off. And her words haunted me, 'what skills, what credit to your name?' She was right, I couldn't answer those questions, not really. I had enough credit from the research study to get on my feet when I returned, but return to do what with myself? And I would have a much longer life to live and pay for now. It was both a blessing and a curse.

The only thing that popped to mind was what I used to do before I had Becky, and then Laurel. I was a scheduler, for people who didn't want to use the A.I. for maintaining their lives. The rich had plenty of credits to get implants without signing up for an exchange program, and with it came easy access to a personal A.I. scheduler, but many people, even people with an average amount of credits, still chose to hire people like me to speak with them and even drive them around to their appointments. That was ages ago, twenty years to be exact, and I wasn't sure being a scheduler really qualified as a talent or skill that made me special.

I didn't know what I wanted to do with myself when this research program was over. It didn't take long for Becky, Holden, and I to reach the shuttle port, and I still wasn't any closer to knowing who I was or could be. A new wave of depression tugged at my insides, weighing me down.

Laurel was busy today, so I didn't get to give her one more hug as I stood within the lobby, waiting for my time to board the shuttle that would take me out to the research vessel. The girls spent the night at Holden's condo with me, doing one last date night with pizza, and root beer floats. We watched a classic that was recently remade with a sci-fi twist. I laughed and cried when the lines were adapted for the fact that we were now part of an intergalactic universe, "I'm just a human standing in front of a trill, asking them to love me."

They did a humorously awful job with the CGI for the trill, because they used a human in a green suit, instead of trusting a trill to be an actor. There was still quite a bit of backlash on giving Earth jobs to aliens even when many of the jobs we had today were with the H.E.T., Human Exchange Trade. Many jobs were already taken by A.I. programs.

I still didn't know if my species was fully ready for joining the universe, but here we were.

Some humans embraced the change and others rebelled. There were always multiple facets to humanity.

Holden wrapped me into a hug, and I was brought back to the present. "You know I'd come with you if I could," he said and squeezed me tighter.

"I know," I rasped. He had applied to join the same program but he wasn't cleared on the health exams to withstand the travel there due to bone density. I was going to miss him, and the ache in my gut was just another reminder that this was what I should have been feeling for my husband, for the nothing but kind-hearted Tyler. I sighed. I didn't deserve him, and this was the only kind thing I could do for him and for me. Leave.

Here I was waiting to leave the planet, and I wasn't worried about not seeing Tyler... The sick feeling in my gut had nothing to do with him, but how guilty I felt that I wasn't sad, or near tears for spending so much time apart. I squeezed Holden, and sniffled, pulling back to take another good look at him. I was going to miss having someone listen to me like he did, but Holden was the kind of guy that people gravitated to. He'd be fine.

Pivoting, I went to hug my daughter when my assigned case worker approached to lead me to the shuttle. Joel was a bit of a crotchety old man, but there was a kindness about him.

"Did you not read through your manual?" Joel quipped as he stared at the backpack and the luggage at my feet. I blinked at him in confusion.

"Two bags—"

He cut me off, "One bag per passenger."

Then my daughter picked up the backpack and smiled at him awkwardly as she said, "This one is mine."

I gaped at her as she averted her eyes from me. All yesterday, I was baffled by how my girls found out what the trip to Trillume was about, and what program I actually was accepted into. They knew because Becky knew...

Becky knew because she, I stopped my train of thought and gripped Holden's shoulder to steady myself. He was pressing his lips together and smiling awkwardly like internally he was saying, 'surprise!' He knew!

She didn't tell me, and I think that hurt more than knowing she was risking space travel so young. Joel nodded and motioned for both of us to follow him.

"I don't know what to say," I prompted for her to help me understand. She said she got into a college program to study psychology abroad. Abroad was a bit of a stretch. This was off planet, into the universe, and a little check box that said you understood the risks that you might never return to Earth.

"I didn't lie," she finally said as we took our seats on the shuttle that would take us to the transport ship. "I'm part of the intern staff for studying human and interspecies' relationships. I'll get college credit for my time on Trillume and be trained by top scientists in studying behaviors. I had to earn this spot with top grades and having my essay chosen amongst the candidates that applied." She took a deep breath and continued, "I lied to Laurel when I denied not seeing the distance between you and dad. I don't talk much, but I see things. You and dad can walk right past each other without saying hello. When you're sick, dad has to be reminded that you might need medicine or water."

"Your father does everything for me," I countered.

"If you ask," she added softly. "When I'm sick, you held me when you could, gave me medicine, made sure I had water and that I drank it, asked if there was a movie I wanted to watch, or if I had any requests before you reminded me sleep was the best healer. You'd check on me and didn't care if you got sick by kissing and hugging me, then you'd bring me ice cream and read a book while I slept on your lap," she paused a pained expression, "Mom, do you have any idea how guilty I felt when I was five and I wasn't big enough to do more than hug you when you weren't feeling good?"

"Oh, little bean, I—" I wanted to wrap her up into my arms but she stopped me with a shake of her head.

"Not because you were sick, but because I knew, when I was five, that dad wasn't going to do it. Laurel wasn't old enough yet, but you were so sick you were puking, and you needed medicine, but it was days before you admitted to yourself that you needed help, and you told dad to get you medicine, and sure, he got it for you... but that was days after you asked. You were sick for over a month. To me, it felt like you were sick for a very long time, but you were the one that drove me to school with a cup in the car, just in case you needed to puke on the way."

I gave her a hug. "Well, you're my everything little bean. I'd do anything for you."

"You deserve to be someone's everything too," she choked on a sob.

"I didn't realize you were already a therapist," I joked, feeling uncomfortable that my daughter was hanging on to all of this and shouldering this hurt on her own. It felt like failure, that I had failed to protect her.

"You're deflecting," she reasoned, and I wasn't that far off. My little girl was grown up. "Don't worry, I won't be assigned to your group or any group that interacts with you, so you can feel out whatever you might find on our adventure without thinking I'm judging you. I'm not, by the way. I hope you find someone that thinks about you without being asked to, but even if it isn't within this program, I think the distance from dad will give you some perspective to move on and find it eventually."

"When did you get so wise?" I teased but then added, "I think you were always more aware than other kids, even at four years old. You were more adult than most adults and said things like, 'I think I'm having sad thoughts, and that's bad.' I'd hug you and say, 'That's okay to have sad thoughts, it isn't bad to be sad or upset, it's being mean to others that's bad, so let yourself feel and think whatever you need to, I'll be here to listen and eventually the feeling will fade and there will be room for happiness again.'"

"So, I guess you're the therapist. Because of you, I wanted to help others make room for happiness again when they are feeling sad," she said with a smile, giving me a big hug. "You're the reason I wanted to help people, like you helped me. You can make room for more too, and I'm glad that I'll still get to have mother-daughter night on another planet together," she paused in consideration and asked, "We are still having our night, right?"

I chuckled, wiping away a tear before it fell. "Of course, we are."

"Good, because I hear Trillume has sectors for different cultures, and I'd be a bit freaked out to check them out on my own."

"You know they don't let any humans wander by themselves; we would have an escort."

"Yeah, I know, but escorts are usually like ghosts, following you like a creepy stalker, and it's unsettling. I'm also an intern that most of the trained anthropologists and psychologists are reluctant to talk to for fear that I'll become a parasite that they can't get rid of and be forced to train themselves."

"Well, that's what they signed up for," I reminded her, my annoyance at the scientists building up into mama-bear mode as we spoke, "Be annoying if you have to, it's a disservice to yourself and to the program for you to stand back and let them ruin your learning experience. Worst thing you can do is not ask questions and miss opportunities while you're there."

"I know, I know," she smiled, covering her beautiful teeth with her hand, "Please don't go around telling them what their jobs are. I can handle it myself."

"I know you can, it's just you don't always speak up..."

"Just because Laurel is a loudmouth doesn't mean I need to be. I pick my battles," she said with confidence, and I nodded.

"You got this," I said while bumping my fist in the air.

Her eyes widened and she coughed. She gathered my hands up in hers and brought them down to my lap. "Don't do that when you meet the aliens, especially the trill."

I stared at her in confusion, and she continued, "I know you didn't go through all the training programs for this assignment, they didn't want bias in the observations, but just be careful with your hand gestures, or even the way you sit. That shouldn't be a problem, but as part of the research team, I went through the training. You'd be sending the wrong signals. I shouldn't even be telling you this, because it might be messing with whatever research they are trying to conduct, but you're my mom and you've gone through enough."

"What does it mean?" I whispered.

"A fist pumped out like that for a trill is like saying fuck you, for humans it's a you-get-em encouragement, but not for the trill. And for the necia warriors that guard us, don't uncross your legs because they might think you want them to service you and they aren't really into humans, but they take signs of needing to be relieved seriously. It's a life-or-death thing for them, and they forget it isn't that way for other species. I'm going to be training under an unGor scientist, and they tap fists with those that are in their tribes. Offering a fist is a sign that they wish to court you or fight you. I'll be keeping my hands to myself," she advised, and I smiled at her with pride at how seriously she was taking her internship.

"I'll try not to offend them, but there is a reason why they didn't put us through training, and I'm sure even the aliens aren't trained about humans to see how we handle the discrepancies of our cultures, right?"

"Right," she agreed with a sigh.

I whispered back to her, "But I'm glad I have the inside scoop on a few tips to avoid having to figure some stuff out." I winked at my daughter and squeezed her hand, infusing it with my love.

The ride to the ship was faster than I anticipated, but it was the process of being transferred and all the protocols of being latched and system checks before boarding that took the longest once we were floating in Earth's orbit. My stomach was doing anxious flips and I wished I could see outside and watch the Earth from above, but there was no observational window in the shuttle. I would have to wait until we were processed on the ship and settled in first.

Several hours passed and the airlocks hissed with the change in pressure from someone finally coming to escort us aboard. The shuttle filled with murmurs of everyone's relief that we'd be starting our journey soon, an electric excitement could be felt down my arms. This was the unknown, and I had no idea what to expect. I had no expectations, really. This wasn't about being attracted to aliens for me. This was space, and time to think about things.

We filed out, large necia warriors flanked and guided us through the ship while a trill explained next steps of leading those who wanted to see the observation deck in groups scheduled throughout the rotation. They wanted us to be aware that time as we knew it on Earth would be in terms of rotations since hours and minutes were subjective constructs based on Earth references.

Once everyone had a chance to view space then groups would be selected for who would go to stasis first and who would like to have the first phase of staying awake, if at all. Conserving resources was a balancing act, and they planned how many humans were accepted into this transport based on a certain amount being in stasis the whole time, while some rotated out with each other, sharing the same pod throughout the trip.

"Which one of you is the hooman Becky Grady?" a gruff deep voice asked, stopping us both in our tracks. I looked up to find a large necia warrior scanning the group of us, and I couldn't take my eyes off him. We had broken off into smaller groups for our tour of the ship, and he was an intimidating presence when compared to the trill escort. He wasn't wearing a shirt, and all of his muscles were on display as well as his spikes protruding from his skin that made him a literal walking weapon.

I hadn't even processed that he had been asking for my daughter as I stared at his muscles, and his white hair tied behind him, a few strands wisped across his face and I found myself captured by his amber colored eyes, like two suns making my skin burn.

Becky squeaked, "Me." And I held her hand reassuringly. The warrior watched the movement and flared his nostrils at us, making my smile faulter. I'd been staring at him like he was dessert, and I had an unquenchable sweet tooth, but by his demeanor, the feeling wasn't mutual.

"Did you bring your mate with you to keep your health optimal for your travels?" he asked my daughter, not sparing me another glance, but she snatched her hand from mine quickly, his eyes following the moment keenly.

"No," she snapped. "I'm happily unmated," she corrected him, but his gaze still flitted from each of our hands with curiosity at why we had been holding on to each other.

I debated if I should tell him I'm her mother, because I didn't know if she'd want people to know that we were related or not, so I remained quiet. Not to mention a small part of me didn't want him to know that I was old enough to have made a fully-grown human. There was a tempting voice in my mind that liked that he had thought I was young enough to be her mate, though directly after thinking those words I cringed, my nose wrinkling at the thought.

The necia warrior turned to me and stared as if I should be saying something, and my daughter elbowed me like he had asked a question. I grunted and just repeated what she said, "I'm unmated."

Becky's shoulders relaxed and I figured that meant I had replied correctly, and she didn't want people to know I was her mother. But it felt odd to say the words, unmated. Almost like a lie. I knew my marriage was over the moment I stepped on the shuttle instead of rushing back home to Tyler for forgiveness, but unmated... It'd been so long since labels mattered in that way. This was a research trial about attraction, so I guessed, for this trip, I was unmated.

He said nothing to me and eyed my daughter again to say, "Should you need anything for your human wellbeing, you may seek out the medbay where our medics have agreed to assist in whatever your needs are."

Becky cleared her throat, clearly uncomfortable. "That won't be necessary," she mumbled, and I felt my cheeks flush with irritation that I had no idea how to protect her but to cut into the conversation.

"She's an intern, and nineteen years old," I proclaimed incredulous at him potentially hitting on my daughter.

"It's okay," Becky squeaked, taking a step back from the large warrior, and instinctively she hid behind me.

I stepped forward to put myself between them and glared at the brutish warrior.

"Neither of those facts are relevant," he replied calmly. "There is no reason to defend her honor, as the medbay is available for every species on this ship. I am already aware of her human cycles and position on this ship, as I am her direct supervisor in charge of training her before we arrive on Trillume."

Becky lifts a brow in confusion and stated, "I thought my trainer was unGor?"

"On planet, you will be assigned to Pryxus of AsunGor. He rarely leaves the research facilities. Many have refused to train you due to the newest reports about humans circulating the base."

"Oh." Becs bowed her head, averting her eyes. Clearly, she knew what he was talking about.

"What reports?" I asked, and Becky puffed out her cheeks like she normally did when she didn't want to get her sister in trouble. I repeated it again but to the necia warrior, knowing Becky was not willing to say anything. His white hair was pulled back and I stared up at his deep amber eyes. Why was I thinking about how handsome his chiseled jaw was? "What reports?" I repeated.

He lifted a brow, a very human thing to do, before he decided it didn't matter if he told me or not. "Human pheromones have been shown to have a higher reaction in many species, triggering their barbaric ancestry, and none of the staff wants to risk interrupting their research because of a human. This, of course, is a precaution on their parts, as any researcher would know none of those claims have been verified, or even tested without bias."

"What about another human?" I asked, thinking perhaps Becky could train under someone else that was a bit less intimidating.

"None of the humans signed up to study with their own kind. If you'll follow me to your quarters," he said turning his back on us. I supposed that was the end of that conversation, I thought as my eyes trailed down his backside.

I turned to Becky and whispered, "He seems like a serious guy. Maybe you'll learn a lot from him since he's answered every question we've asked?"

Becky nodded and gave me a weak smile.

"You told me the necia warriors aren't interested in humans, you should be fine," I tried to be positive but added, "but if you need me to run interference?"

The warrior stopped and turned once more, a grin revealing a sharp canine as he corrected, confirming he heard every word, "I'm not interested in spawnlings, and the only interference here is an intern failed to disclose they were involved with a participant."

Now, I was puffing out my cheeks in annoyance, and struggling to keep my relationship with my daughter hidden.

"I'm sorry, little bean," I then turned to glare at the warrior, alien or not, he was out of line, "She is my spawnling, and you'll do well to answer her questions and do your job without using human pheromones as an excuse to do anything outside of that. Do I make myself perfectly clear?"

"Mom," Becky warned, and then I saw the change in the warrior's eyes, the insufferable smirk faded, and he nodded.

"I'm not sure I should be leaving you alone with him, will you have other colleagues with you?" I asked with my arms crossing over my chest. If I didn't know better, I'd say those amber eyes flicked to the top of my shirt and I turned away slightly like that would change the swell of my breasts. It was ridiculous to think he was peeping at all, and it was just as likely that he was amused at a human thinking they could stand up to an alien with weapons sprouting from their skin. He had sharp bones sticking out of his forearms, as well as his shoulders that could skewer me like a shishkabob.

He took a step forward and it took all my willpower to hold my ground as he got closer. "You've made yourself perfectly clear," he finally said. "I will teach your spawnling as if she were my own." He took a whiff of the air around me and grunted. "You're producing your human mating odor. We will deposit your young in her quarters and I will bathe you as honor dictates for speaking out of turn about your spawn. I can see now the resemblance between you both, though most humans look the same. Follow me."

He turned and walked away. Becky slipped her arm through mine, and she dragged me along behind him.

"We aren't seriously following him?" I muttered to my daughter.

"Mom," she hesitated but pushed through to tell me, "I'll check my messages when I get to my room and—"

"And you will find for the duration of your travel, I am to be your direct report," the warrior with exceptionally great hearing interrupted. "You may call me General Sou-el, General of the research sector, not to be confused with the general of the commanding forces of this ship, General Tensel, future commander of this ship once we arrive on Trillume for his promotion."

I gaped at that silky, long white hair pulled at the back of his head. He didn't even turn to speak to us, as he continued walking down the halls that blended into one another, making me lost.

"General..." Becky squeaked, while tugging on my arm like I should know what that means. "It's an honor to have you agree to teach me."

He did turn then and gave her a curt nod of acceptance. I was about to object to her giving him any honor at all, when she pinched me to shut me up like she did when she was a kid in junior high telling me not to kiss her goodbye in front of her friends.

"Honor is achieved in many ways. My elder taught me this long ago and after the death of the trill queen, I will not allow my sector to repeat the sins of the past towards humans. No matter how vulnerable your species is, I will train any that show a true interest in knowledge that can benefit our galaxy."

"I thought most warriors served in the military and the protection of the treaties," I voiced out loud, finding it fascinating to see a warrior be in any other position besides using their natural physical advantages.

"It is true that every tribe requires us to be vigilant with our studies of mastering our own bodies," he ground out, sounding irritated. I'd definitely offended him with my observation. And without any shirt to cover his carved muscles, he was definitely as in shape as the warriors that served as bodyguards and natural weapons of compliance within the ship. They were protectors, and dangerous predators. The spikes on his shoulders were proof enough of that.

He fisted his hand and pressed a scanner on the wall, that beeped, and flashed blue. That would normally mean clear on Earth, but on this ship, filled with aliens, blue didn't mean approved.

"These are your quarters," he glanced at the way my daughter clung to my arm and added, "It is already programed to allow your personal implant access. Only the Commander, General Tensel, and Head of Security can gain access, but even they must go through necessary protocols to do so." He was explaining that she would be safe in her rooms from everyone, including him, and I appreciated it. So did Becky, because she smiled weakly at him and nodded as she reluctantly released my arm and took a step forward as he stepped back to allow her access. She waved her hand in front of the scanner and it must have connected to her implant because the door opened to a room no bigger than a closet.

I wasn't sure what I was expecting, but as I glanced inside from the hall, the whole room was visible. There was a bed bolted to the wall at eye level and below it was a small desk and a secured chair with a two-seated cushioned couch next to it. The room was barely bigger than the bed inside, and nothing else.

"Food is available in the common area, as well as a sanitation station. Most of your time will be in the observation wing and my offices. Use the call button should you require an escort; the nearest trained staff will come to retrieve you from wherever you are."

I noticed he didn't say that he would escort her, and I was having trouble letting go of my shy baby girl, panic was already building as I thought about how as an intern, she was going to be awake the whole trip to Trillume and I'd be in stasis for at least half the journey, if not more dependent on the stasis pod schedules.

As if General Sou-el could sense my unease he distracted me as he tapped behind my ear. He was so quiet as he approached, I hadn't noticed as I stared at my daughter walking into her room.

"What did you just do?" I asked, startled.

"I uploaded your files, so that I may direct you to your own quarters and verify what division you are assigned to."

"Oh." My face flushed with heat as his fingers touched my neck before he backed away, all business. I glanced around him to my daughter once more as she peeked her head out of her room, her eyes were sparkling with more excitement than I would have anticipated for seeing what kind of room she was to stay in for the next few months of travel. She'd be alright, I assured myself. She was a grown woman and could take care of herself.

"I'll see you on Thursday, right?" she asked with a smile and winked at me. Did she think I'd already be hitting on her supervisor? I doubted that was how the program worked, they wouldn't be setting me up with the researchers themselves, and he had made it perfectly clear he wasn't interested in humans, I thought with a huff. But I knew what Thursdays were, even if days didn't work the same on the ship as on Earth. Thursdays were our day, mother-daughter date night, and I wouldn't miss it for the world. No, the universe, I thought with a bright smile.

"I look forward to it," I told her as I watched her twinkling eyes explore her new room.

"Food is on me," she called out before the door slid closed on her room. I laughed, because the food was provided by the generators in the common area, and her room was just big enough for us to squeeze together on the cushioned couch under her bed for a movie on her tablet. I was thankful that I chose to pack cozy sweatpants and a blanket, despite the tight amount of space in my personal carry-on bag.

My face fell, now thinking about the fact that I had thought I had two bags of space, and wondered if Becky tossed the things I packed in that bag she claimed as hers and put her own things in it, or if she was able to stuff those things into my carry-on. Holden must have known all along, because he was persistent in making sure I stuffed my bigger bag until it appeared near to bursting. I shook the thought from my head, it didn't matter. Anything in the bag didn't matter as much as the fact that I got to have my daughter with me as I traveled the galaxy. It was a gift I never thought I'd get. I was fully ready to embark on this adventure alone.

General Sou-el grunted and I was brought back to the present after staring at the closed door of my daughter's room for who knew how long. He waited there patiently, or impatiently, I wasn't paying much attention until his grunt. With her out of ear shot, I pleaded with him once more, "You don't become a general without being good at what you do. Please take care of her. She has a good heart and told me once that knowing our biology and our minds is like decoding a map of peace between ourselves and others. She won't let you down."

"I'm aware of her file. She has top scores in her studies. It will be my pleasure to add to her studies of humans with that of other species and cultures. Human faces have so many muscles just below a thin dermis that your expressions come with many variations that take on many meanings. I'm still learning myself as I correctly uncovered a connection with your spawnling, but mistook this connection for mating interest as your scent clearly indicated attraction."

I coughed on my own spit as he explained his misunderstanding with such clinical detachment about how he could 'smell' me. A gross shiver tickled down my arms at the thought of attraction to my own daughter. My tongue came out of my mouth in a dry heave, and I patted my own chest as if that would clear the distaste. But the only other explanation for my scent was the alien standing before me, and I had to admit, I was admiring his backside only minutes before.

"She's my daughter," I clarified once more just to make sure he understood that there was no attraction to be misconstrued there. I didn't know if aliens were okay with relationships among family, and I didn't want to know.

He nodded. "Forgive me, I'm not used to females being interested in me for relieving their biological needs, as I have not been fertile in some time. I do not produce adequate enzymes to assist with balancing a healthy warrior's appetite, though I've been informed that humans need relief but not for their homeostasis, but mental wellbeing."

"Excuse me?" I was still processing what he had said. Was he saying that I had somehow told him with my scent that I wanted to fuck him?

"This is why I had no issue with taking a human as an intern. With no overactive adrenaline glands and lack of enzymes, no matter what pheromones you produce, I will still remain logical in my duties," he said matter of fact while I stood face-to-face with the alien's muscled chest. When did he get so close? My heart hammered as I could smell him, and I was beginning to wonder if it was necia warrior pheromones that should have had a warning label and not humans.

I licked my lips, and a low rumble came from General Sou-el that made me clench my thighs together. What was happening to me?

"Logical," I repeated with a rasp.

35

The word seemed to wake us both up and he took a step back and grunted.

"Humans," he groaned.

"You can call me Renee," I snapped back.

"I know your name, it's in your file. As well as your placement with the Blue District."

My cheeks heated with embarrassment.

"How much is in the file you have?" I asked him, wondering if he even had access to know I was married, or how old I was?

"You'll be placed in the communal living quarters, where you will be observed for your interest level in freshly awakened participants from the stasis pods. You'll find your accommodations are much more comfortable than the research staff to promote more favorable conditions for mating practices. Your scent indicates you should do well in the studies and given generous credits upon arrival on Trillume," he replied tightly. It was true, there were tiered incentives based on participation levels of the study, but that wasn't where my mind was at.

I blinked at him, unmoving as he walked away. When he realized I wasn't following him, he stopped and turned to see the thin line of my mouth as I ground down my teeth.

"I was under the impression that any interactions were my choice," I finally said while glaring at him for insinuating I was going to fuck every cock that came knocking. Was that what aliens thought of humans? Simple animals willing to fuck anything for credits? Sure, having extra credits were nice, and some humans were willing to do it just for that, but we weren't animals.

"Of course, all of your needs will be provided for," he grumbled back and my eye twitched at how I still felt like he was saying the same thing he had before. That I was some human slut with overactive pheromones. I stomped past him, even though I had no idea where I was going, and every hallway looked the same. The same as he thought our human faces looked undistinguishable from one another.

"You are upset," he stated the obvious.

"What gave you that idea?" I snarked. And for someone who was supposed to be highly ranked within his field of understanding behavior and researching something like attraction between species, he was pretty clueless when it came to humans.

"You are displaying signs of distress, and though I have read up on human behaviors, I'm concerned that our reports of how human needs are not as vital as my own species, you are displaying concerning levels that have me questioning their validity. Perhaps, I should change the subject for the upcoming study for my sector..." he mused to himself.

"You're unbelievable," I scoffed. I had thought aliens with their advanced technology wouldn't have the same issues our own people had in understanding others. He's already stated that aliens think humans are less than their kind, and that our needs are not as vital. I forgot what I was upset with him about before and now I was simply upset for all humankind.

"Goddess help me," he said under his breath. "I'll bathe you, Human Renee, I had already said I would be honored to do so as a way of amends for my misjudgment. Though I'm unpracticed, I do not wish for your tiny human heart to thunder any louder."

He grabbed my hand to stop me from running off, and I was going to yell at him, but my words caught as I watched his spikes on his arms retract into his skin and the ones on his shoulders seemed to grow larger. Heat rushed up my arm from the wrist he held, and he moved forward until my back was up against the wall.

"I can," I stammered, "I can find the bathroom on my own." I didn't need his help washing my pheromones off, and I wondered if he kept some kind of tranquilizer in his pocket to knock out humans who he thought were hysterical. He was definitely going to take me to the medbay at this rate due to all of our miscommunications. I whimpered as he lifted my wrist and placed it above my head, his body so close I inhaled his scent. Fuck, he smelled so good. What was that smell? I couldn't put a name to it, it didn't smell like anything I recognized.

He groaned as his nose trailed up my arm and then his tongue flicked out to lap up my wrist as his hand slipped through my fingers. What was he doing? I shivered and when I reopened my eyes, he was staring at me with those amber pools. He slowly lowered his head to my face and licked my cheek and my knees grew weak as jelly. He had to use his other arm to keep me up right and his brows furrowed in what I'd call confusion if he were human, and his nostrils flared as he sniffed me.

There was a wonder in his voice as he commented out loud, "I've never had a female react to my enzymes before. Fascinating." His tongue ran along my neck and his teeth grazed my shoulder as he pulled my cotton t-shirt over one side, stretching the fabric to where I knew it would never recover.

I'd been on the ship for less than a day and already I had my answer. A whimper escaped my lips that I hadn't expected as the emotion of this revelation struck me cold. My body reacted to this stranger more profoundly than I had ever reacted to the man that gave me the greatest joys of my life, my daughters. I sniffled, and felt my eyes swell up with guilt and self-hatred for myself, for how my body was reacting to someone I didn't even know.

General Sou-el's body stiffened and he backed away to observe the tears threatening to overwhelm me. He shook his head, and he released my hand to gently wipe at my cheek. My fresh tears on his thumb, he licked the salty betrayal of my feelings, and I didn't know what to say. I was embarrassed and confused. He closed his eyes and then backed away farther but kept his other hand on my hip to make sure I was steady on my feet.

"You wound me, Renee of Earth. I'll take you to medbay." His amber eyes traced down to see how my legs still trembled and he scooped me up into his arms. "I will note this possible reaction in your file and warn other researchers of the possibility with other humans interacting within the Blue District project. No further harm will come to you," he assured.

Oh fuck, I thought, my own emotional hangups are going to mess up the research for the whole program. I knew how important this study was for interspecies equality and future integration with the universe and humanity. I had to swallow my pride and privacy to explain to Sou-el that this was a me thing and not a human thing, but my words were choking up in my throat making more tears come out. I was an emotional wreck made worse by how comfortable being held in his arms was making me lean into it more. My head rested on his shoulder, and I suddenly realized that I wasn't skewered by spikes, the bones that were protruding before were gone as he quickly rushed through the halls to get me to the medbay.

I had to say something.

"Sou-el," I said through a sniffle, and he froze as if I'd shocked him. I buried my face into his neck, so I didn't have to look him in the eye as I confessed, "Please don't put this in my file, or any file for that matter." I was practically begging, and I knew I'd have to explain why, he was a scientist first and wouldn't keep it from any record without a reason that made sense to him. How was I going to explain that he made me feel things that I'd never felt with my husband? That I shouldn't be feeling this way about a stranger, and someone not even consenting to be in the program at that. He was a researcher in charge of a different group than mine, probably a different program entirely, and I thought I would get to know whoever I found attractive first before revealing whether my body felt something for them too.

He stayed still, and didn't say anything, and I was thankful. I took a deep breath and forced myself to continue, even though I was now rubbing my wet tears into his skin.

"This isn't human specific," I mumbled. "I'm sorry. This is me. I don't think I'm ready to do this. I'm so messed up."

"Technically, your observation does not begin until you enter the communal living quarters," he said, allowing the breakdown I just had to not be recorded in my file or ruin the data for other humans participating. I sighed in relief.

"Thank you," I said, wiping my nose on my sleeve. He probably thought humans were gross with all of the fluids I was producing in my hysterics.

I didn't realize I was going to act like that over how much his tongue on my skin made my whole body react. All he did was lick my wrist and my neck and I was a puddle of goo.

After all these years, I didn't think it was possible. I fully anticipated that I'd come here and be confronted with attractive aliens and humans alike, only to feel the same thing I had before... nothing.

My breathing now under control I felt so tired, and as I swayed with the rhythm of General Sou-el's steps, my eyes closed, and I couldn't bring myself to open them again.

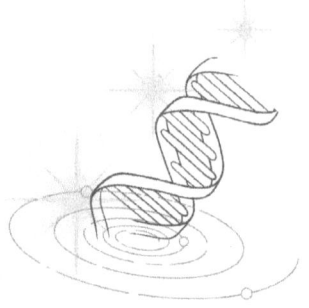

Chapter Three
General Sou-el

My hearts were erratic as I tasted the salt of her skin, an abnormal occurrence with my glands as damaged as they were. The act of retracting my epul was normally a painful endeavor that required a trip to the medbay for an injection of nanobots to help with healing my second skin, but I felt nothing as they receded so I could carry this human female while her legs were uncooperative.

Her reaction to the enzymes in my saliva was remarkable, considering how inefficient my glands were... this was unexpected. I had thought bathing her would go as well as it could given my deficiencies, and as humans didn't need enzymes to orgasm, I thought it would cause no harm in assisting her.

I had been so wrong. As I tasted her neck, I'd felt my fangs lengthen and whatever enzymes were in my saliva had a severe reaction within her that made her shudder with pain. It was always known that I would find another way to honor my tribe, and any female that came to me for a bathing would never be fully satisfied, but, for a moment, as this human moaned from my touch, I thought...

Stupidly, I believed that perhaps there was a hope in the studies of humans for warriors like me. If they didn't need a warrior with active glands to be healthy and cared for that I could have both. I could gain honor in more than my occupation, but with a mate.

Renee, her name was both soft and powerful, a mixture of what it would mean to be both human and necia. When I said it for the first time, my bones ached, and I wanted to say the name many times to feel it on my tongue.

Her body was limp in my arms, and the distress she had faded along with her consciousness. I had no need to bring her to the medbay now that she was no longer in immediate danger, but I had no desire to bring her to her designated living quarters. Soft brown hair fell across her face, and she had long hidden her strange silver eyes from me that seemed to contain all the colors at once. My skin still vibrated from the feel of her tears on my neck as she burrowed herself into my shoulder.

I had to bring her to the communal quarters and avoid her group activities so I could not cause her harm again. It was my weakness and hope that put the whole study at risk. When I scented her arousal and attraction, at first I was jealous and irritated that she had brought her mate with her. The relief was palpable when it was clear the connection was of a spawnling and guardian, and it was shock that stunned me into ignoring protocols to taste and offer myself to bathe her.

Irrational behavior that I didn't think I was capable of. I'd never had any need to take any of the supplements to block my glands from going into a rut. I was sterile, with barely enough gland production to heal minor wounds. My hair had faded to white while still a spawnling myself, a sign of many elders who had obtained true balance of self from being able to master complete control over their gland functions. I had not earned my coloring, and many believed me needing to prove my honor more thoroughly than others.

I did not blame them for their distrust in the honor of white hair being given to a spawnling who was no better than sterile and incapable of contributing to our tribe in every way.

I should have known nothing good could come of being gifted the right to bathe her. It was an honor I was not called to receive. Her tears still tore at my gut, making me sick that I had been the cause of them. But even still the taste of her made me think for a brief time that I was worthy of this gift to be needed by a mate in this way.

As I walked, I found my feet had been taking us back to my own quarters. We were almost there when General Tensel spotted us across the way. He was young, but well suited to lead our tribe with his passion and controlled resolve. His reddish-brown hair was a strong coloring that the elders called the goddess granting him the fire of our tribe's strength and a sign of great achievements to come. Upon seeing me, his shoulder epul lengthened to display this acknowledgement of me, and with my epul already withdrawn, I had no need to show my approval of his rank as he wished to speak with me.

I glanced down at Renee and held her closer to me, unwilling to part with her just yet, but unable to deny that as my superior, I had no choice but to confront General Tensel with her in my arms.

"General Sou-el," he addressed when we met up. I bowed my head as best I could, and his eyes landed on Renee with amusement. "You know how some feel about humans."

"I do." I didn't wish to say more about it, as I didn't know his own stance on the issue and he would become commander soon enough.

"Good for you, Sou-el," he dropped my title, which was either a sign of disrespect or that of a warrior expressing their equality with one another. I would not know which until it was accepted for me to drop his own title, and I would not dare to do so without more data to analyze his actions.

He continued after seeing I wasn't going to divulge more than necessary. Some more youthful warriors might take the pause in conversation to fill the silence with their own voice, but that was not me. General Tensel chuckled and it unnerved me how informal he was being. "I want you to be comfortable around me. We're both generals here, and I don't want to spend the whole trip back listening to people blow dust up my ass because they know I'm being promoted when we get back."

He wished to be friendly as equals it seemed, and he had yet to address the female I held in my arms fully. I was still apprehensive to drop his title or to confess that I had tried to bathe her only for her to collapse after distressing her body.

"I have no intention of giving you dirt of any kind," I finally settle on for a response.

"Good, because I fully intend on using your research to help our tribes integrate with humans more, as there are a few warriors on Necias Prime as we speak that have found not only successful mating with humans, but have claimed the mate markings of a Pulsunne. The implications of humans being that compatible with our species lead me to believe that perhaps a few of our kind have broken galactic laws to hide themselves on Earth many years ago, or humans are a rare universal species. I want you to find out which it is, whether it's only certain humans that might have had contact with our species before, or perhaps they are compatible with all species."

"And how do you suppose I discover this? I am a researcher of behaviors, not a scientist of biology."

General Tensel leaned in, his epul coming uncomfortably close to my human, and a growl rumbled from deep in my chest in warning. I blinked in confusion at my own reaction and he merely smiled at me like I hadn't offended a ranking tribe member with my actions.

"As I was saying before, Sou-el, I'm glad you've found an interest in humans." His eyes pointedly roamed over Renee, and how the shirt she wore was stretched and hanging from her shoulder revealing her tender flesh normally used to mark a mate. When the epul were withdrawn the skin around our necks is more vulnerable than the rest of our body, allowing for our fangs to sink into it with more ease.

But Renee wasn't a necia warrior, she was human. Every part of her body was vulnerable and susceptible to harm.

Did the general not read my file? Did he not know that marking a mate was not a possibility for me? My fangs hardly ever lengthened, and I had no need to drink blood to calm my glands.

"I'd like for you to work with Medic Valmeh should the human show signs of compatibility with you or any other warrior. We have representatives from different planets onboard with us who you should allow to have a chance with any compatible human to confirm our theories for or against universal or previous interspecies contamination."

"General, are you ordering me to disregard cultivating a bond to see if one forms with another before the bond is accepted?"

"You're a warrior of science, the goddess will forgive us for helping confirm our theories that humans with a certain gene marker are meant to mate with necia warriors and no other species."

"Are you telling me the whole pool of humans in this study have already been preselected for a known marker?" I held Renee closer to me and a soft whimper fled her lips, reminding me to be gentle.

"I didn't think it would be so successful that even someone such as yourself would be effected, but I'm pleased to see even if you are not mates that it's clear she has an effect on you. A few humans have been cross-checked after displaying their mate's marks, and our scientists have found a commonality that we used as a basis for accepting applicants regardless of their other qualifications or lack there of. Keep up the good work, and I look forward to seeing your reports as the experiment progresses. Take the human to your quarters if you think there's a chance she begins bonding with you. If not, put her back in the communal quarters to try with another warrior."

"As you request, General," I said, remaining as calm as I could while feeling my blood boil. I would not be placing Renee in the communal living quarters knowing that the observation of her group had different parameters than the others. I was not in charge of her research group, and it was clear that only warriors with active glands would have been assigned to it. It was strange that there were so few from other planets aboard, and now I knew why. I would bet all of my credits that the humans assigned to stay in stasis until we arrived on Trillume were the ones that didn't have the genetic marker they found in the humans who had bonded with warriors.

It was against the goddess to not honor a bond between mates. If one formed, even partially, it was not our place to deny the bond, only the mate should choose to accept or not. I cannot imagine the other warriors would so easily allow a potential mate to begin the bond and then seek the comfort of another without challenging the other to death.

Did the other warriors know this was the plan for this study? I had no place as Renee's mate, and I certainly wasn't capable of forming a bond with anyone, but after seeing her cry from my touch, I didn't think this was the right placement for her.

This was bound to cause her more pain if she bonded with a warrior, only for her mate to be taken from her to see if she could bond with another. I was sure that if she did bond with another, they would snatch that mate from her too, only to start the painful process all over again with another species.

It was unconscionably cruel, and I couldn't bear to see those tears again. She was one human, and I'd be doing right by my intern to keep this one safe, I reasoned with myself. I'd take her to my quarters as the general requested and find a way to get her into the next available stasis pod so she can participate in the study she signed up for in the Blue District.

My quarters were big enough to have a guest due to my title and the type of assignment I have, but they were both my room and my office. Eventually, I will have to explain to someone why I had a human in my quarters if I couldn't get a stasis pod right away.

I activated my comm., to contact medbay. They had access to the stasis pods and could prepare one for my human.

"Medic Velmeh, speaking," the comm. was answered and I paused. They repeated themselves upon only hearing my silence. This was the medic that knew the truth behind the study and I doubted they would allow me to place a human in stasis that was part of their experiment.

"My apologies, I was expecting someone in charge of stasis pods," I said, risking revealing what I needed in hopes that General Tensel hadn't spoken of involving me, and that I would be transferred to another medic. The humans from my group are most likely not involved in their genetic theories.

"I can assist you," they replied, and I debated if I should ask, now that I wasn't being transferred.

"One of the humans is showing signs of distress. It would be best to place them in stasis and then transfer to a health pod upon return to Trillume," I explained. It wasn't a complete fabrication, she had been distraught, and my action would save her from further distress caused by being torn from her future mate many times over.

"Can you describe the human's distress? I have been trained on human health and it is a common thing for them to have periods of adjustment during travel. It can be more stressful on their fragile forms to place them in stasis during this time of flux. Emotions can also trigger physical responses that will pass with time. If their eyes are leaking, this is merely a sign of sadness at leaving their homes," the medic rambled.

"Yes, there was considerable eye leaking," I admitted.

"I will prepare a stasis pod just in case but give the human a few rotations and let me know if it persists, or new symptoms occur. What was the name of the human?"

"Thank you for your assistance. I will inform you if it worsens," I said and ended the transmission without naming Renee. The door to my rooms closed behind me and my human stirred in my arms, but only to press herself deeper into my hold, her head resting on my shoulder. I won't enjoy when I release my epul again, but I would be lying to myself if I said I didn't enjoy the feel of her softness against me. The feeling of knowing a female had allowed herself to sleep in my presence filled me with a pride I never thought I would experience, if only for a short while.

She would leave, and once she woke, she would realize her mistake in allowing me to protect her, a male with inactive glands, and enzymes that caused her pain. I didn't dare lick her skin again, though my gums ached like her taste would ease them.

It was foolish of me to take her tears in my mouth after I knew she didn't like my touch. If I were capable of a rut at all, having her fluids in me, though tears were not as potent as tasting the arousal between her legs, would mean that I sought her out to prove myself and court her as my mate. Why did I do that, knowing it was meaningless to do so?

This could all be explained with a quick scan at the medbay, perhaps when Medic Cenkul was on duty. He was someone I could trust to keep this between us, as what I was experiencing could be a sign of further deterioration of my glands, like the final notes heard upon the ear drums when a warrior's hearing was damaged from battle, it could mean a complete shutdown of my system, and potentially life threatening.

Leaning over to place her on my bed, her arms latched around my neck as she mumbled in her sleep, "I'm not broken..."

Another tear pebbled free from her dark lashes, and she clung so tightly that I could feel both my hearts throb in answer to her. I was the one that was broken, and I hated myself for breaking a fragile human into thinking my faults were her own. Any other warrior would have been able to bathe her with no issue, but she had the misfortune of having me around in her time of need, instead of them.

I laid down with her on my bed and stroked her hair from her face as she settled within my arms. The fit of her against me made me pull her in closer, and I pressed my nose into her soft strands inhaling her scent while I still could. Fucking human pheromones, I thought, she smelled like elder berries and the fresh dew bloom after the morning mists triggered their pollen. It was intoxicating, and, if I were a full necia warrior with working glands, I knew I would rut for her if I could.

But all I had to give was this, and so I held her through the rest of the rotation, wishing that I had been born worthy of claiming such a gift. Her soft breaths against my skin warmed me, and as she relaxed more, I could finally take in the shape of her face. Humans all appeared so similar to me, unable to really tell most of them from one another aside from their varied coloring, but this face... Her face. There was no comparison.

I had trouble looking away from the moment I laid eyes on her, and when I saw her holding someone else's arm, I had acted irrationally unable to see their similarities of being related.

My time with her was limited, and I wanted every second I was granted, but I couldn't risk harming her. She would wake soon, and I'd have to explain how she had to go into stasis. I tried to slip my arm from under her head, and she groaned, before she grumbled, "Tyler?"

Another male's name on her lips? There was no strength left in me to be gentle as I yanked my arm with no caution.

I winced as her head bobbed with the movement and she jerked up right, startled fully awake. She rubbed at her eyes as she snapped, "I get it, you overheat when I try to cuddle. Hell forbid you hug me back first." She grumbled further, "Too much to ask that you suck it up and overheat every once and a while..."

I was unsure what this hell was, but my translator popped up with a rough translation of a land of fire and brimstone. Did she have a mate on Earth that did not wish to hold her while she slept? With how thin her skin was, this seemed like it would be unideal for her comfort, especially with how tightly she held me for my warmth. Did she seek out this Tyler for heat? Was this who she thought of when she latched onto me while she slept?

A low growl rumbled in my chest, and I tried to temper it, but she opened her eyes and her mouth fell open.

She said nothing so I made sure she was aware it was me who had held her by saying without a doubt, "You are not on Earth. You would not let go of me, so I took you to my quarters."

It was perhaps a stretch of the truth, but it did not matter the order of which the events occurred, but that they did occur.

Who was to say that she would have let go if I had taken her to the communal quarters? Perhaps she wouldn't have? And we would have ended up here regardless?

She closed her mouth, and a fresh pink color blotched her neck and down her chest. I furrowed my brow in concern, was this a skin condition that I should seek the medic for? She followed where my eyes were and she slapped a hand to her chest like that could cover it, the action made me certain she didn't feel cause for alarm at the coloring and so neither should I. It was more of a response similar to embarrassment for my eyes gazing upon her. She did not want me to look on her flesh, and I nodded my understanding. I was not this Tyler she sought out, and my touch, nor my gaze were needed.

"Due to your weak constitution, I've asked the medic to arrange for a stasis pod should you not improve within a few rotations. Until then, you are to stay in my quarters."

She folded her arms over her chest, squeezing those soft mounds into plump crescents that remind me of freshly baked rolls from home and my mouth salivated at the sight. How would her flesh taste if I were to continue bathing her with my tongue between those delightful peaks?

I turned from her, not allowing myself to continue those thoughts when my enzymes caused her to tremble and cry. Tasting her was out of the equation. I would not risk harming her.

This was exactly why the goddess had made me with inactive glands, in her wisdom she knew I would do better honoring my tribe with my hard work and dedication towards knowledge. She made sure I would not be distracted with honoring a mate instead of honoring my purpose.

This was as it should be.

My commander would have me mate with any willing female, human or otherwise, but even General Tensel was an oddity among warriors to celebrate a union with a human. His motivations were for science, but many would dishonor me for claiming a human mate without proof that she was my Pulsunne. I used this knowledge to soothe my disappointment, that my growing interest in this human was doomed because of our laws, not because of my failures. It was a small lie, that would have to hold the weight of a lifetime of more disappointments to come. How could I have let myself hope for even a moment? I knew my fate long before this rotation.

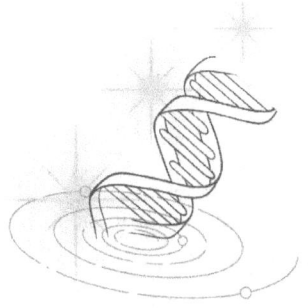

Chapter Four
Renee

Torn between mortification at talking about my husband while in the bed of another or being upset that my emotions were inching me closer towards being kicked out of my exchange contract as defective, I settled for staring at the attractive alien warrior.

His silky white hair was down and reached just past his shoulders, which were still absent of any spikes to impale me. Aside from the rough spots on his skin that appeared like snakeskin and turned more purplish-blue towards where his spikes would normally be, he was like a giant human. Albeit a very well-muscled, handsome silver fox of a giant human, but scaley. I recalled Joel saying something about how the reason they were so cut regardless of if they trained or not was because their second skin could harden like a resin that was stronger than bullet-proof armor.

A deep rumble from the alien I was eye-fucking brought me back to the present to deal with the mess I'd made for myself.

"Let me get this correct, if you place me in stasis, I won't wake until we reach Trillume?"

"Correct."

"No," I said with resolve. I didn't care what I had to do, or who I had to talk to above his authority to make sure I stayed awake to be with my daughter for whatever rotation was equivalent to Thursdays. What was higher ranked than a general?

"No?" he repeated, probably not used to being told no in his whole life with those looks, and his honored position as general.

"No," I said again for good measure, but this time I scooted to sit on the edge of the bed with my feet firmly planted on the ground, only my feet wouldn't reach, as his bed was deceptively bigger than I thought. Of course, it would need to be given how large he was.

I was practically a child swinging my legs in the air. To him and many of these aliens I might have been late in human years, but I was as old as what some considered a spawnling to some species such the necia. This was why I wasn't too concerned about my age when joining this exchange. To them I was still young, and whatever new wrinkles I discovered would just be a strange feature of humanity, like staring at scales on his skin. Normal. I was different but accepted.

"While you were sleeping, I reviewed your contract," he began, and I cut him off with incredulity.

"You did what?"

"I reviewed your contract for remaining out of stasis during your travel to Trillume. It has come to my attention that many humans do not value reading their contracts through before agreeing to them. Staying out of stasis is contingent on being part of a separate study from the one you will be in upon arrival at the Blue District."

"That was explained," I agreed. I'd be staying with other subjects of the study to see if I was attracted to them during my flight. It was considered "flight" to propel through space, right?

"Was it also explained that should you find another subject attractive, that they will remove that species from your grouping after you've rutted with them? You will not see them again."

"I don't understand," I stammered, clutching at my chest where my heart beat vigorously against my rib cage. That created a whole new layer of mental obstacles for me to overcome. I knew going into this that it would just be a one night only kind of situation, but I had really thought it would be my choice to continue to see whoever I chose the whole time before returning to Earth. None of the participants wanted to have a relationship, but it terrified me that I'd get to know someone, and they would just disappear. Could I do that? Did that change how comfortable I would be in being intimate with someone if they would be gone the next rotation?

I should have known that was how the experiment was going to be. It was a study on attraction and if the attraction is confirmed then it was time to move on to the next species to test attraction with them too. This wasn't about connecting with someone, I reminded myself. This was about finding out if I was broken physically, and it was clear by how I responded to General Sou-el that my body could respond even to strangers. I wasn't broken, at least not in that way. I could go the whole experiment without committing to anything more, now that I knew.

Maybe it would be best to go into stasis like he suggested, but there was no guarantee that the same rules wouldn't apply when I got to Trillume. I might as well prepare myself for it and stay awake to spend time with my daughter.

He gave me time to process the information before he continued to explain, "Any connection you make within the study will be taken from you and you've already displayed strong emotional distress within a single rotation. You may stay in my quarters until a stasis pod is ready for you, or I will be forced to bring you to your assigned grouping for you to form bonds that will be cycled out regularly."

"And what would convince you of my stability to continue with my contract?"

I held my breath as he watched me.

"Show me you can be touched without leaking. I can take you to the medbay when you feel you're ready. If you can be bathed without incident, then I will reinstate your contract to remain outside of stasis for the remainder of the travel to Trillume."

My mouth dried as I forced myself to ask, "You want to watch me be licked by someone else?" That's what he had been doing before, licking me like he was going to devour every inch of me clean. I wasn't sure how far a necia warrior bathing ritual went, but I hadn't expected him to actually wash me with his saliva. I really should have asked Becky more questions about the different cultures on the ship.

"I wouldn't dare touch you again," he said fiercely, and I winced. Did I taste that bad? Or he was completely grossed out by my snot and tears. He was actually a decent alien if he never wanted to see someone cry after they touched them again, but that didn't lessen the sting of how adamant he was not to touch me again that way.

"Right..."

"The medbay has a list of on-call warriors who have agreed to honor human bathings, you have your pick of any that catch your interest."

By his tone I could infer he was not among the list, and that was a good thing. I wasn't ready to feel that kind of guilt again. It would have been so much easier if he had touched me, and I felt nothing. If he had licked my wrist and I simply giggled because it was ticklish and ridiculous to slime me with his tongue. That I could have handled. That was normal for me, to feel like I'm giving my body because it was healthy for me to give, and that it was needed by them. Like fulfilling an obligation that helped them stay connected with me.

But that wasn't what I felt as his tongue traced up my tingling flesh, making my whole-body tense and heat. His simple touches as his breath teased my neck and he tasted my skin made my thighs clench imagining him seeking out my swollen labia and swiping between my slit. The image shocked me because I'd never felt my nerves down there seek out pressure and touch, I had nothing to compare that feeling to. It was like every touch of him as he finally pressed his body against mine triggered a need to feel more of him.

And my mind caught up with my body, reminding me that I didn't know him, that he was a stranger, that if I continued, I would not survive rejection. Fuck, I thought with embarrassment, this was what people talked about with women that were stage-five clingers after sex. Like they felt that high, that connection and craved more of it like a drug and it was purely physical. Feeling like this after a simple lick to my neck was a dangerous sign.

I thought with my head, not my clit, and now that I knew my clit wasn't broken but simply uncaring of knowing who was touching it as long as they were a sculpted alien god with saliva that made my skin tingle, I was certain I'd be alone forever or a sex addict.

That wasn't why I signed up for this exchange. I didn't come here to become a lusty sex fiend. I had hoped that I'd have sex, realize it was all the same, and move on. As I stared at the tall general of research, I couldn't help trailing my eyes down his torso and almost landing on where his cock would be, but I quickly diverted my eyes before I got too far. I'd never stared at someone like that before, with nothing but interest in his body and what it could offer me, what I would feel if he touched me again.

It was frustrating and filling me with guilt. I didn't want to make someone else give to me out of obligation like I had done for twenty years. For him this was clinical, his species had a whole list of warriors signed up to assist human needs as they believed it was part of a healthy maintenance of our bodies like it was for theirs. I didn't need sex and I grew exhausted of providing it without getting that same feeling of satisfaction others seemed to have.

I had wanted that feeling, this feeling, the need, and yet now that I felt it, I resented it because I didn't want to be my husband. Taking that high without giving it at the same time. I didn't want to feel this way about someone who felt nothing for me.

I was used to giving, so I nodded and told myself that having my arms and neck licked to prove I was alright would be easier than the routine I'd settled into over the years. "Sure, I'll look at the list." I hopped off his bed, and it lifted up into the wall, giving the room more space. The room had a couch, and a large screen with labeled tiles in a different language. He saw how I was taking in how big his space was compared to my daughters, and he told me it was also his office.

The door opened and my daughter walked in with a stunned look on her face when she spotted me here. I brushed at my bedhead of hair, and smiled awkwardly, but she obviously got the wrong idea because she smiled with a glint in her eye. I shook my head and tried to let her know it wasn't like that without saying the words, but she just smiled bigger and gave me a thumbs up.

I was probably growing red and rashy with embarrassment again. My skin always got blotchy when I was nervous.

"Did you want me to come back another time, General?" Becky asked, and I could tell there was a bit of a teasing tone to it that I didn't miss, but wished I had.

"No need," he dismissed, obviously unaffected by whether I was here or not, and it made me feel even more foolish for having my clit think with my eyeballs and not my brain. "Your guardian will be using my offices until she is cleared to rejoin her study group, or a stasis pod becomes available. We will begin your studies with observation of the communal spaces from here." He waved his hand to the large screen that took up the entire wall, and one of the tiles expanded and showed a room with food dispensers, lounge chairs, and even a workout area where a few large warriors sparred with one another.

"What do you notice?" he asked my daughter, and she stepped forward to observe the room.

She pinched her lower lip with her forefinger and thumb before I saw that her eyes widened with an idea, but she hesitated to say what she thought. You can do it little bean, I thought, rooting for her as I watched.

He prompted her, which eased my worry that she would start off too shy to let him know that she knew the answer, "No question is dumb, no observation is without merit, and you can't focus your efforts without first starting somewhere. What do you see?" His eyes left the screen and instead of watching my daughter and awaiting her answer, those amber orbs stared at me. I knew exactly what I saw there, he was a competent, smart, capable man and I was just a human barely good enough to be researched.

"Uh," Becky cleared her throat, "they are barely interacting with each other, and we want to test their attraction, which can't be done if they keep to themselves."

"Correct, and how do you suppose we can promote their interaction without influencing who they bond with?" He still didn't return his gaze to the screens, and I fidgeted in my seat wondering what he was thinking.

"You can't," she said with disappointment.

"Also true," he motioned for us to pay attention to the screens once more, "but there is still something to be learned from placing them in situations that promote an opportunity to bond. Let us observe as the first influence is added to our subjects." He strolled over to his desk and tapped out some commands on its surface, then sat back as another screen split the wall, to a side room and a human was brought into the room with an alien sitting in the center, strapped to the chair.

I gasped, wondering if the warrior was okay.

General Sou-el assured us both that he willingly participated in this experiment.

The human male groaned but proceeded to approach the necia warrior in the room on the screen that took up the whole wall, making the room feel like we shared it with them. General Sou-el spoke and his voice echoed in the room asking the human to touch one of the warrior's epul while he was immobilized. I could now understand why they had the warrior restrained, because I doubted a human would touch one of those spikes otherwise. They were walking weapons, but though General Sou-el had large epul from his own shoulders, they hadn't harmed me when his tongue was on my neck. I shivered at the memory.

The human being observed touched the base of the epul, where he thought he wouldn't be injured, and the necia warrior shuddered, his nostrils flared, and the human backed up.

"Excellent," the general praised and then asked him to lift his wrist up to the warrior's mouth, but out of reach. He did so and the warrior strapped down, licked his lips and parted them to reveal fangs. Sou-el praised the human male again and then another human came in and did the same steps with the same necia warrior.

While the experiment progressed, General Sou-el would glance back at me and watch as if I too were being observed for some purpose and then he said, "For every study, it is to gain an understanding. With the current stimulus, what kinds of information or understanding could be inferred? We've asked our participants to touch briefly, and have a warrior smell them, then leave. Think on it, and I'll ask again when we've finished with Mouvdeh, the warrior participating currently."

He was so thoughtful, and I smiled at how he was going to be a great teacher and mentor for my daughter. I thought about his question as well, and how the warrior reacted to that first human's scent and touch. His fangs extended, and it was like he wanted to eat them. My imagination went back to how Sou-el touched me, and his fangs dragged across my neck as he licked me. I clenched the chair I sat in, and my heart rate spiked. I could feel my blood pumping and making my ears pulse, possibly causing a rash of nerves like before.

Though General Sou-el's eyes were on the screen and directing my daughter on things to observe about the interaction, his nostrils flared as I watched him. I crossed my legs, and licked my dry lips, hoping I was imagining things. But another part of me hoped I wasn't. Was I crushing on my daughter's mentor?

The whole morning, they repeated the experiment with the same warrior and different humans, until my stomach was growling, and both my daughter and the general turned to see I was still there, and very much hungry. I had sat on the couch watching in fascination at what I could expect when I rejoined my group. Much of the time, I simply stared at the way Sou-el moved, his attention to details, and the way he patiently explained things.

Some humans refused to follow the instructions and Sou-el did not force them to comply. He simply gave them the same praise for being honest about their instincts and asked them to return to the communal room to continue enjoying themselves.

The more I watched, the more my fear faded, and I wouldn't be forced to do anything that I didn't want to do. I could rejoin my group if the researcher in charge handled things the same way Sou-el did. I stared between my daughter and Sou-el just as much as I watched the screen.

He rolled his shoulders multiple times like he was uncomfortable, and I wondered if that had to do with his secondary bone structure that the epul spikes came from. They were still hidden beneath his skin, those large shoulder ones were probably hidden within his back muscles, and he'd rubbed at his scales, multiple times during the experiment.

"We will resume the observation with the next warrior after we allow them free time to explore the ship or consume energy from the food dispensers," General Sou-el said while stepping away from his desk and the screen showed the restraints on the warrior in the room release him.

"General," the warrior spoke out into the room knowing he could be heard, and the General stopped to listen.

"Yes, Mouvdeh?"

"Who was that first human?"

"I've secured our comm," Sou-el said first and then added, "Do not complete your bond until you reach Trillume if you wish to see that human again. May the goddess bless your bond."

"A name?" the warrior repeated.

"William," Sou-el informed, and then cut the line, the screen going back to a tile on the wall as it was this morning.

"General?" my daughter questioned what just happened, and I was curious as well.

"I will not disgrace the goddess by keeping mates apart from each other. A warrior knows when they have met their mate. What I'm looking for is finding bonds that are not more than physical. This experiment is about attraction, but a mate is more than attraction for a necia warrior. I will allow him the chance to prove himself to his mate. Many do not find that bond, and what they feel is merely physical. For those, I will continue with the study, but what did you see when he interacted with the other humans versus the first?"

Becky hesitated but then sighed in resignation. "After the first one he had no visible reaction."

"Exactly, for a necia warrior this is a rare thing for a healthy male. We have no expectations of bonding with anyone, we mate for honor with any warrior that needs to balance their body. We fight to prove we are worthy of our genes being passed on, and if a warrior accepts our offering, we bond with them through rituals. They become our mate, and we dedicate our lives towards their happiness, but it is not the same as what that warrior experienced just now. They will have no reaction to another mate opportunity now that they have found their true bond. It is up to them to prove themselves to their mate and keep them, but he will not seek another even if he fails. This is the difference between a fated bond, and the study of attraction. We can be attracted to many different warriors, and beings, but to not respond to any of them except one...

"We were lucky, or some would say fated to choose his mate first, because if we had chosen him last or in the middle of the experiment, we could not be as certain about the chances of them being fated. As he would have responded to other attractive participants before his mate touched him. At least, many of my tribe would believe this an absolute. There have not been many studies on these types of mates, not since the decline in spawnlings across many planets, including Necias Prime."

"So, you're saying that they will only react to them physical-ly now that he's met them?" I asked, and the general nodded.

"This is what our elders have told us, but that is not based on any valid studies on the subject. There haven't been enough claims to this kind of sacred mating to conduct a study."

"That's actually very romantic," Becky said with a beaming smile. "I wish humans had that kind of instinct."

"Who's to say that you don't?" he questioned and told us he would guide us to the food dispensers shortly. "With the recent reports of fated matings increasing among humans, I have plans to conduct a study on this once I'm promoted to Commander of Research." And if the bond was as rare as he said then it's possible even humans have it, but we don't acknowledge it the same way the necia warriors did if that was the case, right?

He sat down at his desk, and Becky came over to me with a smile. "Fascinating, isn't it?"

I nodded, but my eyes were on Sou-el and the way he rolled his shoulder again. Something was wrong and I had the urge to go ask him if he was okay. "Just a second, I'd like to speak with Sou-el before we leave."

"Sure," she said, but she was already distracted with what-ever she was reading on her tablet. We hadn't opted for eye im-plants, or lenses, preferring the more tactile feel of using our fingers on a tablet. I glanced back at her before I approached the general, and her eyes were glued to the screen.

I cleared my throat to get his attention, but when I turned back to him, he was already watching me curiously. "I, uh," I stammered with what I was going to say. "Your shoulders... Are you okay?"

He grunted with amusement. "I'm not as young as I used to be," he dismissed.

I lifted my hands but stopped. This was probably a horrible idea, given that he could stab me with his epul, but I offered anyways, "May I?"

Lifting a curious brow, he wasn't sure what he was agreeing to, but he nodded anyways. I touched a finger to his shoulder first, just so he knew I was going to touch him, and make sure he wasn't going to startle and stab me with spikes. He sensed my tension and chuckled, "Contrary to popular belief of other species," he mused playfully, "our epul are actually a voluntary response, and only warriors who have trained significantly can summon them on instinct."

"Right," I chuckled nervously, and placed my palms around his shoulders and rubbed around where he seemed to be sore. "Does it hurt?"

He sighed and sunk into my touch. "Perhaps your fingers were just what I needed after a rotation of craning my neck."

I smiled, knowing he was just saying that to ease my worry. "You shouldn't ignore your pain." I'd never seen any of the other warriors flinch at being cut or harmed. They healed so fast, and if he was in pain, perhaps something needed to be checked out by a professional? There were advertisements to assure humans that they were safe while traveling with the H.E.T. program, and in all of them necia warriors got injured and they merely smiled as their wounds healed like magic. The protectors of the universe, they were purported to be.

My daughter's stomach grumbled next, and she quickly glanced back down at her tablet like she hadn't been watching us.

"Shall we?" I asked and squeezed his shoulder one last time.

The general spoke very little as we walked the halls towards the dispensary. His amber eyes watched me, and even when we sat with our food, he said nothing. He pierced his food gel with his fangs and sucked down the solid space goo from his reusable sleeve that he quickly tossed into the recycling incinerator. He was clearly used to eating quickly and leaving, but he did not move to leave us to our own plates that were a lot more appealing to stomach than black gelatin. Our food was shaped and colored to be appetizing to humans, even the texture was similar to eating food on Earth, but some of it had a grit to it that was difficult to get used to, and the flavors were as bland as dry chicken. I made a face, and my daughter moved her food around her plate after a while, unable to finish.

I could see the appeal to swallowing down a nutrition pack quickly and moving on.

"The food dispensers start all humans on basic meals that include additives to help acclimate your digestive systems to other options. Force yourself to eat the remainder of your plate if you wish to be cleared for something more palatable later," Sou-el explained.

So that was what that grit was? I gulped and hesitantly lifted another spoonful and forced it into my mouth. He nodded his approval and then looked to Becky expectantly.

"Is there something tasty to wash it down with? Like a chaser?"

"Becky," I intoned my surprise that she knew anything about a chaser.

"I'm old enough to be sent to another planet, I'm old enough to have a drink, mom."

Right, I tried to calm myself. Anyone who qualified for the exchange was considered an adult in every aspect, including legally being allowed to drink alcohol. Which meant she was granted access since she was accepted into the program. "How long?" I asked with a wince, trying to remain neutral.

"Once," she said, "to celebrate and experience it before I left so I had something to compare it to."

"It is wise to have a control set for comparing experiences," General Sou-el approved, and I glared at him. He paid no mind to my irritation but spoke as a true researcher of knowledge. "You have the makings of an honorable seeker of truth, but you must temper bravery of experience with learning how to understand the same information without being a participant yourself."

"Right, what he said," I quickly added, "Learning from other's experiences. No need to do everything yourself, right?"

Becky rolled her eyes and reassured me, "It was once, and I won't make a habit of it." She picked at her food, pushing it around.

"I'm uncertain of what a chaser is on Earth, but there is a spray in the medbay that can numb your tastebuds to make the meals easier," he offered, and I was thankful for the change in subject.

"General Sou-el, this is the first time I've seen you stay in the dispensary for longer than it takes to grab a pack and go," the woman warrior teased, standing behind us.

"Commander," he bowed his head to her.

I took notice of the tall woman, and her brown hair had streaks of silvery white to it, but her eyes were golden like the rest of the necia warriors. She wore a plated armor over her neck and shoulders, but spikes protruded from her shoulder blades around the armor in a curve that could stab a person if they tried to hug her. The only cover she had was a strap of leather dangling from the shoulder armor on either side that barely managed to hide her nipples. She wore a flap of leather for a skirt with a metal inlay and carved tribal design. If Sou-el hadn't addressed her as the commander, I wouldn't have guessed based on how little was left to the imagination.

"Don't be like that, brother. I came as soon as word got back to me of this rare opportunity to catch you when you do not have your duties to distract you," she said and then eyed both my daughter and me with amusement.

"I'm still attending to my duties of guiding my intern on her first rotation, Commander Rovka. This is Research Intern Becky of Earth, and her guardian Renee of Earth."

"Of course you are, General. I'm pleased to see that you are assisting the integration of humans on the ship, but as this space is considered leisure time, you are not to discuss business, and allow your intern to have her freedom without being intimidated by her superior."

"Are you intimidated by my presence?" Sou-el asked Becky and she smiled awkwardly, shaking her head.

"Brother, for someone who observes behaviors for a calling, you are clearly incapable of seeing things in your own purview. She wouldn't tell you if she were uncomfortable, you are her superior. I'm ordering you to allow her the day to explore the ship and resume her duties next rotation." The commander turned to my daughter and smiled at her. "You are dismissed. Meet your fellow workers, check out the observation deck, or go to the lounge."

Becky pushed from her seat and picked up her tray of half-eaten bland starter gruel. I grabbed my own tray to leave with her when the commander eyed me and used a single finger in a sit motion that had me placing my butt back down with haste. She smiled to indicate I had interpreted her unspoken request correctly.

We left on a Tuesday on Earth, so today was a Wednesday rotation if I just kept track based on when I slept and woke up. Tomorrow would be Thursday for our mother-daughter date. "I'll see you tomorrow," I asked hopefully, and my daughter nodded, glancing back and forth between the commander and me. She was obviously struggling with leaving me alone, and I put my best mask of confidence on before initiating a conversation back to the commander to show my daughter I'd be fine. "I wasn't given a lot of information before joining the exchange, but is brother a spawnling relation like on Earth or a title of respect within your tribe?"

"See," she nodded between Sou-el and myself, "even Renee of Earth can have a conversation not related to work, I'm sure you can do the same with some effort," she nudged Sou-el and then addressed my question, "Brother can be used for both contexts within the tribe, a shared guardian or close bond within the tribe. This one was raised by my guardian, Elder Edilm, after his guardian was challenged for endangering a spawnling."

"What do you mean endangering a spawnling?" I questioned with concern.

General Sou-el stared straight ahead as he monotoned something he'd probably told people many times because of the commander, his sister, "My guardians were sacrificing me to the goddess before my epul could form."

"You don't have to tell me if you—" I tried to give him a way out of revealing his personal business to a stranger, but the commander interrupted.

"They did not go through the proper rituals to end a spawnling's life," she said and took the seat my daughter had vacated, and I wondered why she was telling me any of this. "Elder Edilm found him tied to the rocks just before the tide came in to swallow him up, but he had almost chewed his way out of the bonds himself. He is a survivor."

Sou-el rubbed at his shoulder and averted his eyes, not daring to look at me while his past was divulged.

"Get to the point, Commander," he said standing up from the table, but she gave him the same look she gave me, and he reseated himself.

"As I was saying," she eyed him with authority, "he survived, and his guardians were challenged. Instead of dueling, they agreed that they would be banished from Necias Prime until the death of their spawnling proves them right. He successfully completed his warrior trials, and if his guardians are ever seen by the tribe they will be forced to duel for their life. I would happily end them for claiming pride in what they tried to destroy.

"He is a strong, capable warrior in mind and body—" she stopped abruptly as she noticed where his hand was about to knead into his shoulder again and her smile faded. "General, is there a reason why you've withdrawn your epul? They are large and impressive to any warrior with eyes and a mind of your accomplishments." She unlatched a canister from the belt of her skirt and sprayed something over his shoulders. He nodded at her and his epul pushed out slowly until they stood proudly and lethally like many of the warriors on the ship, but they were quite large and intimidating. The commander nodded at me towards his epul as if to say, aren't they attractive?

Everything about General Sou-el was attractive, but I wasn't about to admit that when he said in no uncertain terms that he would never touch me again.

I smiled awkwardly, and knew that nothing I could say would help him with whatever trauma he had as he was growing up because of his parent's mistakes that almost cost him his life. It made sense why he decided to be a behavioral analyst if he wanted to understand why his parents did what they did.

I settled on saying, "I'm glad you fought to find your true family. Commander Rokva seems to hold a great deal of respect for you."

"I do," she praised, "He's on the road to being a commander of his own research team, a prominent position among the tribe. Worthy of respect and mating." Her statement was an obvious attempt at endearing myself towards her brother, and I cringed a bit knowing she was trying to play matchmaker with the wrong girl. He had no interest in me.

General Sou-el closed his eyes and his nostrils flared in what appeared to be an exasperated annoyance that he kept locked down as his sister was also his commander. That must have been a tough balance to work through being so close with a sibling that was also a superior at work. I wondered why he chose to work on the same ship as her?

"If we are done discussing personal matters, we are both ranking officials on this ship and should allow Renee of Earth to her own free time to explore the ship and finish her nutrition," he clipped, and even with the glare he received from his commander, he pushed off from his seat and bowed before walking away.

Commander Rokva glared after him and then turned to me with a smile. "Humans value passion in their choices, do they not? He will not say so, as he is a warrior of honorable discretion, but he only avoids females that wish to have spawnlings as he can not have any. As you have already had a spawn, you will not be needing more, and he would make an excellent mate."

"Oh, I'm not—"

"No need to lie to me, I was gifted by the goddess with heightened smell, better than our greatest trackers. Many with my skill become matchmakers, not commanders, but for my brother I will be both. This ring," she pointed to the bone bar pierced through the bridge of her nose, "has holes drilled through it that if I turn it, I smell more, and turn it again and I block most of the scents. Created by the first matchmakers of our tribe," she explained, "I smell the faintest of changes in odors when I am this close to a match, and when you look at my brother, you like what you see. You are a good match, and if you wish to see that he can be both attentive and honorable, then consider following our mating traditions and offer him a token of your interest.

"Many of our tribe start with bathing rituals to confirm there is a compatibility of enzymes to balance our gland production, but as that isn't an issue for my brother and you, a simple offering of your own fluids should suffice."

I choked out, "Excuse me?"

"Something he can keep with him that smells of you, so he may lock in on your scent and build up a bond with it even in your absence. He will seek you out on instinct no matter where you are on the ship if he accepts the offering."

"That is a very, uh, generous offer. I'm sure General Sou-el will make someone a wonderful mate one day, but I'm part of the Blue District studies."

Commander Rokva's eyes narrowed, but it was more a look of concentration than annoyance, I thought. At least until she slammed her fist on the table and growled. "Our laws over rule that of your Earth contracts, this ship is under Necias Law, even your contracts include a clause about prevailing laws of the territory you are stationed. This ship, my ship, our laws. If you want to be with my brother, I will terminate your contract and you will be part of our tribe, protected by our law."

She stood and placed her fist to her chest with a thump and said, "It is settled, Renee of Earth. Show me an unne mark before we arrive on Trillume and your contract is void. My brother is an honorable and wealthy warrior, you will want for nothing.

A drop of your blood in a bead for his hair is an ancient art of Rakne to prepare a warrior for a battle of Rakture in tribal mating rights. You can get a specimen bead from his office, or any of the research facilities on the ship. I'll catch up with you after confirming all programs are running smoothly aboard the ship."

Commander Rokva rushed through the aisle between tables and she was fast. There was one person who got up from their seat and the commander seamlessly pivoted around them before the person even noticed they almost collided. The wind from her movement fluttered the fabric and hair of the man, and he blinked in confusion before looking at the back of the commander just as she disappeared out the door. I had no idea how fast a necia warrior was until then.

I sat there stunned for a while, mindlessly swallowing the rest of my not-chicken grainy food substance. Eventually, I was spooning up air, and left the spoon in my mouth, its handle hanging from my lip.

What just happened?

Did the commander of this ship just set me up with her brother, who very clearly said he'd never touch me again, and asked me to gift him with a vial of my blood?

Well, I certainly wasn't going to be doing any of that, but I smiled anyways.

General Sou-el was lucky to have a sister who cared so much, but I doubted any mate prospect would override the trauma he must have had from surviving parents that tried to kill him. My smile flattened. Now that I knew that about him, I was the last person his sister should be setting him up with. I was married to a human, and this was only temporary for me. He deserved someone that wouldn't abandon him, that knew what they wanted.

I was too much of a mess.

Chapter Five
General Sou-el

"I don't need, nor want, your matchmaking," I said through gritted teeth. Without prying eyes, I could finally speak freely with my sister, instead of who she was among the tribe, my commander.

"I have a nose for these things," she insisted.

"Your nose is wrong!" I lost my temper, my breath heaving as I whirled on her, even my epul jutted from my arms and fingers as if I would fight her for shoving a hopeless dream in my tired hearts. This was cruel to keep pushing a mate on someone like me, who would never have the honor.

Her own epul lengthened, ready to defend herself should it come to how we dealt with fights as spawnlings. Her eyes alight with mischief, but then they sobered to pity that I couldn't stand to look at for a second longer.

"What are you not telling me?" she asked, taking a step back to give me space. She did not become commander for being reckless, she was fiery, but fair, and wise.

I was no match for her in a fight, she would win, but she didn't want to send me to the medbay over this.

Rokva had already saved my honor today by spraying my shoulders with a numbing agent so I could extend my epul without pain. Keeping my shoulder epul inside was uncomfortable, and eventually I would have had to go to medbay to release them again. She carries that spray with her everywhere, so she can help me cover my weakness, but it wasn't much of a secret among our tribe.

"My enzymes harm her," I groaned out with frustration.

"They what? That's ridiculous, you hardly have any enzymes to grow a thorn on great Horve's Vine."

It was an expression, no amount of enzymes could grow a thorn on a vine, but it was to say I was harmless and incapable of having any sort of effect on anyone in that manner. I couldn't regulate another female's glands better than they could do of their own efforts. The enzymes in a warrior's fluids are meant to help balance the adrenaline in their mates. I don't have enough enzymes to help a necia warrior, but I had enough to harm a human. As my commander, she should know that this was a possible reaction with humans, so I gathered my resolve to tell her.

"I attempted to bathe her, and she trembled and leaked from her eyes before she collapsed in my arms. Mating her is not an option."

"Horve's Vine..." Rokva sighed. Pacing the security room that she'd emptied in her haste to drag me here after we left the dispensary. "You are more hopeless than I thought," she finally huffed. "You are blind when it comes anything outside the office of your research. Perhaps your brain turns off when you leave?"

"Enough, Rokva. I've long since accepted your matchmaking attempts are wasted on me."

"The reports from Necias Prime have stated humans are more sensitive, possibly due to their thin skin and how their blood is easily accessible, or even their singular heart. Sou-el, have you not thought perhaps this is caused because you have not courted her properly? Our traditions are not to be dismissed. Rumors have said one of the humans is mated to our future king, making our future queen a human. Do you not understand what great news that is for you? A human queen means great honor in having a human mate! Times are changing."

She wore our tribal dress, ignoring the uniforms befitting a commander of a ship. The trill aboard the ship avoided her with their conservative robes but did not dare to question our traditions and laws. Our bodies were natural weapons, and most clothing got in the way or ended up destroyed by our epul.

"And what would you have me do?" I said with exhaustion. It would please me greatly to have a chance with Renee of Earth, but I would not risk her health for my happiness.

"Carry a token of her with you, acclimate your body with her scent, her offered fluid. It has been done for many generations before ever bathing with an intended mate. In fact, brother, it is only recent generations that have skipped this step because warriors have become distracted and wait until the last possible second to regulate themselves.

"Now, they take their supplements to avoid rut. They ignore their needs until even the supplement can't rid their adrenaline and they are forced to be restrained or bathe with whoever is around," she was on one of her rants, and by the sounds of it she would go on for a while yet if I didn't divert her attention, "You know, warriors used to take care in selecting their bathing partners, giving a token of interest before they touch them. They are all thirsty sodenmars exposing themselves to whoever accepts, it's a shit throwing mess out there, and you're one of the only decent males out there and not even you are willing to make an effort."

The image of a sodenmar resting in the sun with their legs lulled open exposing their genitals was not appealing, the animals were odd looking creatures that threw their own feces around at other males, hoping to ruin their competition's chances with a female during their own rut. Being compared to one in the context of mating was an insult. They baked in the sun's heat surrounded by food, and shit, with their cocks erect during mating season for any female that passed to jump on them for a deposit and then leave. For a lucky sodenmar, they were visited by many females as their seed plumes. They did not take mates as we do.

"I'm not unwilling, Rokva. She is asking for the list of warriors agreeable to bathing and wishes to rejoin her Blue District study."

Her mouth closed from what she was about to say, and a familiar glint appeared in her eyes that could lead to no good. It wasn't until she was promoted to commander that she cut back on her mischief, but when it came to me, she held no boundaries.

"If that's what it will take, brother, I will make it happen."

"Make what happen?" I tried to sound disinterested because if I outraged too much it would only cause her stubbornness to harden.

"You'll see." And then she called the security team back in. "Olben," the head of security glared at my sister, but she smiled at him regardless, "add General Sou-el to the list of bathing candidates for medbay, then send the list to the human Renee of Earth's implant. Remove him from the list directly after."

"If this is one of your matchmaking stunts, this is a gross violation of my clearances," Olben said with an eye twitch.

"Of course not. General Sou-el, do you wish to be placed on this list?"

I could not deny that the idea of knowing Renee would choose someone from that list, and I was not on it had me cursing my fate to honor only with wisdom. The silence that consumed the security hold while both my sister and head of security waited for an answer was heavy. If I said yes, I would be putting Renee at risk, and there was no other option.

"I do not qualify for this list," I told him honestly. All applicants for the medbay must pass all optimal physical standards for a bathing ritual, no matter for human or warrior.

Olben's eyes lowered, he understood what I meant. He had forgotten and since he had access to all personnel files, he was fully aware of why I would not qualify, but he did not wish to go against my sister's order directly so he freed us both from the burden as best he could, "Go to medbay and be cleared for the list and I'll add you when the results are sent to me."

"Perfect," Rokva surprised me with the ease in which she accepted this compromise because it would lead to her not getting what she wanted. "General," she smiled at me, her fangs on full display, "I expect you to follow through with your duties should the human pick you from the list. The medic will confirm the safety of what we discussed earlier. Warriors, I have business to attend to, my free time is spent for the rotation."

When she left, Olben spoke again, "I shouldn't be saying this, but the commander has been acting more strange than normal.

You are her brother, perhaps you can find out if something is upsetting her?"

"I wouldn't call this her most mischievous of displays," I countered, and he didn't appear convinced.

The other security officer chuckled, and Oblen growled at her to stay quiet.

He cracked his wrists before he turned in his seat. I thought that was the end of the discussion, but he spoke with his back to me as he typed on his screen. "She has marked the security room with her blood like an elder hut over a sacred dwelling as if the goddess will protect our ship from outlaws or security breaches. Her blood will no more protect us than the elder's blood protects the tribe from fire. It is nonsense and distracting for the real reason this ship will be safe, which are our efforts here, looking for loopholes and detecting viruses."

"What he means to say is he likes the smell of her blood, and he is having trouble concentrating," the other security officer, whom I was not familiar with teased. "I've seen him salivating to lick it, but he is a prude that doesn't want to risk rut or using the medbay services."

"Novek," Olben warned. "She is our commander; we will honor her by respecting consent."

"He won't let me lick it either," Novek fake pouted, then she licked her lips like she'd attempt to merely to get a rise out of our head of security.

Olben spun in his seat and then glared at me, an easy target for his troubles.

I hadn't even noticed the scent of my sister's blood until he made mention of it. It did permeate the room, but I was so used to her scent that I had dismissed the difference between her being here recently, and her blood dried on the threshold.

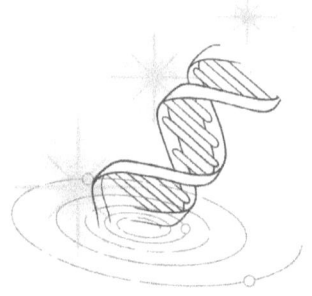

Chapter Six
Renee

A minor headache was making concentrating on anything difficult, and I didn't really have much I needed to be focused for. I couldn't even enjoy watching Earth from the observation deck, without feeling the queasiness of staring out into space and needing to close my eyes despite the beauty of the planet. We would be disembarking from Earth's rotation as soon as every shuttle was accounted for, and I wouldn't get to see this again for a year, but it would feel like only a few months for me, as some of that time would probably be in stasis, especially for the return trip.

Briefly, I thought about returning to General Sou-el's office to rest, since I didn't have an assigned living space yet, but an image of him walking off after saying he didn't have need of a mate, and his sister clearly making an effort to set us up squashed that idea. My next choice was to go to my daughter's room, but I saw how cramped her space was. That closet was just big enough to have two people sitting butt-to-butt cheek on her couch to cuddle for a movie, and her bed atop that was big enough to fit one large warrior if they didn't move.

That should have been enough room for us to cuddle up, and might have worked if she were Laurel, but Becky was not an easy sleeper. I learned fairly quickly that no matter how big the bed was... Becky would make sure I either fell off the side, or ended up kicking me in the back. Sleepovers would have ended when she was five years old if I didn't discover the secret pillow technique of wrapping my arm around a pillow and her until she passed out, and then using that forcefield to stop her from kicking me out of the bed. I hoped her bed came with straps to make sure she didn't fall off the bed herself.

A passing trill officer was kind enough to greet me and show me the way to the medbay. I wouldn't know their name to thank them, as they rarely gave their names to anyone unless they felt they would be communicating with you frequently. Even the trill who facilitated at the exchange office only showed a clearance card when going about their business. Joel said it was better to simply refer to them all as the trill and do my best to avoid their snobbery. This one was very kind and spoke in poetic reference to eyes and something about the forest, then proceeded to tell me the next time I see them to place my pinky to my forehead and fan my fingers just so as a sign of greeting and gratitude for the goddess.

It was becoming a commonality that the trill and necia warriors referenced a goddess often and had a belief system that I should probably learn more about as I wasn't sure if they were referencing the same goddess or different ones as they were different species.

"Ah, you got my summons," a necia warrior dressed in white robes said without even lifting their head from examining something on the table. He straightened, and I could see small spikes poking through their robe, they were barely more than an inch of spike from their shoulder unlike the size of General Sou-el's, which were substantially bigger.

I wasn't sure why I was making a comparison, but ever since the commander made a note of it, I'd been paying more attention to the size of epul on every warrior I passed.

"I didn't get a summons," I corrected him, "I'm here because I have a headache."

"How odd, please come, sit." I took a seat, and he waved a pen over me, before tapping at the air and grunting. "Yes, there is the problem."

"What?"

"Easy fix," he said without a thought and before I could ask, 'what' again, he stabbed me in the neck with a needle. "There you are. The latest model. Don't worry your old implant will dissolve. You'll pee it out in nanobits after it's filtered through your blood stream."

I rubbed at my neck and glared at him.

He continued talking like there was nothing wrong, "This is why I keep telling the trill to let us administer the implants ourselves. Humans keep slicing open the skin and causing scar tissue to build up. Never great for implants to have scar tissue since your bodies are so slow to heal. This implant is better anyways, they give everyone those basic models for language processing, and they aren't built for message relays because people think they are just overhearing a conversation they aren't part of. They end up adjusting the frequencies and then there you go, headaches."

"So, you're telling me I caused my own headache by trying to mute background translations?"

"Messages, not translations, you can tell by the ding before it starts speaking."

"I thought it was an intercom error on the ship..."

He sighed with exasperation, "Humans."

"It's fixed now?"

"Better than fixed. Newest model, more languages, messaging interface that can connect with an eye implant, or lenses. When you hear the tone, you can press behind your ear and activate the message without getting a headache. It's even capable of muting background noise, if you press just so," he demonstrated on himself, "you can increase or decrease the noise buffering. Sometimes I turn it on to tune out someone particularly chatty. Did you want an eye implant while you're here?"

"Uh, I've had enough excitement for the day."

He leaned in and whispered, "Between you and me, you've been approved for whatever you want and that isn't something every human gets, so I'd think about coming back for one before your permissions are removed. On to why I summoned you. I have to retrieve samples of every warrior on the list that you are potentially interested in for bathing. As you have been flagged as potentially allergic to the enzymes in our saliva."

My face flushed with an image of General Sou-el licking my skin. He must have added a note to my file because of my reaction to him, if only he knew it had nothing to do with allergies.

"Is that normal?"

The medic stared at me and then carefully smiled without showing his fangs. "What is normal, really, but undiscovered data? I'll collect samples and have you come in to test them safely as a precaution. Do you have a preference to narrow down the list?"

"Aren't they just going to, uh, lick me? Does it matter beyond that?"

"It matters a great deal," he said aghast like I had said something ridiculous. "There is preference of skill, enzyme compatibility, rank and honor among the tribe, interest level of bonding or strictly for assisting with yours or another's adrenaline saturation." Seeing my confusion, he shook his head in disbelief and mumbled about how no one ever listens to him when he says more training should be given to humans. "I'll take care of it, and make some selections for you, come back next rotation. I'll message you when I'm ready."

The medic stabbed me again, this time with a canister that took a blood sample, then swiped at thin air, like he didn't even see me anymore as he grunted and nodded. More hand flicks and he smiled to himself muttering to himself, "Yes, that will do nicely."

My headache was gone, but a new type of annoyance built as I tried to think through next steps of where I was supposed to go after I left the medbay. Surprisingly, the meal from this morning kept me full throughout the day, and with how big the ship was, I lost track of where I was, or even how to find my way back to where I started.

Everything looked the same, every hall was filled with sliding doors that led to more halls, small living quarters for ship staff and I wondered when I'd come across something different like a communal space or even the medbay, observatory, or an office.

I'd passed several humans, warriors, and even some other species I wasn't familiar with. Didn't see the helpful trill again, but I finally spotted a double-wide slider that usually meant a communal space of some kind.

When I entered, there were rows and rows of stacked stasis pods on a conveyor system that I couldn't even see the end of.

A trill was dressed in a similar robe to that of the medic I saw earlier, she turned to see me and lifted a brow ridge.

Her green skin was lighter than the other I saw in the hall earlier, but I did remember the odd pinky greeting I was shown and attempted a recreation of the gesture now, to temper the awkwardness. She did the same, and said, "Small is the sight when focused on one instead of many, human of Earth."

Scales fluttered along the outer ridge of her head, a golden sheen glinting off them in the dim light before she closed her eyes and tapped her pinky once more to her temple.

I wasn't sure if I was supposed to say something in return, but she was definitely watching me expectantly, so I replied, "That's very admirable to give to others."

I was pretty sure that was what the translation meant in my head, and a ding sounded in my ear. I tapped where the medic had shown me, and a pleasant voice that sounded a great deal like a popular actress on Earth said, "A traditional greeting of the trill, commonly followed with the phrase, 'In many we rise.'"

That's useful to know. I quickly placed my pinky back to my head and said, "In many we rise."

For the first time, I saw a trill smile, and I was both relieved and terrified as all of their teeth were carnivorous.

"A polite human, how refreshing," she said. "How may I assist you? I have all humans accounted for from the last transport.

The next shuttle should not have cleared for processing yet before we exit Earth's orbit."

After having a compliment from a trill, I didn't want to disappoint her with the reason I made my way here, but there was no changing that I was lost, and I'd have to swallow my pride.

"The ship is as large as a city, and I got a bit turned around."

"Ah, you need guidance to your living quarters, or perhaps the lounge that is much too loud to fit the name humans call it? Lounging is a state of relaxation, and yet that is not what happens there. I cannot leave the stasis pods, someone must always be monitoring them, but I can upload the directions to your implant as only the latest models would have had access to enter this room." She flicked through the air like the medic did before and then turned from me, signaling the end of our conversation.

As I exited the stasis pod room, the same notification sound beeped, and I tapped my implant. The voice returned and navigated me through the halls. My implant must be able to track where I was on the ship, because it was precise to the step on when I was supposed to turn, and the door I was standing in front of at the end... was General Sou-el's office.

Whatever file was on my implant had his room listed as mine, and curiosity got the best of me as I lifted my hand to be scanned for entry... it opened.

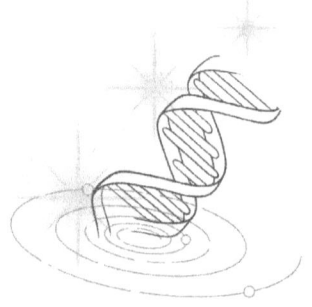

Chapter Seven
General Sou-el

All medics had implants in their fingers or a disrupter tag to scan nanobots, upload or download information from implants, and carry out their tasks. Medic Cenkal was servicing the medbay, and he was not one for pleasantries before administering my exam, though he was particularly chatty while he proceeded.

"I thought you would be by sooner than this to pick up your supplements, General. As a warrior of research and knowledge, you should be aware that there is honor in accepting science's help to be our best." He shoved a finger into my mouth and rubbed it along the inside of my gumline. "I'm surprised that the reason you are here is for a re-evaluation for bathing consideration. Are you experiencing symptoms of oncoming rut?"

"You know I am not," I confirmed for him, mumbling through my lip being pinched before he let go.

"You know I took this shipment's assignment to stay by your side, and yet you hardly visit. I was beginning to think you had forgotten I had claimed you as my brother, and that comes with honored courtesy of your attention from time to time," he continued to ramble on, and I grunted my acknowledgement.

"You owe me nothing," I released him of his burden many times, but he has yet to accept it.

He stabbed a needle in me with unnecessary roughness that I had schooled myself to ignore. My face remained unflinching, though he quickly sprayed my arm with numbing agent anyway, knowing I felt it more keenly than other warriors would have. Cenkal was upset with me, but he did not truly wish me harm.

"I owe you my life since we were spawnlings, but you are right, I've paid my debt that same rising. Together we survived the tribal rites, and together we will continue to thrive. One day, I will mate and you will be there to show my spawnlings what strength and honor look like."

I nodded my agreement; he had proven he would always be there for me, and it was my honor to be there for him and his future spawnlings. It didn't go unnoticed that he did not include me as having spawnlings in the future. He was a medic, he knew this was unlikely, and gave me the gift of having his own spawnlings be my own one day. It was the greatest honor that I never thought I'd have.

"Are you waiting until you are promoted to General Medic to honor me with spawnlings to raise as my own?"

"Don't be ridiculous, brother, they are still my spawnlings, you will guide them and protect them, but I fear they will come to honor you more than myself if you don't have someone else to honor and attend to."

"Have you been speaking with the commander?" I grumbled, not in the mood to be ambushed by Cenkal about being mated.

"She may have messaged about convincing you to join me at the lounge one of these nights to look into options, but I was not expecting the request to re-examine your bathing needs. There are mate options that are uninterested in spawn or have damaged their glands and are in want of a companion. You don't have to worry about what your exam will show us. You are well honored in your field."

"I'm aware. I'm not here to find a mate. We both know what my results will be."

Cenkal grabbed a testing paper and rummaged around his desk. "Ah, I used the last of my primer vials for this exam. I've done many bathing readiness exams, and I will have to collect more primers for the future."

"It should not matter; the results would be as they have before. We can skip it and I can return to my office."

"Not quite," he opened a drawer and smiled, "This will have to do. Normally, I have the subjects provide their scent of arousal for priming a bathing candidate, but blood can work as well. Since you have such a low enzyme level, it should be fine to use it as a primer. It can be risky with warriors that have a high level already, leading to a rut, as you well know."

"I've had blood before, it did nothing to help my gland production. If you're pretending to be out of primer to boost my exam chances, I will find out. I have access to supply lists, as General," I warned him, but at least this way there would be no doubts of my failing the exams when the primer was blood.

It should be more potent than arousal fluids.

He grabbed a glove and picked up the small vial no larger than a teardrop of blood.

"If you feel any symptoms at all, you must tell me immediately. I'm required to remind you by law of assent that this subject gave her permission to use this offering for purposes of finding a bathing mate only, and should you feel any draw, you are to lock yourself in your rooms until the feeling passes or until permission has been granted to proceed. Do you understand these conditions? Your answer will be recorded by implant."

"I consent."

"Very well." Cenkal pinched my nose and I opened my mouth for him to rub the small drop of blood at my gums. It was to prevent me from smelling the blood first, which was unnecessary for someone like me, but he would follow protocol. As the liquid absorbed, my fangs lengthened, and Cenkal jerked his hand back, quickly reaching for his elder root spray, every medic had this on hand to knock out a warrior should they show signs of rut.

"Your eyes are dilating. Your breathing is labored, and this is the first time you've displayed immediate lowering of your cuspids," he said with fascination. Quickly, he snapped the glove off his hand and cautiously approached. "What are you feeling?" His elder root spray was readied, just in case.

My hearts thundered in my chest, and I was reminded of that same excitement I had when Renee allowed me to taste her skin, but stronger. My fangs throbbed, and I looked around the room as if I would find her standing there.

"Sou-el," he prompted once more, before he grabbed a disruptor instead of using the implants in his fingers. He extended the cylinder and shoved it in my mouth. My immediate response was to growl at him, and he laughed. Mumbling to himself he said, "Never thought I'd see the day. Incredible."

Cenkal worked on his private screens that only he could see in his eye implant, hands swiping away, and he chatted all the while, though I stopped listening to the words. My whole body tingled, and my epul throbbed, but it was not in that familiar ache of uncomfortable pain. I felt... like I hadn't just stayed up all night staring at a sleeping human but was a buzz with— Cenkal interrupted my thoughts to say what I had not, "Adrenaline spike! Sweet Horve's Vine, your glands are producing adrenaline! Fuck, fuck," he said excitedly as he paced back and forth, "What do I do? Should I spray you with elder root even though you're finally showing normal levels? No, it seems premature. What if I fuck this up? What if I spray you and it shocks your glands and damages them when they are finally working? But," he swiped his finger across my forehead, and I bared my teeth at him, feeling territorial for the first time. I did not wish for him to touch me. Only her. The only touch I craved was from Renee.

Where was she? I had to find her. Would it harm her for her to touch me? If I kept my tongue to myself, would she be okay with me tasting her with my fingers instead?

I stood up from the seat, my nostrils flaring.

"Remarkable," Cenkal said studying some results on his implant. "Even your enzymes are finally coming to the surface of your skin. You'll finally be able to heighten a mate's response by touch. These levels are promising, and—" He touched his finger to my skin again and I yanked back my hand, his touch was like a threat, a challenge, and my epul protruded more from my shoulders like I would fight him.

"Sou-el... your levels aren't balancing. I can't let you leave—" he said with worry.

I snarled, and knocked his hand before he had a chance to secure the elder spray. Cenkal fumbled with the canister before he clamped down on the nozzle, spraying himself in the face, "Fuck..." he said as he stared at me through the mist. He swiped through the air one final time, before he grabbed at the table for stability. The elder root would knock him out for a while in that high of a concentration. It wasn't until I reached the door that a notification on my implant initiated. The door slammed closed behind me, just as I reached the hall.

Every door I passed was triggered into a lockdown procedure, preventing me from entering any spaces on the ship that were not my living quarters. The lockdown on my permissions would stay in effect until the head of security, the commander, or the medic that initiated it, cleared me of suspected rut. Protocol would dictate that I should go to the holding cells and be restrained, but I felt perfectly rational, and of sound mind to simply lock myself in my quarters until the spike in adrenaline passed. All I needed was to relieve myself and get rid of the images of Renee panting in my arms as I licked her neck.

The salt of her skin was intoxicating, and I wanted nothing more than to sink my fangs into her flesh, marking her as mine, giving her my mark.

I blinked rapidly, trying to clear my head. Drinking her blood was one thing but marking her was a violation of her consent. Humans did not have the same defenses a necia warrior had, leaving every inch of them exposed to our fangs. Commander Rokva kept armor plating around her neck to warn off mates, and her epul were specially designed to protect against unwelcomed mating marks without her withdrawing her epul. To retract one's epul was an act of consent to be touched, to be marked, but humans did not have this feature.

Warriors gave a wide girth as they passed me in the halls, and I felt my hearts hammer louder in my ears as I got closer to my room.

As I stood in front of my door, I stilled. For a moment, I thought I felt more than my hearts beating, but dismissed it as hearing others in the hall nearby. My doors slid open and as I entered lockdown protocols engaged and there would be no leaving until I was cleared.

Renee's familiar scent wafted to my nose, and it seemed stronger than the lingering remnants of her sleep the rotation before. My eyes caught on her soft body as it jumped up, trying to reach the lever to bring down my bed. Then she turned, and I stared at those silver eyes that held every color in their depths and couldn't breathe.

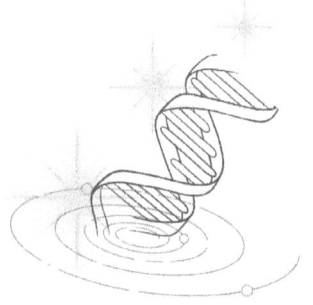

Chapter Eight
Renee

The amber in Sou-el's eyes was nothing but a ring of fire around black pupils like I'd been trapped into a vortex the moment I saw them. I couldn't move. Couldn't breathe. Couldn't think to explain why I'd been trying to get his bed out of the wall, instead of taking the couch. The excuse was on the tip of my tongue to say I was just going to grab one of the pillows, but I knew better. I wanted to bury my face in the fabric of where he slept and console myself for feeling attracted to an alien I hardly knew, who wanted nothing to do with me.

But there he was staring at me as he stalked forward. His epul were intimidating as they seemed to breathe with him, pulsating in and out of his skin. White silver hair flowed freely around his shoulders, no longer pinned back for work, appearing wind-swept like he had been running, or post workout. Even a sheen of sweat glistened on his skin. Neither of us spoke as he never once broke eye contact to lift his arm up, boxing me in against the wall that held his bed.

I gulped my nerves down. His exposed chest was close enough I could inhale the scent of him, that same smell I couldn't put a name to, but was wholly him and exactly what I was searching for when I tried to steal his pillow. A low rumble vibrated from his throat like he could sense what I was thinking. He was warning me that he wasn't interested in me that way, I knew that and it made my chest ache. I broke the eye contact then, looking away with a squeak.

Sou-el leaned down, his nose rubbing the top of my head as he chuffed. I didn't know what he was doing, but I couldn't bring myself to speak or move. My skin tingled in awareness of him, and my heart pounded in my ears. "Can't leave," he forced out.

I blinked in confusion and met his eyes again. All the amber in them was gone, his eyes were dilated.

"Desk drawer," he pleaded with me, his mouth parted as he panted, exposing his large fangs. I should have been scared, but a warmth built up in my stomach, and it spread between my thighs.

"Are you okay?" I asked, stunned. My hand lifting to touch his clammy skin. He was so hot, overly so.

"Desk," he repeated with a groan that seemed to vibrate down to my very bones, making me close my eyes as my body was lost to the way my muscles tensed with the husky noises he was making. Right, the desk, something was wrong with him, I berated myself for being so needy when he was clearly not okay. I forced myself to slip under his arm that he leaned his forehead against while heaving heavily against the wall. Glancing at him one last time, I watched as his fingers dug past the lever for the bed and the metal bent under the pressure. I rushed to the desk, and fumbled for the drawer, but it wouldn't budge.

"It's locked," I said in panic.

"Break it," he insisted as his other hand launched up and gripped the wall alongside his other, creating divots in the metal from his strength. He was breathing so heavy, and his shoulders quaked as his fingers dug down the wall like he was restraining himself. What was wrong with him?

I tried harder to yank at the drawer, but it was no use. What was so important inside the drawer, and why didn't he have a key of some sort?

"Do you have a key?" I begged him as I searched for something to use as a crowbar. "What is going on? Shouldn't we call the medbay?"

"Locked in, already flagged," he said in broken bursts.

Why was he talking so strained? He let out a groan and spun around to face me.

His eyes flitted from where I was to the only other door in his office that wasn't the exit. The light above his door was blue, the sign that it was locked, just like he said, and there was no light above the other door, meaning it didn't lead anywhere. It was probably a closet or a bathroom.

"Renee," he growled out my name and I shivered as heat pooled between my legs. An ache building within me that needed pressure, and begged to be touched. If this was what people felt when they lusted after people then I understood why Holden gave me such pity-filled eyes when I told him I felt nothing. This alien hadn't even touched me and I was already licking my lips, and his dark eyes caught the movement like a predator.

He lifted his hand up behind him, still watching me, as he pulled the lever and walked forward. The bed lowered itself and his nostrils flared as he slowly sat at the edge, his legs wide, making it impossible to miss the large bulge against his thigh.

My daughter's words of warning tugged at my thoughts to never uncross my legs when sitting down in front of a necia warrior. My mouth grew dry as my lips parted, my breathing coming out in pants. It was an invitation for them to touch you, and here he was eye-fucking me as his legs were parted, displaying his interest proudly, but I couldn't bring myself to admit that the same warrior sitting before me actually wanted me, when he had told me that he would never touch me again.

The tension in the room was so thick I felt heavy, and my knees were shaking.

His hands were fisted into the side of the bed, as he leaned forward. Sou-el cracked his neck back and forth as his epul withdrew back into his shoulders, another sign that he was inviting me closer. Why else would he withdraw his lethal spikes if he did not intend for me to come to him? My legs clenched together, my body responding to him and we weren't even touching.

He shuddered, as he groaned. His breathing quickened, and I gripped the desk hard to keep my balance. What was he doing to me?

"Lock yourself in the lavatory or break the drawer to paralyze me with the spray inside. My body believes that I have won mating rights to rut with you as I have bathed in a drop of your blood. With your proximity, and," he growled low as he sniffed the air, "your arousal. I can feel my blood heat. I will lose myself to instinct soon."

His words were strained, as he gritted his teeth and continued, "I've been flagged for rut, and I do not have access to unlock the door. No one does, except head of security, the commander or a medic."

He seemed to have a bit of clarity in his eyes for a moment, some of the amber ringed the black, as he struggled to hold himself back.

My chest tightened with frustration that of course he didn't actually want me to come to him. He didn't want me, this was some warrior biology he was fighting against. And here I was, a fool, letting my body react to him, and thinking he was offering himself to me.

I cleared my throat so that I wouldn't still have that raspy tone of need when I replied, "Will someone come to help you?"

He shook his head.

"No one will believe the flag on my file, and the one person who could convince them is currently knocked out with the only thing that can subdue a necia warrior. He will be unconscious for too long to help."

"I don't know much, but I do know that necia consider balancing their body's needs life or death, and you're saying no one is coming to help you?" Instincts surged through me to protect him, to help him... somehow.

"I'll be fine," he gritted, each word staccato. How could I believe the same words I'd say to myself over and over through my life? I'll be fine... was nothing but a statement I said because I knew I couldn't expect anyone to help me.

I didn't believe him. I watched as his grip bent the metal frame of the bed.

"You could open the drawer," I surmised with the strength he had.

He nodded.

"Then I can go into the bathroom, and you can bust open the drawer for the sedative."

"I won't do it."

"Why not?" I yelled at him, clearly, he was in some kind of medical emergency, and he wouldn't bust a drawer open to help himself?

"If you go for the lavatory, I will try to get to you before I try to get to the drawer. Instinct will make me think you're running from me, and it's possible the door won't hold for long," he admitted with a groan.

"You seem to have plenty of restraint at the moment, so come here and open the drawer while you still can," I demanded.

"No."

"No?" I felt like we had done this dance before, except last time, it was me refusing to be sent to a stasis pod.

Epul pierced through his thighs, ripping his pants. More epul extended from his arms, and he used a claw that came out of his knuckle to slice slowly across his stomach.

A few drops of blood beaded up to the surface in a thin line, following his sharp touch. Sou-el stared at me darkly as he licked his tongue over his fang. Then said, "The only thing I want is to have you on your knees while I bleed for you."

"You what?" I watched as he cut himself again. "What are you doing? Stop!" I ran to him to grab his arm and stop him if I had to, not even thinking about how foolish it was to think I had any kind of strength to stop him from doing anything. But I got there and held his wrist without hesitation, and he grinned at me. I glanced between my hand and his face. His epul should have skewered me, but my hand wrapped around nothing but scales and skin. Surprisingly, the scales on his wrist were soft like suede, and I wasn't harmed at all.

The tang of blood could be smelled on his knuckles where the epul withdrew into. My stomach grumbled, the first sign of hunger since eating the ship's breakfast gruel. He moved his fist closer to my lips, and my own followed, still gripping his wrist, as my heart pounded deafeningly in my chest.

I wanted to lick him. Eyes locked together, we stared until he stilled just centimeters from my lips. Grabbing his wrist more firmly, I pulled it away to examine the blood, it was fresh, but he wasn't bleeding. My lips trembled as I brought his knuckles back up and kissed them. I didn't know what was wrong with him, but I wouldn't let him hurt himself anymore. Blood smeared on my lips, and heat tingled down my throat and deep in my belly. My tongue swept out with a moan, and I wanted to taste more.

Skin tingling, I licked blood off his knuckles, and he growled in response. I paused to think about how ridiculous I was and quickly pulled away to apologize. This was insane, and I couldn't make sense of why I just did that.

"I'm sorry," I mumbled, but he grabbed my hand.

"Are you harmed?" he asked hoarsely.

My hand was trembling, but I shook my head. "No."

"What do you want?" he asked while gently rubbing my fingers with his thumb.

I thought about it, as my body was pressed against his chest. I needed to stop thinking. This was why I came, wasn't it? To make sure whether I felt nothing with everything, with everyone, but this felt like more than nothing, and I was scared.

Scared that I'd get used to this feeling and seek it out when I returned to being numb, when this was over, when he woke up from this strange state he was in, and realized this was a mistake.

He wasn't in his right mind, I thought with a groan. He wasn't part of the program, so I couldn't be sure this was what he wanted.

"I want you to tell me you want me," I rasped.

"I want you," he repeated my words quickly, and he leaned in, rubbing his nose along my hairline.

"No," I pleaded with him. "I don't mean because of this, because of whatever this is," I tried to explain, but fumbled when his nose reached my ear, and his hot breath tickled my neck. "I don't want to use you."

"This," he huffed, "is our biology telling us we are matched. My restraint to wait for your consent to touch you, is my mind wanting you to want this as much as I do." He nuzzled into my neck while holding my hand against his chest to feel his hearts beating rapidly. Every muscle of his was taut with the strain of keeping himself seated before me, his legs spread with me between them. Everything about him screamed touch me, and I wanted to, so very badly. But I doubted myself, my motives, and the state he was in, keeping us at a stalemate of small, heated brushes of a nose against my skin, or the way my thumb gently rubbed his chest absently while tangled with his hand closed around mine.

"You want me," he whispered in a husky low tone.

My only reply was a whimper of assent as his thigh rubbed against my leg, his firm length unmistakable. I did want him. I leaned into his touch, rubbing my face against his as he groaned into my hair.

I'd never been into licking people before. Tyler used to kiss me with his mouth open and it reminded me of a puppy slobbering and the smell of saliva on my skin was unpleasant. The whole process was a waste of time that simply got me dirty and in need of a shower, but as my nose nuzzled into Sou-el's hair, I inhaled deeply, and all I wanted to do was devour him. I needed him in my mouth, and against my skin. Friction, pressure, more. My tongue flicked out to lick at his ear and suckled on his lobe before my teeth grazed across his neck. A low growl rumbled through him, and a hand snapped up from where he held himself to the bedframe, to then wrap around my waist, tugging me closer.

He spun us around, lifting me until my back was on the mattress, and he panted with controlled heaves as he stared down at me. My legs dangled off his hips, they had clung to him as he picked me up and shifted our positions. With my legs opened to him, he traced his knuckle along my shirt, a sharp epul snagging on the fabric, ripping along its wake. As my chest lifted and fell with anticipation, the shirt eased off my breasts and he growled at the sight of my bra. Slow and careful, he pinched the clasp at the center of my ribcage, and he tugged to unlatch it. Cool air hardened my nipples, because it couldn't possibly be the way he looked at me like I was something he couldn't tear his eyes from, or that my skin heated at the very thought of him touching me with that tongue slipping over his lips.

My gaze traveled down his torso, blood smeared across his abs from where I rubbed against him, and there was no sign of a wound anywhere. I lifted a hand to finger over the same line he had cut with an epul before I stormed over to stop him, and there was nothing but the smooth suede texture of his scales. He was healed. Red blood sticky on my finger, but no sign of where it came from. My finger trailed lower, just above the waist band of his torn pants. Slits from where his epul extended on his thighs made the traditional leather skirts the commander wore make more sense for a necia warrior. Though the spikes were gone, his pants were in ribbons, tearing more with every strain of his muscles.

"Is it uncomfortable to keep them in?" I asked, trying to keep the breathiness of need from my voice, but failing miserably. I was looking for an excuse to push him away, to stop myself from indulging in what my body clearly wanted. If he was uncomfortable, I could force myself to leave.

"Most of the time," he confirmed. "But this is the first time I don't feel them aching in every fiber of my body. The only thing uncomfortable is not being able to touch you, to taste you, and claim you with my blood begging to rut you while the whole ship watches with envy and pride. My name on those pretty lips as you come around my fingers first, then in my mouth, before I take you with my cock."

Fuck, I thought breathless, my thighs trying to clench together for friction, but he was firmly between my legs as he bent over me moaning as he inhaled deeply.

"You smell like rak blossoms in winter, and if you were not human, I would have already taken what is clearly mine to have. Tell me, Renee," the way he said my name was dark and sultry, "that when my blood was on your lips, your body welcomed it. That you are unharmed. That I will not see your cheeks marred with tears at my hand?"

A thumb brushed under my eyes, and my hips thrust up in answer to his question, but I knew that wouldn't be enough. I'd never felt this before, this need, and I didn't want to let it go even though I should. I grabbed his hand and pressed the palm fully to half my face and turned into it to press my lips there to erase the memory of my tears and replace it with my touch. I slid his hand down my neck until he cupped my breast, and I pressed it there giving my nipple a slight tug with a moan.

"I've never come before," I admitted to him with a rasp. "I want to know what it feels like. I want to know what *you* feel like with your tongue, your fingers, and—"

My words were stolen from me as he squeezed my breast and filled his mouth with the other, his tongue capturing my nipple.

"It is my honor, Pulsunne," he said between swirls of his tongue tasting my hardening peak.

The word didn't translate, regardless of having the updated implant, and I didn't care. Pulsunne, I repeated in my mind, the word rolled from his tongue in a way that made my back arch up to meet him.

Sou-el's tongue traced down from my breast, along my ribs, and over my curved stomach. I was all squish to his hard muscle, and I tensed as he kissed the same stomach my husband used to quickly glide over with little interest, his lips pressed into my giving flesh. My body never bounced back after childbirth, no matter how many crunches I did to tone my waist. His eyes roamed over the stretch marks that spidered around my hips, and he licked them like the sight of them urged him on.

"Not every human has these markings," he growled as he licked them, his fangs nipping at my skin. "These were made by another, and the next time you look upon them, you will only think of me," he demanded right before he kissed one that webbed out along my hip.

His interest in them had nothing to do with their appearance on my skin, but that of why they were there. A sign that I had been with another man, that I had born someone's children that were not his. He lifted me, pulling off my pants, easing them and my panties around my curves, kissing each new slice of exposed skin. I moaned as he suckled at the crux of my hipbone, leading to the heat between my thighs. My fingers dug into his silver hair while his own found their way between my lips, finding me slick with need.

Sou-el closed his eyes as two fingers pushed at the notch of my entrance, and I clamped down, my inner walls aching to be filled. Hips lifted and moved to force him inside, but he placed a hand on my stomach and teased around my clit with his tongue. His fingers stayed pushed against my pussy, edging at the threshold as he swirled circles of delicious pressure tipping in, then out, in and out. All the while his tongue flicked at my throbbing clit and his other hand held my stomach in place.

I panted as I watched him moving against me, there, but teasing as my muscles spasmed and my hips jolted, needing more. This was delicious torture, and a heat built up, making me feel like I needed to pee. Oh fuck, I was going to pee on him.

"I'm going to pee," I said in a panic, as I pushed at his head, squirming at the pleasure wrecking me with every flick of his tongue and a third finger joined his others as he put pressure at my entrance, but not actually filling me like I so desperately craved.

He didn't stop, even though I warned him of what was surely to come.

My hands flew up behind my head, gripping the sheets of the bed as I bit my lip hard to stop myself from losing control.

"I'm— I'm going—" I gasped out, trying to warn him again that he needed to stop even though my whole body tingled, and heat pooled at my core. I couldn't hold it, the pressure building, as pleasure made my toes curl.

"Fuck, fuck," I moaned as my hips tried to escape before I peed all over him because my muscles were squeezing, and through the haze of pleasure I was riding, the most embarrassing moment of my life was unfurling, and I couldn't do anything to stop it. Everything throbbed and then all three of his fingers thrust inside as liquid gushed out of me. His name echoed in the room from my scream.

As the high flowed through me, releasing the tension in my body, turning to jelly in his arms, I finally had time to be mortified. My eyes were squeezed shut, not wanting to see his reaction. It wasn't until his fingers slowly pulled from my core that I squinted to peek, only to find him licking his fingers like a spoon. My eyes widened in confusion and arousal.

The amber of his eyes returned to a fiery ring peeking out from the darkness of his hooded lust.

"I'm sorry," he finally said, shocking me. What did he have to be sorry for? That was the sexiest thing I've ever laid eyes on. He was the sexiest I've ever seen. "I had promised to make you come with just my tongue first, but I wanted to feel you come around my fingers as I bathed in your release."

I didn't pee?

I must have said that out loud because he smiled and said, "I will enjoy feeling you come around my cock after you've agreed to take my unne mark."

That word created a notification in my implant, reluctantly I pressed behind my ear and in that pleasant actress voice the message relayed, "Unne marks are a mating ritual within necia warrior tribes to show warriors that are claimed in mating, similar to a symbol of marriage."

Marriage... the word struct me cold.

"Unne mark?" I repeated.

"You have my blood inside of you, and your blood is inside of me," he stated like I should know what he's talking about.

"And that means what exactly?" The pleasure of coming ebbed, and only the pulsing of my labia reminded me that I still craved his touch as the rest of me froze and worried about the very real fact that I was still married to a man on Earth, Tyler.

"You will bare my mark once I bury my cock inside you, whether I bite you or not, Pulsunne."

"I'm married," I blurted out.

The silence was heavy between us before the most agonized roar ravaged through his throat once my words sunk in. Black consumed his eyes, and he pulled at his hair, before his epul snapped out from his shoulders.

"No," he whispered in pain as he spun away, leaving me there on the bed. I pulled the scrapes of my shirt over my chest and hugged myself. "You are mine," he said in disbelief like repeating the words made it true.

He stormed to the desk, ripped open the drawer that had been locked and grabbed a small spray canister. He cracked his neck back and forth before calming himself and staring at me with a kind of madness. "I do not care about your Earth customs, mate. In my tribe, when a mate is not cared for by those they mark, their claim is challenged. Your Earth contracts mean nothing to me."

Sou-el licked his fingers, sucking on all three before he moaned and continued with a sharp command, "It is my tongue on your flesh, my blood inside you, my name in your screams of pleasure, and it will be my mark that surpasses all others. I *will* have you, Renee, but not with another male's presence between us. When I wake, I will challenge your bond of Earthly marriage. And when I win, you will take my cock, and my mark, Pulsunne."

"What does that word mean?" I asked, as he sprayed the mist in his own face. His nostrils flared and he held himself up by clinging to the desk, before his knees buckled, and he fumbled over to the wall, sliding down in a heap.

He didn't answer me, and this was not how I imagined my trip to the Blue District going. Of course, I had reasoned with myself that it was a possibility that I might have sex with an alien, but Sou-el wasn't part of the program and this wasn't exactly a one night only feeling, or someone just looking to have some fun. He gave me the best orgasm of my life, the only orgasm I'd ever had, if I was being honest. I wasn't even sure if what that was could be called an orgasm, I thought I was going to pass out from pleasure, and pee myself all at once.

I wanted more, like a newly minted addict. But, I had no intentions of mating with anyone. This was all supposed to be temporary. I'd find out if I was broken or not, return to Earth, live out my days by myself and be there to see my children's lives grow.

And I was afraid. Afraid that I'd like what Sou-el was offering me, accepted it, and have it taken away. I wasn't a spring chicken, as my mom would remind me, and realistically this, with Sou-el, would never be anything more than temporary, no matter what he said about marking me as his mate.

We knew nothing about each other, and this was just lust. I couldn't leap into an alien relationship I knew nothing about. He'd change his mind when he realized more than half of my life was already lived, and aliens lived so much longer.

I wiped at a tear that escaped, running down my cheek. Don't worry Sou-el, this was my fault, not yours.

Chapter Nine
General Sou-el

The most horrendous smell wrinkled my nose and I choked on it until I bolted up right. Memories of my rage and pain resurfaced, knowing I had to knock myself out while I still had my mate's come in my mouth, before the craving to bury my cock deep within her to finish our mate bond overwhelmed me and I made sure to refill those silver eyes with lust until she begged to have me fill her again. That wasn't the way I wanted to claim someone as treasured as Renee. I would do this the right way, without being blinded by rut over having her blood in my system.

I would earn her blood the honorable way.

I groaned, holding my head in my hands at the massive headache from the elder root. It was a chance I took that I would have enough adrenaline to work through the concentrated spray quickly before whatever affect her blood and ello nectar had on me wore off. For the first time, my glands functioned normally and produced enough adrenaline and numbed the second skin where I felt no ache in my epul, only pleasure. My healing was fast, my pain gone, and it was a cruel awaking to feel that familiar tortured thrum beneath my skin.

Cenkal prodded me with a disrupter stick to check my vitals, and I winced. He wasn't risking getting close enough to me to be fooled again, though it was his own fault that he sprayed his own face with the elder extract. I hadn't done that to him, he was just clumsy when he grabbed the canister.

"The commander believes I manufactured your results in your exam," he began without any preamble. "Wouldn't let me take you to the medbay, saying I had no right to dose you with elder root, but I didn't spray you with anything, did I!" He prodded me again for good measure, even though he didn't need new scans.

He continued when I groaned, "You didn't tell me that the human was assigned to your room before being cleared to re-join her testing group. With your little stunt, you're lucky you didn't mark her under the influence of rut. It would have been dishonorable, and you would have been sent to stasis until we arrived on Trillume unless you could prove she gave her blood willingly. Which you cannot no matter what either of you says, she is human, and therefore unable to prove consent when you got your first taste from medbay exams.

"Do you hear what I'm saying? Your blood, your sweat, your saliva, they were primed with more than enough enzymes to influence a human's libido through their pores by simply touching you. Your levels are back to normal, so no one believes a single word I say on the matter. They know we are brothers, and believe I am dishonoring my calling by lying. The fact that you didn't finish mating her supports their claims." He harrumphed with annoyance.

"Which is it, Cenkal? Are you upset that I did or didn't claim my mate?"

"Both," he snapped. "It can be both, brother. I'm so fucking happy for you, and frustrated with you beyond words. These levels can only be explained by her being your mate, and yet no one believes me, and if you had claimed her, it would have been a much more difficult road for you to keep her.

"I happily wear my dishonor because we both know I am not lying, and I'd take any dishonor with pride knowing what it means for you."

"I could not claim her in dishonor," I finally said with a groan, "But I would have if she had freely given me her blood, I would have damned us both. She is mated on Earth, Cenkal..."

"So what? I did not see her mate on the ship's manifest. He has forfeited his Earthly rights."

"I'm aware, but by our laws, she has born him spawnlings..."

"Oh," he sobered with understanding. "You must challenge the claim, then?"

"I have no choice. Even with her blood out of my system, I taste her, and sense her like an itch that I could follow anywhere on this ship to scratch."

Cenkal shifted in his seat that he brought to my side. I knew without even glancing around my office that Renee wasn't there with us. It wasn't normal for him to keep his mouth shut, so I grew wary.

"Speak," I demanded.

"With confirmation that your mate is capable of participating in the testing without worry of harm, she has been reinstated in her group, and General Tensel stepped in as lead on the project."

"Lead of a research team..." I repeated out loud, thinking about the implications.

General Tensel was being promoted to commander of this ship when Rokva transferred to her new post. His purview was not on the research but the running of the ship. At most he should be consulting with the warrior in charge of the project, not running it himself.

Ignoring Cenkal's protests, I rushed to my desk and brought up screens of my own project and confirmed my suspicions that this wasn't just about Renee.

My manifest of subjects has been altered. The human William was transferred to a new team in my absence. How long was I out for?

"What rotation is today?"

"You've been out for two risings. Your bathing ritual with your mate was successful in negating your rising levels of adrenaline. That with the combined paralytic nature of the elder root, your glands stopped functioning for a while. The spray is only designed to last a few cycles of the rotation, but I've been by your side since Medic Velmeh found me."

The medic in charge of General Tensel's initiative behind the research program for the necia gene within humans.

He knows.

"Did you tell the medic about my results?"

"Why wouldn't I?" he said before he could process what I was saying. "Horve's vine... if he believed me and denied my results then they do not want you to honor your mate."

He didn't know about the project's goal. "General Tensel is in charge of an initiative with someone who has enough power and influence to force Commander Rokva to change assignment to this ship and become commander himself. My sister will have no choice but to accept his decisions or risk showing the ship that she did not agree with the decisions of a future commander."

"You should have given your mate the unne mark," Cenkal said with unease. Even he knew that if I had done so they would have had claim to say my mark was invalid and put me in stasis until a ruling could be made on Trillume. "At least then you would prove your mating at trial and not be forced to watch as your mate is matched with others."

"He may be lead of her study, but I'm the highest-ranking researcher on this ship, with the same honorable title as General Tensel. Blocking me completely will cause undue suspicion on his research. I'll have to force my way in and begin the process of challenging her previous mate's claim by our laws."

"It won't take long for him to suspect what you're doing," Cenkal warned.

"My sister is right, traditions are to be respected. If I plan with her help, perhaps we'll all be detouring to Necias Prime for our Rakturan Rites by the end of this."

"May your mate see your honor and bare your mark until the goddess takes us," he wished me well on my Rakturan, and then returned to his training, his knowledge of the obstacles I would face, "Sou-el, you have no way to prove she is your mate without being in contact with her, and humans are unpredictable in their mating practices. There are reports that a human has become a delegate with AsunGor. Though no one has verified the claims, it would suggest some humans need more than one mate."

Cenkal didn't have to finish his thought for me to know what he was leading to. That she had a mate on Earth already, and it's possible she would seek to return to him while also accepting my claim.

It wouldn't be enough to keep her with me.

By necia law, she would be forced to return without me, as the air on Earth was toxic to most species. But that wouldn't be what kept me away. I would allow the air to pollute my body and live out what years we had on Earth, but if I returned I would battle her mate. If she sought to keep him, I would not harm her by killing her mate if she was similar to the unGor females, but I could only guarantee that by staying away.

I patted my brother on the back, only females grew epul there, and said with determination. "With necia blood in her, she will live a long life, even on Earth. Her mate will die before she does, and I will take what time she honors me with."

"I have a contact on the next scheduled ship to Earth," he offered to have her mate taken care of.

A mixture of emotions warred for dominance from relief that if he were gone, I would have greater chances with my mate, and annoyance that there was no honor in not facing her mate myself if I were to kill him, and pain, physical pain aching in my hearts that this male was the guardian of a spawnling born from my mate. I would not be responsible for taking this male from her or her spawn.

"I cannot," I said with firm resolve.

He merely nodded and let me know that there was strength and honor in earning a mate without destroying their past. Many warriors would not agree, even my sister would not hesitate in killing a warrior that would stand between her and someone she believed to be her Pulsunne when she met them. She held our traditions, even the more violent ones, as honorable. It is her dedication to those ideals that allowed her to rise to commander despite being raised by Elder Edilm.

He was our guardian by fate, not birth. And he was only granted the title of Elder because he chose his tribe over his hearts, but no one forgot why he was able to help the tribe.

He took the side of Commander Direl, King Sylve's second, and killed warriors that tried to go against his order to stand down against the trill. To some, he saved lives and bought our species time to gain power within a new era. To others, he was a dishonorable warrior that should have died with our fallen to prevent those from following a queen that was not our own. He lived only because his reputation of killing warriors was exaggerated to the point of being as great as Horve himself. Were it not for the circumstances, he would probably have his own phrase to rival Horve's vine.

Edilm's wrath, to some.

But for those that he helped save, it was not such an easy thing to think of his past in the color of our brother's blood. He would not take life without reason, and maybe one day, he would tell me how he survived all those warriors without a scar to show for it.

I could still hear his reply to my question that I had asked many times as a spawnling.

"The truth is a road to madness when your mind refuses to honor the acceptance of responsibility for your part in it. One day you will understand."

Many times, I'd thought of his answer and thought he had felt madness from what he had done to those warriors, and perhaps that made him guilty of the dishonor others gave him. But on rotations such as this, I think perhaps the warriors had forced the decision on him, and he still accepted the responsibility of the outcome, and did not wish for me to absolve him of his part in the truth.

Whatever that truth was, the truth I did know was he taught me that I didn't need to use my body as a weapon when my mind was so much stronger. They were frustrating words when I was a spawnling unable to do more than pretend that my epul were more than decoration that caused me constant pain. If I had pursued a warrior's path, I would have been dead long ago as my glands did not heal my wounds as fast as the rest of my tribe, and I needed constant appointments with the healer to help make sure I didn't bleed out internally from my own epul.

"Take this," Cenkal tossed a canister of numbing agent with his own blend of nanobots to help keep my health manageable.

"Will they interfere with my bond?" I was a researcher of behaviors, not the science of biology like he was.

"They produce artificial adrenaline to boost your natural healing. You should be fine, but I'm not sure how a human heart will react to consuming your blood when the nanobots are active, given they only have one heart, and your mate's scans show no signs of damage to her own adrenal glands. Avoid needing the boost on the day you want to share blood with her, both because of your reaction to her blood and her possible reaction to the nanobots," he paused and shook his head, "Don't avoid using the spray unless you know you'll receive some of her fluids, you can't afford for your levels to drop too low, you'll bleed out of your pores."

I swiped open my communication module, and my implant automatically connected. Another flick and a message was sent to my sister to tell her that her match-making skills were required. I also needed to know how much she knew about what General Tensel was tasked with doing on this ship. His conduct was suspicious, and my sister would not be pleased about keeping a warrior away from his chance to mate unless General Tensel was seeking to challenge me for rights to claim my Renee.

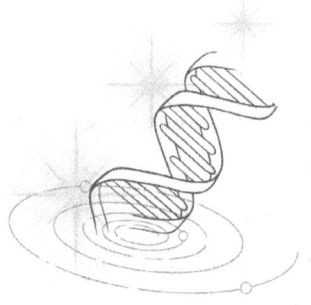

Chapter Ten
Renee

T houghts of the stasis pod haunted me as I waited for word on how General Sou-el was doing. He didn't come to see me, and the medic assured me every warrior woke up after a few human hours from what he called Elder Sleep. The other medic that took care of my exam before had assured me that he would stay with Sou-el while I returned to my research group. But I'd spent the whole day worrying and feeling guilty about what I'd done.

I counted down the seconds in my head waiting for when I could meet up with Becky for our Thursday date night and confirm she had resumed her internship with him. My testing group for attraction was half necia warriors and the other half were trill and unGor, with the exception of two humans, a male and a female.

William stopped punching the sandbag in the sparring area he'd been focusing on, to bee-line for me before I could make my way to grab a food packet. I didn't feel like eating the re-constituted bland chicken for ten minutes, instead of simply squeezing down a tube of the nutrients I needed to acclimate within a minute. He reached the dispensary first, and grabbed two, since he saw what I chose for breakfast and then shoved it at me more aggressively than necessary.

"Thanks?" I said instead of asking him what his problem with me was.

"I heard you talking with one of the necia about getting directions to staff rooms for your daughter," he blurted.

"She isn't part of my program, so she wouldn't know where I was and I have a new implant, so I don't have her contact information to message her. I don't really know how to use the implant that well even if I did," I explained, but I wasn't sure why I was telling him any of this. I guess not speaking with anyone for a day did that to a person. Humans were just programed to be social and blurt our personal information for connection, I guessed. Then I thought about Sou-el, he would probably know more about why we behaved that way, that was his job to research those things.

"Staff quarters are in a different part of the ship that we don't have access to, and they are at the center, so by extension we don't have access to the other half of the ship either."

"The ship is that huge..." I said in wonder. It was so big that I got lost in just the section I had access to.

"All of the necia in the program are considered part of the ship's crew, who are called to serve in rotations of moons or something. I overheard some of them talking about how this group is for humans that already mated before, and more would join them as they sorted through ones showing promise of re-acting to mating hormones of another species."

He downed his food packet, and tossed it in the recycler as I stared at him. He was tall, muscled, and looked ready to punch more than the sandbag. "I knew what I signed up for," he finally said after a pause that was bordering on uncomfortable, but I didn't know what to say to him. "But that fucker doesn't get to run away from me after what he said."

I wasn't following.

"What who said?"

He groaned and waved it off. "It doesn't matter, what matters is they are going to give you access to see your daughter, and you're going to take me with you."

"You are not dragging my daughter into whatever this is," I said while giving him a pointed look to reflect on the way he was acting. He appeared unstable, agitated, and about to cause trouble. My mom senses were tingling, and I sighed to go at this a different way. "I'm not saying I won't help you, but I need to know what you plan on doing."

"I came here to have a good time, no judgements," he began, and I nodded, my eyes softening. "I won't bore you with the details, but my preferences are not approved of in my circle of influence. I did what was expected of me, and this is my fucking time for what I want. When I return to Earth, that's it, all I will have are my memories here, and my family expects me to have this out of my system, and I'm..." he groaned again, like he was struggling with telling me what he needed to, "I'm attracted to one of them, and they transferred me here before I could do anything about it. I have to ask him if this was his way of rejecting me or not, because I wasn't even sure if my preferences were in my head or real until... you get the point, already. Are you going to help or not?"

He was already walking away from me, and I called after him, "Yes."

He stalled for a moment showing that he heard me, but continued walking and we didn't speak again until the warrior that agreed to take me approached.

"I have been studying human culture, and date nights are had during and after the third meal of a rotation. This is the Thursday date you were hoping for with your daughter, correct?" he said with a smile. His epul were large, and his hair burnished, reddish-brown that he had braided in a style that reminded me of Vikings from Earth history.

"Yes, thank you for agreeing to guide me," I said with a returned smile.

"You don't mind if I bring along a friend, do you? It is on the way to the lounge."

"Of course, I was going to ask you the same thing."

He raised a curious brow and William choose that moment to approach, probably eavesdropping as he was shown to make a habit of.

"Impressive epul span," William complimented the warrior.

"You are quite large for a human male, your tribe must be proud," the warrior returned the compliment. "Epul on our shoulders grow with battle and mating, drinking the blood of our victories both in duels and rakture feed their growth to full maturity, a sign of our readiness to lead and spawn."

My eyes grew wide and uneasy at the spawning remark, and he noticed. "You should not worry, none of the warriors in this study wish to have spawnlings, they seek only to relieve their glands from harming their hearts. And even if they wished to spawn, they are honorable, and would discuss the bonding process that is necessary to breed.

"The trill are such prudes that I doubt any of them will find attraction in the study, and the unGor... they want a human who is interested in taking on more than one mate and have been avoiding all the humans who have shown interest in a necia warrior. I've kept the estreld candidates in a separate study because they are actively trying to procreate with humans regardless of mating them or not."

He explained as we walked through the halls. Then added, "Because of this I must add tests within the study instead of letting you all mingle freely and see what happens. Don't get me wrong, I do have a control study in the works with simply having them cohabitate together and see what happens."

He spoke like he was running the whole program and he saw the understanding flicker in my eyes when he smiled at me and introduced himself, "General Tensel, director of the Human Attraction Research Team."

And future commander of this ship, according to Sou-el.

"So, then you're who I talk to about why I was transferred from my original group?" William asked, and General Tensel glanced at him like he had forgotten he was following us.

"It's my job to ensure the study runs as smoothly as possible. I'm sure you'll be better suited to this new group."

"That wasn't an answer," he called him out on the avoidance tactic.

"No, it wasn't," General Tensel agreed, unperturbed by the aggression thrown his way. "It is not my place to disclose private data of other participants, but I'm sure you'll speak with him soon enough to find out for yourself."

He was speaking of the warrior William was interested in. General Tensel did not rise up the ranks of warriors by epul size alone, he was astute and knew more than he said, and he had said a lot.

I was left with my daughter, who threw her arms around me as soon as the sliding door opened to her closet of a room.

"Mom!"

I held her to me as General Tensel and William walked away. Our guide had told him he would take him to the lounge where he would find most warriors not on duty, including one of particular interest to him.

"I haven't been able to get a hold of you, and I was worried," she dragged me inside, "I stayed in my room hoping that you'd find your way here, and I didn't want to miss you."

"You know me, I get all turned around," I tried to make light of it. "My implant was replaced, and they changed my group assignment." On the tip of my tongue, I could feel the question bubble up inside me about how her day of interning with General Sou-el had gone today, or if she'd seen him?

"Request to link with H.A.R.T. Intern Becky Grady," my implant sounded in my ear.

"Accept," I said out loud, not sure if that's how it worked, but Becky's response back was enough to know it worked.

"Just tap behind your ear and say, 'comm. Becky', unless you meet another Becky, you shouldn't need to clarify more for it to message me while on the ship."

"Got it," I said while giving her another hug. It was nice to have her here, even though I was worried I'd signed up for something that I didn't fully understand.

Normally soft spoken, Becky surprised me by jumping into her day with excitement. She didn't meet up with General Sou-el today, or yesterday because she was having the most bizarre

experience with this communication device left in her room that sent her all the way to Trillume's labs to talk with the head of research in the Blue District. The unGor she had listed on her supervisory paperwork before realizing he was staying on Trillume and she'd join him when she arrived.

"The labs there are underground," she had said, but continued to describe the Blue District she saw, "They have a super filtration system through the building, and even have masks for different species to prevent them from being overwhelmed with various heightened senses. There are rooms like a high-tech brothel and aliens can sniff the sensors to see if they are a match, then the species inside will choose whether to allow them in or not. When you go there you basically get to walk down a super fancy building full of rooms, and choose which one you want to check out, and if you're allowed in then you have the night to spend time with each other, regardless of if you just talk or do more. The security is insane, and there are oncall warriors of all species, but they can literally spray the whole compound with the same filtration system used to clean the air, and balance out the room based on species needs, to knock out the room if you're in danger or even sanitize the space after use."

"Should I be concerned about your enthusiasm for a brothel?" I laughed awkwardly.

"Mom," she groaned, "it's not just a brothel, it's a safe space for all species to seek each other out for their needs without judgement, while also allowing scientists and researchers to learn more about interspecies behaviors. Plus, you know that's where you're going, right? They explained that to you? I mean, shouldn't I be asking you if I should be concerned?"

"You're right, Little Bean." I put my hands up in surrender, caught red-handed, or... blue-handed by alien standards. "Should you be concerned?"

"The facilities looked safe from all those kidnapping concerns the activists are rallying against on Earth. To be honest, we are more likely to be attacked during transit by planets that don't agree with the galactic alliance to include humans as members. So go ahead and get laid, but..." she puffed out her cheeks like she did when she was trying not to say something.

"Go ahead," I prompted. What could be worse than my daughter already knowing I was heading to an alien planet to figure stuff out. I bit my lip, really hoping she didn't ask about General Sou-el. My body still tingled thinking about what I'd done, and the way he thrashed after I told him I was married and then sprayed himself in the face with that Elder Sleep stuff.

"It's okay, you know. You tell me all the time that it's okay to go for what I want. That life isn't about failures and successes, it's about living. That's why it was so important that we both told you we were okay with this. Laurel is okay. I'm okay. Don't hold back your choices because of us."

I sniffled, and then laughed. I wasn't sure what I did to deserve them in my life, but it was strange hearing my own words repeated back to me with such seriousness. I had just recently said those same sentiments to them when they told me they wanted to look into schools and options away from home.

"I love you," I told her and squeezed her close before we spent the rest of the time watching Earth movies that were downloaded to the ship's database for humans to have a bit of home during the journey. There were also options for some alien entertainment as well, and we said we'd watch one of those next Thursday. There was a quiet acceptance between us, that we were both going to take chances and live while we were on this journey without thinking about whether the other would be okay about our choices.

"Mom," she asked softly before her eyes started drooping from exhaustion.

"Mmm hmm?"

"Statistically speaking, half of the humans who enter the exchange never want to return to Earth, and either never return, or immediately reapply to leave again."

I knew what she was asking me, without a question being asked. She felt valued being part of a team of researchers. She was excited, and it's possible at the end of her term, which would be longer than mine as an intern, she may not want to return to Earth. Her exchange was not just a temporary subject in an attraction study, she was starting a career, and she'd be on Trillume for at least a human year on planet, with a possible option to extend her contract if she proved herself.

I nuzzled my nose into the top of her sleepy head, inhaling that scent that was only possible with holding one of my daughters. It was pure serotonin squeezing her to me, and letting that feeling go, of never getting to hold her, to feel this love so deeply again, would break me. But I wouldn't hold her back.

"It's okay," I finally said as she drifted to sleep, curled up on the tiny, two-seater couch. Lifting her up onto the top bunk wasn't possible anymore that she wasn't seven years old, but a fully grown woman, capable of dreaming big dreams that might not include me or Earth.

When I exited her room, William was waiting for me. His eyes were bloodshot, and his skin a bit blotchy.

"I wasn't expecting you to wait for me... Have you been out here for long?"

"They don't record us when we're in this section of the ship."

I wrinkled my nose, yet another awkward hang up of mine I had to get over if I wanted to do anything on this ship. Being observed. My face flushed of color thinking about if Sou-el's room was recorded as well, if what we did was observed by someone on this ship.

I bit my lip, and watched William brood. He had something he wanted to say to me.

I waited for him to speak.

"He told me humans are like pets to necia warriors. They are meant to protect us, and like pets, we attach ourselves to the first source of attraction and comfort. He doesn't trust that what I'm feeling with him is more than that and won't go into rut over someone who will cling to the next source of comfort offered. 'Go seek comfort elsewhere', he said, 'then return to your Earth mate.'"

My heart pounded in my ears at his confession. He was married too?

"Earth mate?"

"I told you I did what was expected of me," he said and then cursed under his breath.

Sliding down the wall next to him, I commiserated. "Sounds like someone told him you had a mate, and he was upset."

"You weren't there."

"No, I wasn't," I agreed.

"He was disgusted, I've seen that look before, I just never expected it would be because I was human," he said while rubbing his face.

The anger in Sou-el's eyes when he sprayed himself with the Elder Sleep was still fresh in my mind, and I hadn't heard from him since. But maybe that was for the best. Would he do the same thing to me that was done to William? He'd come to his senses and remind me I was human, and he was necia, and that I was mated, and this was wrong.

"I'm still married," I confessed to him as a distraction from his own worries about being human. Something out of his control, and it wasn't worse than what I was doing.

He fake laughed and shook his head. "Guess that was part of the requirements for our group. Humans already married, but still choosing to leave for a study on attraction."

"Oh," I intoned, realizing my attempt at throwing myself under fire didn't succeed in distracting him at all, but compounded the issue.

"Everyone at home believes I'll be cured when I come home. Scratch the itch and realize fantasy and reality are just that, a decision, a choice to see delusion or what is in front of me."

"That's awful. I mean, if Holden were here, he'd tell us both to fuck that, and be happy."

He didn't even question who Holden was, or even lift his head from his hands to look at me.

"I do love my son. He's ten, and I can't abandon him for long. I will return, and I can't expect anyone I meet here to come to Earth for me. For now, he thinks it's cool that his dad is out in space, and the program pays well. My family is taken care of..."

"But," I added for him in understanding, "it's like being here has lifted a curtain from your head, and even though you'll return for your son, you don't want to return to how things were before... pretending to be happy when you were simply existing."

"I wasn't just existing," he snapped, an anger bubbled at the surface that I knew wasn't for me, so I stared ahead at a screw in the wall. He stood up then. I peeked up from my peripheral vision to see him clenching his fists with his back to me. "It wasn't me. You don't know me."

I could almost hear him in my mind saying exactly how I felt about my own life, "I don't even know me."

Our stories weren't the same, and our hurts were not comparable, but we were both lost and trying to figure out who we were and what we wanted.

"Fuck, why am I even talking to you about this?" He slammed his fist into the wall with a thud. If someone was in the room behind the wall they probably would have come out, but most of the crew was at the lounge, like General Tensel explained.

There was this strong urge to tell William all about my own troubles within the silence stretching between us, but as a mom I'd learned that my job wasn't to unload my burdens, it was to listen and let my daughters process their own life. I smiled realizing that I may not have talked to them about what was bothering me, but they saw it, and when it mattered, they supported my choice to come here, even if they didn't know why I made the choices I did in my life.

That didn't matter, because I wouldn't have changed them. Not when those choices gave me two wonderful daughters.

Eventually, William groaned and sat back down. "I don't know why I thought things would be different here," he began.

"Why do you like him?" I asked.

"Before all this shit? It felt like he saw me, and he didn't just sniff me and want to fuck. We could have, but he didn't. The tension was thick enough to cut, and we spent the whole night talking. He called me brave, when I've been a coward my whole life."

"You are brave," I affirmed. "I don't have to know you to know not many would have snuck out of their programs to go to the lounge on the other side of the ship to see a guy that basically ghosted them. To give them the benefit of the doubt about why they were gone."

"I didn't give him the benefit of the doubt," he denied. "I wanted to force him to face his decision to walk away. To look me in the eyes when he did it."

"You wanted to punish yourself..." I whispered, but he caught every word and shockingly laughed at my assessment.

"Fuck," he bemoaned with a forced chuckle. "Let's go fuck some aliens and move on."

He got up and offered me a hand to stand. I took it and saw the pain hidden behind the smile. He didn't want to do any of that. He wanted the alien that listened to him. The warrior that cared enough to know him first.

I wanted someone to actually listen to me too, I thought with an ache in my gut. I was used to listening, and so was William, as we hid behind our roles assigned to us in life, but it was rare to find someone who wanted to look at what was underneath the titles we carried.

I wasn't special. I wasn't worth more than a microbe within this universe. I didn't have some special talent, or remarkable intelligence.

I was just Renee.

And I was still figuring out who exactly that was. Even at forty-six years old talking to a young man in his early thirties.

I sighed, giving William a nod to return to our common rooms. All the while I was thinking of that fiery determination in Sou-el's eyes as he told me he'd challenge for rights to be my mate and knocked himself out so he wouldn't force some alien ritual on me that I knew nothing about. But those were words said in the heat of the moment, and when his mind cleared of whatever animal instincts his species had to procreate, he wasn't anywhere to be seen. Not even my daughter, his intern, had seen him.

My stomach turned in knots and I wondered if perhaps William was right about confronting what was painful, so there were no hopeful delusions to cling to. Was I a coward to allow myself to hope that what he said was real, and leave it alone?

I laughed without any outward influence or reason to do so, but William didn't question it, or ask why. It was ridiculous to think he meant any of those things. We only knew each other for a day.

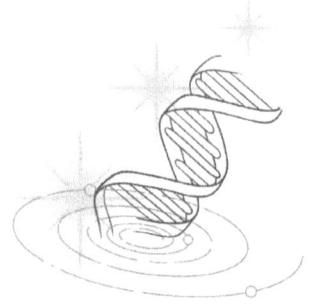

Chapter Eleven
General Sou-el

General Tensel's quarters were empty, or he was ignoring my request to see him. A message popped up on my contact implant informing me that the general was currently working with the research team, and I could leave a message of my own.

As politely as I could muster, I relayed that as General of Research that I would be overseeing his plans for the project, with authorization from the current commander.

That resulted in an immediate summons of direct communication while I stood outside his quarters.

"General Sou-el, you are just the warrior I was hoping to speak to," he said with an enthusiasm I did not relate with. As I had no such compunction for him. "You've done good work with confirming humans with possible necia DNA markers are capable of compelling rut-like bonding."

'Rut-like', he stated like what I shared with Renee was nothing more than a physical response promoting spawning. Perhaps it began that way, I thought logically, but she knew of my past and still she did not run from me. She was a human with thin, breakable skin, and yet she confidently stood before me and told me, 'no' when I insisted she be placed in stasis until we arrived on Trillume.

I'd be a fool to think she stayed because of me, but it was yet another strength of hers to fight to stay awake so she could spend time with her spawnling. I stopped myself from marking her without her truly accepting what was normal for my tribe, because I saw the way she didn't watch me with pity. When my sister explained my past... she saw honor and strength in fighting for family not of blood, but choice.

It wasn't until then that I realized how much I wanted to know a female wished to be with me... not because I had a title, large epul, or a sister that was a commander, but because they saw more.

I felt seen, and knew I couldn't have her. When she appeared disgusted after Rakva said I was a good choice for a mate, I stormed off with irritation for my sister throwing it in my face. I could hear the hesitation in Renee's voice when she said she was not interested, and I left.

General Tensel finished explaining that he had further use for me in the study and was hopeful I would agree to participate as more than a research advisory capacity.

"If you can have your human consent to mating without the influence of your enzymes or blood, then I will remove her from the program, and you may continue your mating rituals without interference."

The only way to do that would be to make sure we didn't touch and spray us both down with pheromone blockers.

"You wish to have me enter her group?"

"Not exactly. Similar to your own experiments, we will have several rooms with different participants, and you'll have a set amount of time with her like others will. Each time we will introduce different requests and gauge reactions."

"And should she choose me, you will capitulate her contract?"

"I would love nothing more than for you to prove that humans are not universally adaptable to matings. Or better yet, General Sou-el, it would please me greatly to know that a bond is not simply a matter of proximity and procreation."

"That is why you chose humans with mates, and with spawnlings. They have mated, and their body's necessity for procreation will not be as strong as humans in their prime," I surmised.

"You will make a fine research commander soon enough, Sou-el. I look forward to seeing the results of our experiment. Meet me at common lab phase two testing at sector 53."

The young general, soon to be commander in his own right, was very intelligent for his age, and I shouldn't have been surprised that he had planned ahead on what kind of humans were accepted on this research ship. I was merely a general of the research itself, and not given purview into the selection process, but only given a group of subjects with an outline of what kinds of questions could be answered within shorter experimental windows. Until I was promoted to Commander of Research I would not have full access to initiating my own theories. For a warrior so young to be leading a project like this was impressive, but he was asking me to suspend my belief that she was my mate, and prove it outside of traditional ritual of our tribe.

And I had only until we reached Trillume to convince my mate that we were meant to be together, while also challenging her previous mate's claim to her. A difficult task for the strongest of warriors, made more difficult with not knowing what it was that humans valued in their mates beyond data collected from obscure reports on the human species.

Not even humans had a full grasp on their own mating rituals. So much contradicting data that boiled down to a theory of proximity, pheromones, and familiarity. Of which, I am told I will have a limited amount of time, and unable to use the second, while the third was based on layering the others over time I did not have. Yet I agreed, as there was no other alternative to gaining access to her within the time we had.

When I arrived at sector 53, General Tensel was waiting for me, and ushered me inside one of the attached rooms to the common area Renee resided in. I was strapped down to a chair, blindfolded, and sprayed down with what I assumed were pheromone blockers.

Then I smelled her enter.

General Tensel's disembodied voice echoed in the room across the intercom unit, "You have as much time as you would like to speak with the warrior in the room. He cannot see you, and it is advised not to touch him, but you are welcome to if you wish. He does not know who you are, and however much time you give him, he will be required to spend that same amount of time with another when you leave."

Horve's vine, I cursed. General Tensel was going to force me to have another human to prove his theories when I had no desire to have anyone other than Renee. He may not have said that was who was in the room, but I knew her scent intimately, but she wouldn't know who I am, if she was blindfolded as well, and she certainly couldn't smell me after being sprayed.

"Okay," she said nervously, but her voice sounded different... altered. They put a modulator on her.

"Do not be afraid," I wanted to assure her, and let her know it was me, but even my voice was not the same, and cursed the restraint around my neck that included a modulator within.

General Tensel continued, "Part of this experiment is not revealing your identity, but you may discuss anything else. The cameras will be turned off, should either of your discussions include names the cameras will resume, and you will be asked to start again with another subject."

He was making this more difficult by the breath. I wanted her to know who I was, to know that I had come for her.

"Are you comfortable?" she asked, and I wondered if she was blindfolded or if she could see who I was? As she showed the same concern for me that she did with the experiment she viewed in my office.

"The restraints are for your comfort," I explained again in the same manner I had before, "we agree to this precaution so you do not fear touching us, as our epul can be intimidating to humans."

It may not have been exactly my voice, but I would hope she could see the similarities of my speech patterns.

"You agreed to see if you could bond with a human?" she asked with irritation, and I could smile if that was jealousy in her tone, but I schooled my features to neutral before replying.

"Just one human," I clarified. "I am of the belief that I've met my mate, but I'm required to prove this theory by having no reaction to other stimuli and earning the honor of marking her."

Her scent became stronger, and then I felt her touch at the base of my epul, just as the other human had done with the warrior in my own experiment. Was she seeing if I would react the same as he had? My nostrils flared with her scent, but with the sheen of nanobots protecting my skin from her and her from me, I wouldn't have the same reaction to her unless she touched beneath my clothes where the mist did not reach.

"So as long as you don't react, then she'll be your mate?"

I nodded, but again didn't know for sure if she was blindfolded as well, so I added, "Yes."

"Awfully bold of you to assume," she sounded... amused, and I couldn't be sure if that was a good or bad thing for humans. For a warrior, being amused while proving honor was considered an insult. This would indicate a steep mountain trial with low probability of success. Very rarely did a warrior come back from a Rakture with a mate that insulted him beforehand. They would return bloody from battle that was not part of a mating ritual but one of reclaiming lost honor.

I would not do such a thing with Renee. If she did not see me as worthy, then I would wait until I'd gained enough honor to try again. And if she denied me again? I didn't care to think on it, because I would lose all title, honor and begin anew within my tribe to seek out a mate that had already rejected me and fail again.

Many have banished themselves after such a blow.

"Necia warriors spend their lives working for honor within our tribe. It is not an assumption for us. It is only the young and desperate that assume."

"Okay," she conceded, her breath inches from my face. If I were not strapped to this chair, with a restraint around my neck, I'd pull her to me. "Then, prove to your mate that you can't react to anyone but her."

This was a dangerous game, I thought, as her finger trailed down my chest with no reaction. If I respond to her touch, then she could say I responded to someone I wasn't certain was her. If I don't respond, then I've proven to her that we are not mates. With the spray insulating my skin, all I have is her smell, and she can't see the way my eyes would dilate for her with a blindfold on.

"How would you like to prove that?" I asked, a possessive growl easy to come at the thought of having her touch me.

"Tell me what warriors like?" There was a shyness to her demand, almost a question lilting at the end. She was nervous, and I didn't wish to spook her.

"My glands are damaged," I informed her as her fingers splayed over my chest. My hearts beat against my ribs, wishing I could touch her, lick her, and take her essence into me. I licked my lips, which made her fingers curl against my skin. "I never thought I'd be worthy of any mate, but when I'm with her, I feel stronger. If you wish to prove something, you can tell me why you left Earth?"

I would never win honor with my mate if she thought all I needed her for was to regulate my glands. My glands have no use for a mate, and before her I never thought I would experience something physical that wasn't simply me trying to give and feeling nothing but regret that my enzymes would never balance another warrior's glands, nor would their fluid set my blood on fire.

"I--" she stopped and then started once more, "I get along with everyone." She sighed, but she did not remove her hand from me, instead she sat upon my lap. Her perfect ass, shifted along my cock to get comfortable, and if she continued, I would not be able to hide my interest. My hands itched to hold her, wrap around her waist, but they were strapped to the chair. Quickly, I withdrew my epul, not wishing to accidentally harm her.

Her hand moved up my chest and rubbed at my sore shoulders where a few drops of blood could be felt where the holes were trying to heal over.

I didn't mean to distract her from answering my question, but instead of talking about herself, she instead asked about me. Not many ever cared to wonder beyond the rumors that my glands couldn't provide for a mate. "Does it hurt?"

"Adrenaline within a warrior's body speeds up our healing properties in our blood. The second skin is normally numb to pain, as a spike of adrenaline heals over the wounds caused by moving our epul," I explained that many warriors do not feel the pain.

"Adrenaline produced by your glands," she read between the lines and there was a sadness in her voice. A warrior with damaged glands...

"You get along with everyone?" I prompted her to return to her explanation for joining the study. I didn't need her pity; it didn't serve me in proving my honor to her.

"It's easy to be liked, when no one knows you, and they feel comfortable with having you know them, listening to them."

My hearts ached for her to be surrounded by humans that gave her their own honor but did not honor her by getting to know who she was.

"What do you seek by leaving Earth? Leaving the ones that have yet to know you?"

"The chance to know myself. To feel something."

"I'm listening," I whispered.

"You are, aren't you?" Renee wrapped her arms around my shoulders and nuzzled into my neck. "How is it that I feel seen, and your eyes are covered?" she asked, a slight sniffle that made me tug at my restraints to hold her, only to be denied.

She was breaking, I could feel it. And I could do nothing.

Before I could say anything, she chuckled and remarked, "You could skewer me right now, and yet I don't want to let go."

"I would never harm you," I insisted. These restraints were preventing me from holding her properly and I growled, a low rumble in my chest making her head pop up, and I regretted my impatience. "I wish to hold you," I explained.

"You smell like disinfectant spray," she wrinkled her nose when she rested her head back down.

"So, my enzymes do not affect you or influence your decision to see me again."

"And how do I see you again?"

I smiled, and her fingers lightly tugged at a few strands of my hair playfully. I liked how it warmed me in a way I've never felt before to have her wrapped around me, with no expectations as she did as she pleased.

"I'll be at the lounge waiting for my mate to return to our room."

"Do you think she'll come?" she teased.

"I would love nothing more," I said with a groan, thinking about her coming on my tongue, clenching around my fingers.

I could feel her thighs flex as she sat on my lap, and my cock hardened beneath her ass. The resulting wiggle told me she felt me there, and her arms tightened around my neck as her breathing quickened.

Her soft lips pressed just under the metal strap around my neck, and there was just enough give on the restraints to shiver with a moan. My body remembered the heat her touch created, and even with the spray, my thoughts made up for the lack of electric pulses that her touch gave me the night before.

Fingers slid down my torso as her ass rotated and rubbed against me, before she pushed away and there was nothing I could do to stop her from leaving.

"When I left," she said absently, like her mind wandered and I was just a bystander to her thoughts, "I was terrified, but also relieved, like I was freed from expectations and all there was left was me and my choices. The problem is I still feel the grip of guilt that these choices will haunt me when I return to Earth."

Return to Earth, the words repeated like stab wounds to my hearts. Of course, she was free to return, but for a warrior like me, my visitation would be limited if sanctioned at all. General Tensel's theory was that warriors had already visited Earth before, and our DNA was within a few humans, generations later, enough to have highly compatible mates, even in a time of fertility decline. Even still, those warriors would have had strong enough glands to fight against the toxic atmosphere of Earth.

I said nothing, allowing her to process her thoughts. It was an easy task to listen to her, even without my training as a researcher, because I was eager to know more of what went on in that mind of hers.

"Does it make me a coward that I don't want to return?"

"No," I said immediately, wishing to solidify this thought of staying with me, of not returning to Earth. "If you are running towards something, then how can it be called running away? In which case, it is not a coward's move, but one of strength and bravery. Returning to familiarity can also be considered running from what could be your future."

"What future?" she asked wistfully.

"Whatever future you want."

"And what about you?"

The question caught me off guard.

"What about me?"

"What future do you want?" she asked.

One with her in it, I thought, but I knew that wasn't what she wanted me to say. She wanted to know what kind of future I could give her. What kind of future we would have would involve her giving up everything she's known.

Doubts about whether I would be a good mate for her resurfaced. Not just about my damaged glands and what I could provide physically like many warriors would demand, but what of our future. Traditionally, a warrior would give up their jobs and follow their mate, caring for their spawnlings, honoring our tribe and teaching the next generation. But I could not follow her to Earth, and her spawnlings are grown, I would honor the spawnling that came to learn by training her for her post at the Blue District labs, but beyond that, what could I give her?

"I'm soon to be promoted, with my choice of placements. With the fertility crisis across the galaxy, I considered behavioral analysis of survival bonds. Placing potential mates who all show similar levels of biological compatibility but putting them in an unfamiliar environment to see which traits are preferred. Evolutionary theories say bonds will be formed with mates that are adaptable and capable of surviving the environment, while mates with no skills will not bond."

"I'd probably fail that study," she said with a laugh.

"I don't theorize we pick our mates this way. I believe, even if the mates do not have strong survival skills that they would still fight and work together to survive and keep their less skilled mate. There will be mates that like being a provider, keeping their mate safe. But more importantly, survival is more than our bodies, because if it weren't then I would have died before ever meeting you."

"Are you saying I'm the more skilled mate in this scenario?"

"You have accomplished more than I ever will," I told her truthfully. She has mated, honored the universe with her spawnlings, and bravely left her own planet to escape the pressures of her tribe. Not once had I ever considered going against my tribe's wishes. Even now, I had the full approval from my sister, the commander, to pursue my mate. I may have been away from my planet, but I had never left my tribe.

"You will help future generations with your research," she defended and then sighed. "I have nothing left to give. No skill to contribute."

"What I'm beginning to understand, even after all my years of research, is that you don't have to give to receive someone's affections. Beyond physical attraction there is an acceptance of being understood. To be seen by someone. I am still uncertain how to prove this theory of shared truth, but in my tribe the elders would say every action in our lives changes our very D. N.A., and it is our body that knows the truth before our minds and hearts accept what the goddess has gifted within each other. This is what mates are, two truths recognizing each other."

I've never spoken so much in my life, but with her, I can't help but share whatever is on my mind. It isn't simply that she listens, which is something she's been forced to do as a guardian of spawnlings, but that I want her to know, and I wanted her to know I could be trusted with her own thoughts as well.

"Two truths recognizing each other," she repeated, contemplating how she felt about this theory rooted within my tribe's belief in the goddess. I was a warrior of science, but even myths and legends were rooted in our minds trying to make sense of the unexplainable. Whether the goddess existed doesn't matter, the truths of what she represented may yet to be explained, but that didn't make them any less true, as they have yet to be disproven.

There was no other explanation for me except that Renee of Earth made a series of decisions in her life that led her here, with me, in this moment for her to understand and see me, just as I had lived through decision that led me here to see her. Some of those actions were out of our control, and others were purposeful decisions including the one to be in this room, instead of letting her go.

Finally she spoke again, "I've been attracted to mates before, felt my body react, and they were not my friend. This was biology seeking to populate the world. My body lied to me about their truth, about who I could trust.

"I chose someone that I could trust with my heart, and my body lied to me again, feeling nothing when we touched. You're telling me to trust the truth in what I feel, when everything I've felt has proven otherwise. If your theory is correct, then I'm an outlier in your data set and none of it applies to me. I wanted everything, and so I will have nothing in my greed."

The sound of the door sliding open and closed was the only indication that she had left me there stunned as something I never thought I would feel since I was a spawnling made the wrap around my eyes dampen with shedding moisture.

I had more work to do to prove my honor to her than I thought, as there was more than a mountain between us, there was a chasm of hurt that couldn't be filled with a single overture. Mates from her past have only attended to one aspect of her happiness, and neglected the others. This was something the elders would say only time and persistence will heal, but I had very little of those resources available and I had to find a way to make it up to her before we reached Trillume.

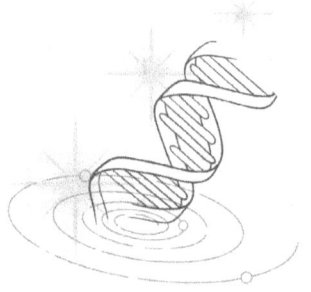

Chapter Twelve
Renee

This was temporary, I told myself over and over again. Getting involved with General Sou-el was a lesson I'd already learned before, and didn't have the strength to work through what ever it was between us. He wasn't officially part of the study, no matter what he did to get in that room earlier, he was a researcher, not a participant. He was promising more when more was never guaranteed. Hormones wore off over time, and what I'd be left with would be mind-blowing sex, and a broken heart. The body lies. There was no such thing as having both, and thinking there was would only lead to my ruin.

This adventure was always meant to be temporary. A free pass to feel something physically and then return to Earth and the security of living out my life in peace. There were known expectations, and no promises to be broken. I was hoping it would confirm that I'd feel nothing for everyone, and my long ago memories of feeling something as a teen would just be memories of when my body was in its prime for reproduction.

General Sou-el reawoken that inner part of me from when I was a teen, that hopeful passion before I met Tyler. That physical craving. And in that room, blindfolded, he knew who I was, and he promised me more. Something too good to be true, and nothing he could prove without first risking that he was wrong.

I don't believe he was lying, but our bodies lie, and by the time our minds and hearts catch up the lie destroys what remains of our hope until there isn't much hope to hang on to for the next blinded victim of our body's lies.

The program was safer. Everyone knew what to expect, which was nothing.

I'd spent a half hour in the room with him, and I was scheduled to spend that exact amount of time with another participant, but this time I'd be blindfolded.

I wasn't required to be strapped down like a warrior, but I sat on the chair with my blindfold and waited until the whoosh of air marked the entry of another participant. Their voice would be altered like mine was, and we'd talk or touch, which ever we wanted.

I was determined to force myself to prove that I could feel the same way about General Sou-el as I did about any warrior that entered, so I could move on.

My arms were folded over my chest and I could hear a chuckle from the male in the room with me. Guess only one participant was blindfolded at a time.

"I imagine your silver eyes are just as fierce under that blindfold to match the set of your jaw, and the strength of posture. Do you plan on fighting me?"

"No," I said trying to relax my shoulders, and sighing. "I'm just wondering what kind of information they get about attraction by only blindfolding one participant?"

"There's a vulnerability in having the senses altered or blocked, forcing the subjects to trust, and search for connection when normally it is an animalistic tendency to seek out things to exclude someone as a mating option," he said in a way I imagined Sou-el would explain things. Would they really put the same warrior in the room again, but switch roles?

What were the chances that all the subjects I was placed with would be researchers on the ship?

When I was the one that saw Sou-el, I was doing exactly what he was saying now. I was looking for things to push him away. And as I was blindfolded, I found I was looking for something that connected us. Was I really that easy to manipulate?

Nothing more than an animal that followed instincts to either procreate or survive.

"Fight, Flight, or Freeze," I whispered.

"In the tribe, we often fight or chase our mates. A mate who freezes is often killed when our epul come in, as they are likely to do nothing when it matters most, when lives are at risk, when mates need us most, and when our spawnlings need us most," he sounded like this lesson came from experience, the pain in his words despite the vocal changer that obviously made his voice sound deeper than it was.

Did this have to do with his own childhood? The commander told me how he was almost killed by his own parents, strapped to the cliffside as the tides came in. Was that their way of proving he wasn't a child who froze, but fought to live? What a harsh lesson to learn so young...

Guilt tugged at my heart for pushing him away. He had every reason to not trust people after being harmed by his own parents, and yet he was trying to trust me with his hearts. I was such a bitch. There was something to this whole being blindfolded thing that he spoke of. Seeking out connection when you are missing a sense you're used to relying on.

I smiled and reached out my hand for him. His footsteps came closer and his hand slipped into mine, squeezing gently.

"Your skin is so soft," he said breathlessly.

I smiled awkwardly and chuckled. "Your skin is soft too."

"Ah, scales are smooth, but if you press them, they are firm as the toughest alloy, capable of withstanding many weapons. When I squeeze your hand, I can feel your skin give to my touch to the bone beneath, and yet I can feel the heat of your touch reach deeper than where our fingers meet."

His thumb rubbed against the top of my hand, and I felt what he meant as my skin tingled until my stomach clenched as I remembered how his tongue had seared into my core until he devoured my come.

He took my hand and placed it on his firm abs to press into his scales that were soft, yet hard as rocks.

"Do you feel this?" he asked with a growl, and I nodded, knowing he didn't mean the firmness of his abs, but the tension building between our bodies seeking for us to touch each other more. "A warrior has enzymes in their pores that activates when touched by a compatible mate. When you ingest our blood, we begin bonding, sensing where you are, feeling what you feel, and seeking to solidify that bond with our D.N.A. inside of you. We only have one chance to create a matebond with the same partner, because we begin creating a compatible enzyme once we are given our mate's blood. It's considered nonconsent within our tribe to bond after giving our blood, we should seek to be given blood first."

My breath hitched remembering how I reacted after licking blood from his knuckles, and how he sat there on the bed cutting himself, bleeding for me.

He knocked himself out because he didn't want to finish something without consent, true consent within his tribe. Me offering him blood first.

"You have my permission to drink my blood, but I will not give it without first being offered yours," he said as my hand, held within his, traced up his chest.

There was something erotic about being blindfolded and letting myself feel, but I wasn't ready. I needed to know that this was more than physical. He just admitted to me that what we experienced in his office was a reaction to taking his blood and couldn't be trusted even in his own tribe's laws.

"I took a sample bead from the office," I admitted, while digging into my pocket with my free hand. I had to stand and I could feel his breath on the top of my head. Holding it up to him. I didn't have the nerve to fill it yet, but he'd know what I was offering.

"Does anyone know that you took this?" he asked, and his nose nuzzled into my hair, inhaling my scent.

I shook my head, and he then lifted my palm up to his mouth. His fang traced along the meat of my palm beneath my thumb, not breaking skin, but my heart raced none the less.

"Are you offering me a token of your blood?"

Nervous, I explained, "Commander Rokva told me about how warriors used to wear tokens of blood in their hair." I had already stripped a bit of black cloth from my clothes to braid a ribbon to attach the bead to, but hadn't added my blood yet.

"I'd be honored," he said before his tongue licked out, tingling my skin, and pressure dug into my palm as his lips closed over. A soft pull made me lightheaded, and I whimpered, falling against his chest as he drank from me. He kissed my hand, and delicately grabbed the bead and pressed it against the puncture, filling the offering. It didn't hurt at all.

"I only grazed your skin with the tip of my fang at a percise angle similar to what humans call a papercut. It should heal much quicker than other wounds. Will you braid this into my hair?" He closed the bead and ribbon into my palm, and I heard him shift to kneel while he leaned his head against my stomach. I took a few strands of hair and braided the ribbon in, with a smile plastered to my face.

I didn't know what would come of allowing him to pursue me as a mate, but for a little while, I enjoyed feeling wanted, and a tiny bit of hope bloomed in my heart.

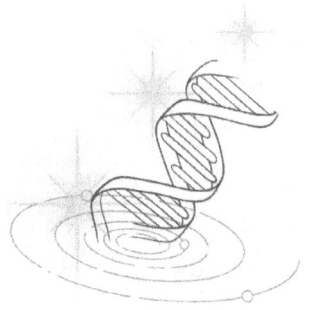

Chapter Thirteen
General Sou-el

I waited in the lounge, my eye catching on every new arrival, waiting for one of them to be Renee. It was foolish to think she would come the first rotation after confessing that I believed we should trust that we both see our truths, and are meant to be together, but slowly, I would bridge that gap between us. My eyes shot up once more to be disappointed in the face that wasn't hers scanning the lounge. General Tensel walked in with an air of confidence and a smile that could make any warrior kneel to serve before his eyes landed on me.

"General," a warrior cooed as he passed, her legs parting in invitation. The lounge was one of the places on the ship where it wasn't uncommon to walk in on warriors bathing each other. With his status, and his promotion to commander soon, he had his pick of any warrior on this ship.

He smiled at her and with a soft chuckle that had the warrior biting her lip, he replied politely, "I've already bathed today, Ginva." She nodded with disappointment and closed her legs lest another warrior think she's inviting them to bathe. "I'm in Rakturan. It is a time of celebration," he called out to the room and warriors cheered. It was then that I spotted the leathers braided through his hair with a mate's offering, and his words repeated in my mind how he bathed already. The bead dangling from his auburn strands was similar in coloring, red. An offering of blood for him to keep near and become accustomed to their scent.

He didn't say Rakture... he said Rakturan, his mate was previously mated. Rakture was a duel of the hearts, either against a competing mate, or to prove yourself to your future unne bond.

My hearts beat wildly against my ribcage and an uncontrollable urge to fight surfaced within me. Whose blood did he take?

General Tensel took that moment, as I gripped the table about to leave, to sit across from me with that insufferable smirk.

My nostrils flared, smelling her on him. Renee? I looked to the doors to the lounge expecting to see her there, but she was not there, and my eyes shot to him, then to the offering in his hair.

I forced myself to calm and asked, "I did not realize you were eager to mate so early in your service. Who is the lucky warrior?"

"I'm glad you asked, Sou-el," he dropped titles once more like we were friends. "She is quite special. Unafraid, her words so pleasantly free, and blessed by the goddess our biomarkers are compatible. I have no need for a mate eager for spawn, as you pointed out, I'm still very early in my career, and she will be a refreshing first mate for the remainder of her life."

My grip bent the edge of the table, the only sign of my annoyance.

"A human then," was all I had to say to prompt him further. He would mate a human he was merely 'compatible' with to amuse him for the remainder of her days, until he outlived her, then chose a new mate. At least he was honorable enough to accept mating a human through their lifespan, but he had no misgivings that his blood would prolong her life, that they would bond so completely their lifespans would merge. They were compatible, that was all, and he found her to be refreshing to talk to. It was true, many warriors were not casual with him, giving him respect, and not speaking freely with him, as I would now do.

"You've dishonored me, Tensel, and you know what you've done."

I stood from the table; the edges bent where I grasped them to restrain myself from harming the future commander of this ship.

"You should be praising this turn of events in our study, Sou-el. The data would not be accurate to offer a rival mating that was less than the one presented to her. A general soon to be promoted to commander, there was no other warrior that fit the study's need to confirm that humans with the gene marker are highly compatible across our species having nothing to do with status or first contact, but simply proximity. She has your blood in her system, I could smell you on her, but blindfolded, she still responded to me, offered me her hand, then her blood."

I growled in warning, other warrior's attention shifted in our direction to see what would happen. Fighting in the lounge was prohibited, but we could take this to the dueling hall. Through gritted teeth I had to ask, "Did you give her your blood, knowing she did not know who you were?"

"Of course not, I'm not an ancient beast," his comment was deliberate as he smiled at me. His unspoken words, like you, rang through my head. It was true, I had been blinded by my increasing adrenaline when I was locked in a room with her. Acting on instinct, I cut myself for her, which was not against our customs when courting a mate, but she was human. There were laws protecting weaker species, their bodies were not designed as ours were, so laws were made even before humans, for warriors that survived into tribal initiation but did not have the capability of withstanding normal mating customs were protected by law, and by extension any species that did not have epul had to be courted with consent unaltered by first blood.

Many times, we resort to the Rakture custom of having the other species duel us, if they win then they are shown capable of making us bleed, and therefore capable of consenting to bath in their victory of drinking our blood.

I had drawn my own blood for her, and first blood was not consented by traditional Rakture, mating duel.

Seeing the guilt on me, he continued, "As she has provided me with her own offering, I am within my right to give her my blood, but as I did not accept her offering merely to prove my theory, I will be courting her as tradition dictates, and removing all claim her Earthly mate may have over her. I will gift her my blood in a token that she may choose to take for herself without being lured by its scent or after having absorbed my enzymes, free of influence. I will, of course, tell her what necia blood can do to a human, how it can manipulate their body into reacting regardless of actual interest in a future."

He was telling me this, because that was what I had done to her. She deserved to know, but that wasn't all it was to me. I stopped myself, and even though her blood had been neutralized in my system, I still saw our future together. This would be yet another blow to her trust in us. She was already speaking of how our bodies lied to us, and she was right, because as her eyes and ears were blinded, she gave General Tensel her offering.

I controlled my features, and plastered a fake smile of my own as I looked down at him still sitting so relaxed and confident before me. "Do not fool yourself into thinking that offering was meant for you," I told him plainly, ignoring that he would soon be my superior. Regardless of our titles being the same, a commander of the ship was always higher than a commander of research within the tribe.

He shook his head, that smile lifting to show me his fangs. His hand lifted to pinch the ribbon in his hair and brought the offering to his nose and inhaled deeply. It was like salt to an open wound as he enjoyed what was not his to take. "I'm on suppressants to prevent rut, but I can feel my glands activating regardless with her blood in my system. My enzymes are adapting to bring her more pleasure when she asks me to bathe her."

I growled, and he stood from his chair in challenge.

"I will take her in front of our tribe," he taunted, "for all to hear her screams." My blood boiled, but if I fought him here, he would win. I would be restrained for punishment while he was free to continue proving to her that he was more honorable than me as a mate. If I were a normal warrior, I would have already attacked him, but I knew I would lose in a fight right now, more likely to bleed out than to prove anything of worth.

He was a young warrior with strong glands, and without the same pain that came with using my epul without a numbing agent, or the help of nanobots to help heal my wounds. Trained for battle, while I was trained for research.

Research that told me his body language indicated he was not lying about wanting to make Renee his mate. Whether it started off as simply wishing to prove he could have what another general coveted didn't matter. It was real for him now, just as it was real for me.

"I accept your challenge," I gritted. "Your Rakturan includes me. As I have officially challenged your claim, you are required by law to allow her the freedom to go where she pleases, with whomever she chooses."

"Of course," he said with a smile and placed his fist to his chest. "Her implant should have access to anywhere she wants to go."

I nodded and left before I did something I'd regret. I had to keep reminding myself that logically there was no reason for her to have made that token for General Tensel. He was trying to convince me that what I was feeling for Renee was simply biological. Something that could happen to anyone, as it happened to him. The goddess couldn't have made us both her fated, so if she went with General Tensel then he was disproving ancient beliefs in a bond so powerful to be called Pulsunne, the song of one's hearts. He was willing to bet his own future of taking her on as his mate for however long she lived to prove a theory that Pulsunne's were myth. He knew what I felt for her, and that's exactly why she was chosen.

A human that triggered a rut-like state with a warrior known for having non-functioning glands. His interest in her, and in me didn't start until after reports from my brother Cenkal. He was determined to prove a fated bond was nothing more than overactive biology, even if that meant bonding himself.

My back to him, I asked one final question before taking my leave, "Will you still seek to disprove the theory when a broken warrior like me is chosen?"

For someone so young, he seemed so certain life was nothing more than instinct and biology. Perhaps, I would have been the same if I hadn't kept proving it wrong test after test. I should have died against the rocks as the tide came in. I should have died again when my epul grew, and during tribal initiation once more. There should be no scientific explanation for why her blood made my glands function, when they haven't worked even with medbots. I was an anomaly that shouldn't be possible, but I was.

I survived, broken, yet alive.

Broken, yet I found a mate.

And he wouldn't be the reason we failed.

He never answered me, and that was also an answer of a kind. My anger ebbed with the surety that Renee was my Pulsunne.

I only had to break down her walls and prove my honor to her, and to her spawnling. My mate held much respect for my intern's thoughts, and I would gain every advantage afforded to me. Renee spoke of the lies our bodies told us, but what she didn't understand was that if our bodies reacted as they should, it wouldn't be me that she responded to, but General Tensel alone.

General Tensel was everything a mate should want physically, and though I didn't like who'd he'd chosen to pursue, he was an honorable warrior. He was who she should want if her body ruled everything. There was no competition logically between myself and him, but that didn't matter. Because we were proof that biology wasn't everything, because if our body's simply wanted to procreate there was no reason for her to pick me.

And yet, everything in me knew she would.

She was my hearts' fate.

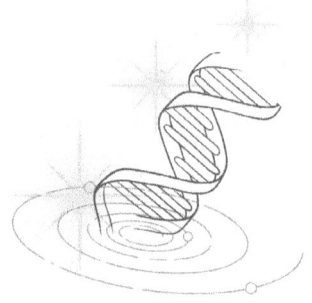

Chapter Fourteen
Renee

Rotating my palm up, I could see a small cut under my thumb where Sou-el took my blood, and I blushed. I'm not sure why such a small act made me feel so giddy, but I wanted him to prove to me that our bodies knew before we did that we were meant to be. When I was younger, I knew what it felt like to be attracted to someone. When I was older, I knew what it meant to be truly cared for by someone. But, to have them both was a nice fantasy to hope for.

Someone that could fulfill me body and soul.

I giggled to myself as I rubbed at the papercut from his fang. It didn't hurt at all, and there was something erotic about being blindfolded and only seeing him in my mind as I held his hand and felt his hearts beating, pulsing through his soft scales.

When he was strapped to the chair the first time, it took all my strength not to tear open his pants and explore what he denied me in his room before. His cock was so hard, pressing up against my ass as I straddled him. It made me feel like a teenager again. Horny and with a hopeful desire that if it felt this good, how could this feeling be wrong?

He hesitated when I was the one blindfolded, and I didn't blame him. Not after I left him so abruptly telling him that our bodies were liars, and this wasn't anything more than lust and attraction.

Nervous, I buzzed at Becky's door. I needed to sort through some things, and she was the only one I felt comfortable talking to about it.

"Oh good," she said as she tugged my arm through the door and closed us into the closet-sized space. "I thought you might be the general."

"The general?" I questioned, since it didn't appear to be a good thing. She looked relieved that I wasn't him. My heart sank at the prospect that she didn't like Sou-el.

"Nothing bad... yet." Becky plopped down on to the two-seater couch below her bunk. "It's just that," she groaned, "I don't want to get fired from my internship."

"Why would you get fired from your internship?" I was getting angry just thinking about it. Thoughts of storming up to Sou-el and demanding explanations made me grip the couch cushions with a bit more force than necessary.

"You know how office romances only work out in books and movies," she explained, and then my heart was stabbing at me for a completely different reason. Was I jealous of my daughter? I was much too old to be having a relationship with an alien, and she was young and beautiful, with a talent for research.

I bit my lip and made myself listen, because if she liked Sou-el that way, I couldn't bear to have her be heartbroken because of me. It was natural for students to get crushes on their teachers, or figures of influence.

"I doubt he'd fire you from your internship for liking him," I assured her. He didn't seem the type.

Becky rubbed her face. "I'm hiding out here, so I don't accidentally run into *her*. I only saw her in passing a few times, but I tingle all over when I do. I know, I know," she shook her head, "General Sou-el told me that humans are more susceptible to alien pheromones, which is why I'm avoiding her all together."

"Wait," I stared at her with confusion, "Who are you talking about?" She clearly used the pronoun 'her' and wasn't talking about General Sou-el...

"Uh, no, weird. I've seen him eye-fucking you when you weren't looking, and I'll have no part of that."

I sighed with relief, and Becky grinned at me in recognition.

"Leave it to you, mom, to pick someone not even in the program to be interested in."

"I'm nervous," I admitted. "But, let's talk about who this general is?" I wanted to know more about who she was interested in, and I didn't realize she was interested in girls the same way her sister was? That was news to me. She never really seemed interested in anyone before, male or female.

Becky's elation sobered. "You thought you wouldn't meet anyone you liked, and return to dad? Mom," she sounded like she was chastising me, the roles reversed from parent to child, "I talked with dad," she began, and I knew she was going to say what I already knew going into this, her hand landed on my knee in support, "He just wants you to be happy."

I choked on a sob. Why did Tyler have to be so fucking perfect? He was a soft place for my soul to land after so many heartbreaks. The reason I was so healed to even be here at all, was because he loved me. My best friend, and I was betraying him. Why did my daughters have to be so perfectly understandable and supportive? She was focusing on me instead of telling me more about her interest in this general.

"No, no, no," Becky soothed, trying to wipe at my cheeks, and I felt even more awful for putting this on her shoulders. What a mess I was. She should be able to talk to me about anything, and I was here talking about my own troubles. "I didn't mean it that way. He loves you and told me he should have let you go a long time ago, but he was selfish and comfortable. He gave me a big hug and told me he wants all his girls to find passion in life and not settle for less. He was what you needed to be ready to love again, and you're still his best friend. Make mistakes, be passionate, and maybe one of those times you'll find the kind of love we all hope for."

"When did you become so wise?" I hooked her head with my elbow and brought her into my chest to squeeze.

"Whatever," she said with a chuckle. "Just stop crying. You're probably getting snot in my hair."

"Gross," I joked and rubbed my chin into the top of her head to pretend I was wiping my snot on her. She pushed away and playfully batted at me to stop.

I took a deep breath and asked her seriously, "Tell me more about this general of yours?"

"Later, I'm not really ready for that. Hence, hiding out in my room. But maybe, if I still see her when I'm on Trillume... when she's off duty, maybe?"

I assumed this general was a necia warrior and instead diverted to what we would both have interest in, "Do you have a file on necia customs? I was wondering how you go about dating a warrior?"

"You've come to the right place," she boasted, confirming my suspicions that this general was a necia warrior. "They are a very open species when it comes to mating. I've been observing some of the other groups and it gets hot in there when a couple decides to bath each other. So, you have to be okay with public displays of affection, and please for the love of my future eye-sight, make sure I'm nowhere near your activities with General Sou-el. I'd like to still have eyeballs by the end of my internship, and I'd rather not pluck them out by seeing you do stuff."

"How do they handle children in these scenarios?" I wondered.

"Ah, spawnlings," she said with a nod, "Everything I can find so far makes me think they have a designated area for bathings and during ceremonies they are kept with elders until they are initiated into the tribe, like a coming-of-age ceremony. But they certainly don't hide their activities from the spawnlings, it is considered normal like it is in the animal kingdom on Earth. Privacy is a social construct, and many of the rooms here are never locked, excepting offices that may have sensitive information or supplies.

"They even accept more than one mate for procreation if their chosen mate is the same gender. Apparently, warriors think it a great honor to be chosen by a same sex mated coupling and give their genetics to their offspring."

"Being a species with honor, they have a lot of trust that their tribe will respect their laws," I mused, thinking of the trust that would take to not lock their doors, or share their mates with another.

"Most of the ship's warriors are on some kind of suppressant that holds back their instincts to rut when around a compatible mate. Even the attraction studies have warriors on suppressants, so that they comply with their laws involving consent of species that can't defend themselves against ancient rituals of courtship."

"Have you already seen warriors in rut?" I asked in surprise.

She giggled. "Sorry, that's not very professional, is it? I have access to a bunch of videos and files on mating and attraction that I'm allowed to study. When the commander dismissed me, I came back here and studied. They have a ritual called Rakture where the mates fight each other and it's meant to prove the male can defend their mate, but also prove the female is capable of strong offspring. It goes until first blood, where if the female mate makes the male bleed first, they have a choice to bathe in their victory, but if the male makes the female bleed first then they can claim their right to bathe in their victory. Females are known to be stronger than the male warriors, so for a male to get first blood is a sign they are either strong or the female approves of the mating match.

"Pretty remarkable, right?"

"It sounds like a documentary on animals," I admitted with concern. I was not a warrior with any skill to battle for a mate like that, and if that was a tribal expectation I was screwed.

"They also have Rakturan rituals where they prove themselves to already mated warriors. It's a less violent practice, where they make offerings to one another, and eventually do a claiming ritual in front of the tribe where the warriors prove no one could take care of the mate better than them."

"And how do you do that one?" I asked, a little too eagerly.

"They trade tokens of blood with one another, so their connection grows. When both have traded in blood then they prove the bond is formed by having one of the mates run away, and the other must hunt them. They claim them with the tribe as witness."

My heart raced thinking of Sou-el tracking me through a forest while I had no intention of hiding from him. A smile tugged at the sides of my mouth and though I'd never been chased before the idea wasn't all that unappealing. But we weren't on a planet with a forest, and I'd known him for less than a week. Thinking about rutting, and mating are two very different things. Was I ready for something like that?

Maybe?

It'd been so long since I've felt anything with anyone that way. If I was being honest with myself, I've never felt that way about Tyler. He was safe. He was kind. And he loved me. His love and safety were a balm to my soul, but there was never passion, never that need in my gut that drove me to see how he was doing. No drive to go see him, like there was with an alien I hardly knew.

He said he'd be at the lounge, waiting for me.

I smiled at the thought.

No one had ever waited for me. Tyler would be there for me when I asked, but he never did anything without being asked. Unless I asked him to wait for me, he wouldn't.

Sou-el was waiting for me, I thought with giddiness. Squeezing my daughter's hand, I stood up, and told her, "I have somewhere I need to be."

"Go get him," she encouraged while swatting at me to get out of there.

"I'm going, I'm going," I said with a lightness I hadn't felt in a long time for someone other than my daughters.

With access to see my daughter, I was also granted the ability to go to the lounge the ship staff used as well, and I was thankful, I wouldn't have to detour to get an escort.

I could see crew members coming and going from the double doors that led to the chatter and sounds of various aliens relieving their stress with socializing, and other activities. Moans could be heard from inside, and I paused, considering if I should keep going.

The social concept of being so free with things such as pleasure regardless of audience was new to me, considering on Earth we would get arrested for indecent exposure. I didn't think we even had any nude beaches anymore, though I did see such things mentioned in movies as being allowed before.

With a deep, strengthening breath, I took another step. This was okay, I repeated to myself, this was natural for the necia warriors, no need to be embarrassed.

"Human?" a warrior grunted as they passed me.

Another bumped into them and said, "There were a bunch of them added to the research teams, most of them stick to the labs."

"Skittish creatures," he grumbled as he assessed me.

Awkwardly smiling, I tried to pass, but the other warrior female growled, "Its baring its teeth at us. Like their blunt, brittle fangs would do any damage to us." She scoffed, and dragged the warrior around me, disappearing down the hall.

"Ignore them," a deep voice commanded. I turned back to see General Tensel smiling at me from the doorway. His red hair was braided back on the sides, loose behind his shoulder epul. "Many warriors still hold onto the honor that humans are much too fragile to be considered more than pets we care for. It is our duty to protect those weaker than us, and they find it dishonorable to take advantage of your species by pretending you are not vulnerable without our help."

"And your thoughts?"

"There is more to your species than your packaging. I was trained as a warrior, but my curiosity was never sated with simply testing my body limits. Come, sit with me for a moment," he insisted with a charming offer of his hand.

"Uh, I was--"

"Looking for someone else," he finished for me, and wasn't deterred, "I will wait with you, should he come. I have a story to share, if you'll listen."

I sighed, and nodded politely, taking his hand. It was something I was used to, listening to people, what was one more added to the list?

When we walked through the doors, I immediately scanned the room for Sou-el, but I didn't see him. My eyes took in a lot more than I ever thought I'd see. There were tables of crewmembers drinking and talking, but there were also warriors propped up on the bar with their legs spread and another warrior between their legs as they panted, grabbing their hair as they grinded against their face. Other warriors watched them with their hands in their pants, touching themselves. Turned on, other warriors grabbed those warriors to put their hands to better use on a partner, as they licked each other's skin. Moans filled the room, as I was led to an empty table to sit at.

I squirmed in my seat, oddly tingling from the atmosphere of lust surrounding us.

"If you're uncomfortable, we can talk somewhere else?" he offered.

I leaned over the small table bolted to the floor to ask, "How do you ignore it?"

He laughed gently. "Why would I do that? It pleases me that my tribe is keeping up their health and attending their needs so they may focus on their tasks more efficiently. If I were not sated, then I'd join them."

"Oh."

"Do you not feel the pull in your body to join?" he asked, and I felt my thighs clench as I averted my eyes from what was creating the moans echoing beside us. He sniffed the air and smiled. "I'll take that as a yes." Seeing my wide eyes as my shoulders tensed up he added, "No need to worry, no one will force themselves on you. You are free to do as you please."

"You said you had a story," I diverted the conversation, while I glanced over to the entrance to see if Sou-el had come in. He didn't.

"Necias Prime had some more barbaric customs in ancient tribes that displaced warriors that never grew epul."

I cringed thinking of what Sou-el had gone through as a child.

"By displaced, you mean--"

"We killed them," he finished for me with a straight face, no emotion one way or the other about it, "We have since adopted customs of warrior's rites, and banish those that try to kill a spawnling before they are tested. But that is not my story.

"I have a theory that some warriors with this condition some-how made it to Earth many centuries ago. They may have been considered giants by your species being larger to accommodate epul, but not having anything beneath their second skin. Your ancient myths of gods and monsters may have included species that made it to Earth and found themselves without resources to leave once they arrived."

"Did you have space travel even back then?" I wondered about the possibility of aliens having made it to Earth in our own ancient times. History has had some strange events that were unbelievable at the time. It was possible.

"Our tribes did not," he said with disappointment, "this is why many would not believe my theories that any of our kind would have escaped being killed and somehow been found by a spacefaring species to then somehow land on Earth. Many ifs and not enough evidence, but it's been a few centuries since we've joined the Galactic Alliance under Trillume rule, and I'm firmly of the belief that the trill had come to our planet well before they invaded and challenged our king.

"Any smart ruler would observe our customs and plan whether to attack, trade, or challenge us. It is entirely possible a trill came to our planet and helped outcast warriors that might have been killed or had spawnlings at risk. I have no doubts the trill were on Earth well before they decided to trade with humans and create the exchange instead of battling your species for dominance."

"Why are you telling me this?"

It was all fascinating, and believable, but why tell me?

He was going to be commander of this ship when we arrived at Trillume, so he knew what he was talking about. I was just a human, part of a temporary research project.

General reached up and pulled a strand of his braid over his shoulder where a familiar leather trinket dangled. I gasped and stared at him.

"How did you get that?" I whispered.

"You gifted it to me," he said with a smile. The way he spoke about his planet's past and a theory about warriors having been to Earth was beginning to resemble the same speech pattern I'd heard before but through a filtered voice modulator. It wasn't Sou-el...

My whole body ached and felt nauseated. Bodies did lie. My body was a lying piece of shit, and Sou-el was not here waiting for me. This was all a delusion of a desperate person vulnerable to seeing and feeling what I wanted from coming here. You get what you look for, and when the fog is cleared you see reality once more.

That was what this was...

I was a fool.

"Renee," he brought my attention back to him and his amber eyes that were more like fire that matched his hair. "I believe some humans have trace D.N.A. of necia warriors and are more compatible with us than their own species. It's possible you have this trace D.N.A. and it would be perfectly natural for you to be attracted to more than one warrior. It's nothing to be ashamed of, and I have other theories that the warrior D.N.A. will activate more similarities when you are mated with a warrior worthy of honoring you. I would be honored to earn this right and prove to you I am a capable and worthy mate."

"I, uh—" I gaped at him.

"No need to decide this moment, the Rakturan Rites are not a rushed process. I keep your token close, but do not dishonor you by consuming its contents until the ceremony. I do not desire to hold the ceremony on the ship, but on my home planet, Necias Prime. Let us instead get to know each other and prepare you for being my equal in commanding this ship."

"Your what?" I squeaked in panic.

He furrowed his brows, but nodded in a kind of understanding before explaining, "Mates are not the same on Earth. When a warrior mates, everything that they are is their mates as well. As future commander of this ship, you would also have authority to command what is mine. That is not to say you are forced to do so, you may defer to my second, or any of my generals, but what is my honor will also be yours. It is also my honor to provide anything that would bring you happiness, should you have a different calling to serve the tribe in your own way."

I gulped, feeling my anxiety climb with every moment. "You," I started again, "You want me to be by your side as you explore the galaxy on your ship?"

"Of course, but I do not spend all my rotations on my ship. As my mate, I wish for your happiness, even if that means taking shifts on whatever planet you wish."

"Earth?"

He cringed but schooled his features quickly enough. "Earth would drastically reduce our lifespans." Seeing that I didn't respond he continued, "But I see no reason why we could not visit."

"I wouldn't do that to you or any other warrior," I told him with a shake of my head, and I could see him visibly relax. "If I were mating with an alien, while out in space, it's unreasonable to expect them to go to Earth."

"There are tonics we can take, and filtration masks that remove the poison in your planet's air," he tried to soothe the ache of knowing mating with an alien would mean rarely seeing Earth again.

"Why me?" I asked him, while folding my arms over my chest.

He smiled, and he was certainly charming, but I had no delusions any more about this being anything more than lies told by my body to procreate with a hot alien that I might share D.N.A. in some distant way. This had nothing to do with me, or with him.

"We are compatible, and your disposition is refreshing. I like that you do not try to impress me because of my honored title and strength. You speak freely, and without worry of displeasing me. It is honest, and your history of raising spawnlings shows your leadership and honor capable of being my equal in command."

I wasn't expecting it to be so thought out, and yet all those things meant nothing to me.

"I do not wish to command," I stated plainly.

He chuckled. "See, no other would admit as much to me. Many would like to share the honor of my title but not admit that they did not wish to take the responsibility that comes with it. They would use the power, without heeding the consequences. I do not wish for a mate that would use my warriors under my command for their own benefit."

"There are plenty of mates that would honor your title and not abuse it. That has nothing to do with me."

"Not as many as one would hope," he denied my claim and added, "It is a good start, no? I make no claims of your human 'love', but I am a man of science and strength. This love is simply a biochemical reaction created over time between compatible mates. We are compatible, this was confirmed with the way our bodies reacted under the blind testing, and I find your blood pleasing to the taste. I'm becoming accustomed to your scent, and over time I will seek to be near it more and more. I will honor you and seek out your happiness. It is your choice, but I assure you, allow me the time to prove myself during our Rakturan, and both your body and mind will be more than sated, but we will both crave each other's attention."

"What exactly is a Rakturan?"

"The severing of your bond with a previous mate," he stated simply. "If you were not previously mated, then I'd simply chase you, prove your body reacts to me, and then give you my knot to see if your body bonds with mine. But as there is another bond to compete with, our mating is more likely to be successful by spending time together and exchanging gifts of each other until our ceremony on Necias Prime.

"I am on suppressants, so you need not worry I will rut before our ceremony. But I will stop taking them before we arrive there after dropping off our exchange candidates on Trillume. As commander, I will have authority to detour to Necias Prime before our next assignment."

He had this all planned out, and his bravado was strong enough to see he had no assumptions that I would turn his offer down. He was a future commander with title and honor, probably had the pick of any warrior on this ship and beyond that would have gladly accepted his offer of mating.

Again, I asked him, "Why me? You could choose anyone that was compatible with you to build feelings and biochemicals with..."

He grinned, leaning back in his chair. "The better question is why not? We all have needs, and is it not exhausting to be searching for who to fill it with? We are sexually attracted, and we can be honest with our thoughts to one another. We all wish to be with someone who will be what we can not to ourselves while also trusting they will remain honorable to one another. We have both proven our honor to be trustworthy, you with waiting to leave your mate until your spawnlings were cared for, and me with earning the trust of my tribe to lead them as commander. Feelings are nothing more than chemicals that we will build together with proximity, and touch. If you do not develop these feelings you crave for mating then we speak no more of it and move on.

"But I will say, I waited here for you." He said pointedly, and the absence of Sou-el was felt more deeply.

"What do you mean, you waited for me?"

How did he know I'd come here?

"Do not think I didn't overhear your conversation with Sou-el, it was my experiment, and I oversee its management. He said he'd wait for you here, but I am the one here waiting for you. Sharing with you my confidences of what I hope to prove with these experiments, that we may have found the strand of DNA that is linked to necia warriors having visited ancient humans. I will not lie to you, and I will not hide things from you. I seek you as a mate and my equal, and I will continue to seek you out until you dismiss me."

He didn't come. General Tensel was here, and Sou-el was not. I was indeed a fool.

"It's flattering to have someone of your honor show interest in me," I said with a forced smile, not wanting to offend him. But he didn't have interest in me at all. I was a checklist of compatibilities to him, and he firmly believed that feelings would grow with accepting that we were attracted first then spend time together. My heart ached at the idea of simply being a series of reactions bouncing around the universe until a compatible chemical rotated around me and wished to bond. It was merely chance and acceptance, nothing more.

Was that all there was?

Was this the answer I was looking for?

I meant nothing.

Was that my truth?

The truth of all mammals such as humans, and warriors alike?

It seemed so bleak, just animals seeking pleasure, or avoiding pain and fear.

"If you'll excuse me," I pushed up from the table, and I couldn't even hear the noises of the warriors fucking around me. My vision was blurring at the sides as I hung on to the edge of the table that had the perfect set of grooves for my fingers to clamp around. A warmth surged through my skin, tingling up my arm, and out of all my instincts the one to flee surfaced. I needed to leave. I couldn't do this. Sweat beaded at my collar, and my breathing labored.

"You do not look so well," he agreed to my leave, and offered his arm to lead me out of the lounge. We were coming up on my daughter's room and I insisted I could take it from there and wished to see her before returning to the community quarters.

The door slid open on her room and water finally leaked down my cheeks.

"Mom?"

"I don't know why I'm so emotional..." I wiped at my tears. It felt like all my hopes were crushed and I had my eyes pried open with rusty clamps to see the truth that I was right all along... my body lied and who gives a fuck about this dumb organ inside my chest?

"What happened?" she asked while climbing down from her bunk, she had probably been sleeping.

"I didn't mean to wake you, but I think I need a bit of separation from the program for a bit."

I gave her a big hug, and told her what happened, at least what she needed to know before I took the easy way out and ran away once more. I knew I was running, but it was better than what awaited me if I stayed. If General Tensel was right, then it was only a matter of time with him before I lost my own freewill and mated with him. I didn't want to be an animal that mated because we were compatible, and if he was going to be the one that showed up, and Sou-el kept on disappearing then I needed to remove myself from the equation.

If I go into a stasis pod, then I'll wake up when we arrive on Trillume, and General Tensel will then be a commander and stay aboard his ship to find another compatible mate. General Sou-el was bound to his research and as a future commander he wouldn't be overseeing the research center I'd be woken up in. I'd see my daughter again and try to forget about both of them. The Blue District would be a great place to do that. As the saying went, best way to get over someone was under someone else.

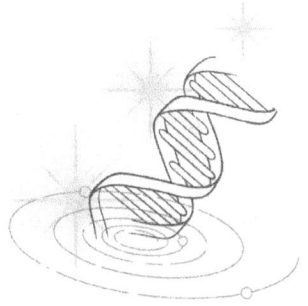

Chapter Fifteen
General Sou-el

When my intern Becky came through the doors, I glanced over her shoulder with a hopeful expectation to see her guardian following behind. The door slid closed with no sign of Renee, and it must have meant she decided to stay with her research group, though I was assured that she had clearance to leave at any time.

I had been disappointed to not find her there when I left the lounge to seek her out, but I was certain she must have been with her daughter. The very spawnling that glared at me from my office doors. I grunted with the obvious signs of her sudden disapproval of my presence. This was not a good sign, especially when honoring her with my wisdom was one way to prove my worth as a mate to her guardian, and my future mate.

"What has you in a state of agitation?" I asked, hoping that perhaps her display had nothing to do with me, but of some other cause. I could assist her in solving her discomfort, though Elder Edilm would say not all things are to be fixed but felt. I have yet to understand his words. Perhaps, today would be the day, and I could be thankful there would be nothing to fix.

Becky lifted a brow. "You don't know?"

"Speak plainly. I will not hold your displeasure against your internship."

"You and General Tensel humiliated her. Mom came back from the lounge crying, and talking about how all you cared about was your stupid research about how humans were nothing but malleable mammals reacting to bodily stimuli. You know, I actually thought you'd be a good change for her, but you're worse than dad."

My hearts stopped beating as I processed her words, this was not something to be felt and forgotten. This was something that had to be fixed immediately. I had hoped Renee would come to my office last night, I had clearly invited her to rejoin me in my room. I would have explained that General Tensel may have been trying to prove fated mates didn't exist, but we were proof that it was real. That we were more than merely animals seeking out our continuation of our D.N.A. but a bonding of our being that no other mating could replicate. It was too soon to rely on our bond to be stronger than her doubts, but she had to feel the draw between us.

"I have never related us to beasts, but I do not doubt many matings are nothing more than companionship and biochemistry as General Tensel describes." Seeing her displeasure at my words, I amended, "I have stated plainly that I consider her more than that."

"What exactly did you say?" Becky was not convinced at my sincerity, and if the circumstances did not involve my Pulsunne thinking I had dishonored her I would praise the loyalty she showed to her guardian. As it was, every nerve in my body was on fire and in need of seeing my mate immediately to calm my anxiety that I may never see her again.

"I told her she was my Pulsunne, and I would earn her honor the right way," I ground out with my irritation growing at the very thought of Renee thinking I had considered her an experiment. This was not a topic of discussion with a spawnling. If Renee had not already had a mate, I would have taken her as our old customs dictated and there would have been no doubts about our bond. She would be wearing my mark, and she would carry my D.N.A. which has been shown in other human mates to increase their life expectancy.

My epul throbbed, and Becky's words caught up with my scattered mind. She had said Renee spoke with Tensel, and that meant she also saw her offering dangling from the wrong warrior's hair. She would double her efforts in hiding behind her previous hurts in life, repeating to herself about how the body lies, and her draw towards me was false.

"Pulsunne..." Becky repeated the word with confusion.

"My fated, the song of my hearts, my mate, *mine*," I growled out as I paced the office, growing more riled up.

"Are you okay?" she asked, taking a step back. Her instincts were correct to be wary. My hearts were pounding, and I felt this before after I had Renee's blood. Horve's vine, how was this possible? I was at the beginning stages of rut? It wasn't possible...

"No," I snapped, then softened my tone to add, "I'm not okay. I may not see it, but you'll probably notice that my eyes have dilated, and if a medic were here, they would see elevated markers of adrenaline. I can feel my skin itching, and my hearts beating faster. My enzyme production is seeping from my pores to attract my mate to help balance my levels. I'm most certainly at the beginning stages of rut where I still have my faculties, but if this continues, I will not remain in my right mind."

"What do we do?"

"*We* do nothing. You are staying here, and another research lead will assist you with your studies. I am going to find my mate."

"Uh, that's going to be difficult," she said with unease.

"Why?" I gritted back, trying to hold back my uncomfortable itch crawling along my scales that begged me to find someone to fight or rut, anything to stop the ache. As she hesitated with her answer, I roughly swiped at the table connected to my screens and contacted the Head of Research at the Blue District, the only one I could think of that didn't have an issue training a human. It was above his duties to train others, but he was the one who agreed to train her from the beginning, chose her specifically from the batch of applicants.

Message sent, approval codes added to my office, and he would have complete access to run the experiment from here remotely. All Becky would need to do is observe and listen.

The spawnling chewed at her lip nervously, debating whether she should say anything, but decided after I was finished securing her training to say something.

"Stasis."

One word, and that was all it took to strike me cold.

"Stay," I commanded of her with a stern look before leaving. Protocols for stasis were started for her because of me, and it was possible a pod was prepared. Even still, she would need to be sedated, monitored, then the stasis pod would fill with the fluids as her body was prepared for long sleep. If she went this morning, I had time to retrieve her before things were too far in the process.

By the time I rushed through the doors of the stasis chambers, I was heaving, and baring my fangs. Fight or rut. Soon, I would lose my ability to communicate beyond action.

My eyes adjusted and focused on the trill stationed here. She turned and lifted a quizzical brow ridge at my frenzied state.

"General," she addressed calmly. "The medics have already been alerted to a possible rut on the ship. Everyone you've passed on your way here has been alerting them to your location."

"Renee," I demanded.

Her large reptilian eyes crinkled, and her second lid fluttered in some kind of recognition.

"She's here," I gritted out as best I could. My restraint waning as I sniffed the room for that familiar scent. It was here, in this room recently.

"It's too late to remove her. You'll have to wait until Trillume. We have limited resources, and removing someone from stasis early isn't an option. Even if we made an exception, you'd be risking her health to shock her fragile body."

My eyes caught movement of her hands digging into her robes.

"Elder spray?" I huffed at the entrance, my epul in my hands flexed uncomfortably. Blood trickled down my chest from my shoulder epul, as well as down my knuckles from my claws.

I would bleed out if my rut continued without a medical team, or my mate's blood. It was a theory, but one drop of her blood removed the pain when I bathed in her ello juices, and I healed much quicker than I ever had before. She was my salvation.

The trill revealed the canister in her hands and smiled, rows of sharp teeth like needles shined back at me. She may not have been a warrior, but if my rut forced me to fight her, she would win with one calculated bite to my neck. Any warrior would survive the bite, but the trill were known to be poisonous. And I wasn't any warrior, I was flawed. The only time I trained to fight was with Commander Rokva, or Cenkal. They both were easy on me, merely playing up the show of training with me so more warriors respected my position as general, even if it was for research and not for leadership.

I collapsed to my knees, straining the epul along my thighs that had protruded. This was what defeat, true failure, felt like. There was enough of my mind left to not rage needlessly against the only being in here that I could fight. It was her duty to use the elder spray and secure me until the medics could arrive.

Did I well and truly lose my mate, the moment she stepped into that stasis pod? My sister would no longer be commander of this ship when she awoke, and she'd have no authority to end Renee's contract with the Blue District. Newly appointed Commander Tensel has shown he doesn't believe in true mates and will not help me reach her.

There was only one last chance...

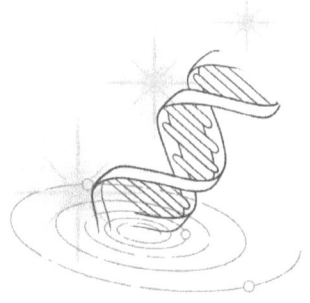

Chapter Sixteen
General Sou-el

When I woke from being sedated, Cenkal told me that I shouldn't go to the stasis chambers. My glands were unpredictable, and being around Renee had somehow given them a life that was never thought possible. With an unprecedented rut building within my system, I was on a regular dosage of suppressant to keep my glands under control, but soon I wouldn't be able to hide the nose bleeds, or the blood in my lungs. Active adrenaline didn't mean my glands were functioning properly to help heal my wounds from my epul shifting under my second skin.

Soon, I would have no choice but to stop taking the suppressants as they were stopping what little healing my body was capable of. Then the rut would take over.

"You're going to visit mom again?" Becky asked as I tried to turn towards the door to hide the blood dripping towards my lip. I wasn't done teaching her what I could for the rotation. It was my honor to train the spawnling of my mate, but I would need to be under sedation again if my body could not make it until Renee's return from stasis.

"Who told you?" I wondered if perhaps she was spending a bit too much time with Cenkal with his constant monitoring. He's aware that my healing was compromised with the suppressant, but with medbots he's been doing what he could to balance it. If he knew I was bleeding regardless of the medbots, he'd have placed me in stasis until we could reach a healing unit on Trillume.

"I followed you, but even if I didn't, Medic Cenkal knows where you are at all times and has asked me to convince you to stop going."

I growled as if she were an obstacle between me and my mate, and I knew my time was short.

"I'm not going to stop you," she added, but not before I turned and she spotted the blood, but this time it was from my forehead where small epul sprouted like a crown. She scrambled to the wall and opened the med hatch with clotting spray and emergency supplies.

Becky patted the chair, and I sat as she tended to my open wounds from breaking through my second skin. Moving my epul at all was a risk, but my control was slipping.

"General..." I thought she was going to tell me she would make sure Medic Cenkal knew about this, but instead she asked, "What do you talk about when you go? There are rumors that stasis is similar to a coma and some people can remember the sounds they hear while they were sleeping."

I smiled at the thought of Renee listening while I confessed my need for her and told her of my plans for us. For a future I may not ever get to have.

"I speak of my home on Necias Prime, and my wish for her to visit for our mating. I've spoken with Cenkal about a filter I could use to visit Earth without damaging my glands further. As her mate, I would have temporary access to visit, and meet with your sister. You've said you are not her only spawnling, and I have desire to know more of your tribe and Renee's preferences which would bring more happiness to her life."

"That's really sweet, and honestly unexpected from you," she said with a smile that was the opposite of my own expectations when she believed my 'sweetness' was out of character from her perceptions.

"For humans this sweetness is appreciated but you did not expect this from me?"

She chuckled and continued smiling despite the scowl I knew I was giving her in return. It displeased me that the spawnling of my Pulsunne did not think me worthy of her guardian's honor.

"No, it's not that. It's just you were teaching me how it was unhealthy for any being to ignore their own happiness for the happiness of others, yet you're willing to risk your own health to visit Earth to see my mom smile?"

This made sense why she was confused, but what she didn't understand was that they were directly connected. "The happiness of my Pulsunne is mine to claim. For every smile, I am filled with pride and honor that I had a part in placing it there upon her lips. You are correct, as animals ruled by our biopsychology, we function in our own best interests, but it is in my best interest to share in the warmth created from being around her and knowing that happiness is mine. Her smiles are mine to care for."

Becky wiped away the blood from my forehead where a few of my epul crown poked through. "You don't even know my mom, though, not really."

"You've had your whole life to know her, but not even you know more than what you feel for her," I tried to use this as another opportunity for learning that what we did had everything to do with studying behavior and finding correlations that could be used to predict attraction and compatibility.

"I know her favorite foods, what she does for fun, why she's here, and..." she paused to repeat, "and..." A confused furrow between her brows as she tried to think of more that she could encompass what it meant to know someone.

"And all of those things can change. I'm sure none of those are the same things they once were before you were spawned, or even how they once were in recent rotations, and I'm certain if you thought about what it meant to know who you are, you would struggle with identifying what you want beyond your desire to learn and be respected within your job. Have you not had times where your guardian has done something for you that you used to enjoy, only for you to say you're not a spawnling anymore? How much does your own guardian know you beyond the feeling they have that tells them you mean more to them than any other?"

"Are you still trying to train me, even now?"

"It is my honor to do so."

She laughed and threw the cloth she was using to wipe at my forehead at me. "You're saying no one really knows anyone, just what they feel?"

"No, I'm saying how you feel about someone is separate from learning how they react towards things. Feelings dictate actions. Those actions lead towards reactions that either reinforce or dissuade those actions being repeated. Feelings are reactions to how our brain reacts towards stimulus. We observe those reactions and make theories and assumptions of how the world works from that data. It is either more or less compelling based on how the data is collected."

"So, then how can you know for certain about your feelings? If they are simply our brain's reaction to chemicals we produce? Wouldn't our feelings fluctuate, and or fade with time?"

"To explain feelings is something we still study, because like all science there is a probable answer, but at any point further study could disprove what we thought was truth, and new truths are discovered. That is to say, all I have are my feelings, and the proof is in my reactions to them. It is for my mate to decide to accept them as fact or not."

"So... you're saying you love her, even though you don't know her?" Becky seemed displeased with this, and I sighed.

"What is knowing someone?" I asked and left the spawnling to think about what it meant to feel without understanding fully. Every being in the universe lived and died with their feelings and their actions without needing to know everything there was to know. What was important was having a certain amount of acceptance for the things in this life that brought us joy.

For me, that was my mate.

And I could only honor her as best I could in hopes that she'll feel the same for me. When she woke from stasis, I might not be in my right mind, but I could hope that my efforts to honor her spawnling while she was gone will bring her some modicum of peace that Becky was cared for in her absence.

Liquid dripped down my temple, and I wiped at the blood before it reached my chin. I was still bleeding, and yet I felt my hearts hammering in my chest. The suppressant was failing, my glands weren't producing what I needed to heal properly. Time was not on my side. I'd go to her one last time. My legs took me down a hall that didn't lead to the stasis chambers, and it wasn't until I saw General Tensel that I understood why. My mate's scent had long dissipated from the stasis chamber, sealed away in her pod, but for the bead of her blood dangling from another male's hair. He glanced up from speaking with the commander and taunted me with lifting his red hair to his nose, bringing the trinket with it for a sniff of her scent.

A growl erupted from my throat, and I lunged without a second thought. My epul lengthened from my knuckles and I cut the strand of hair from his head before he could react. Everyone in the room was stunned, as I snatched the falling leather braid that held my mate's blood from the air and clutched it close.

General Tensel had goaded me, but he did not expect my restraint to crumble in seconds. Neither did my commander and sister as she watched wide-eyed. Her reaction a bit faster than General Tensel as she rushed to block his attack while I inhaled Renee's scent from the offering.

"Are you claiming Rakture?" Rokva hissed over her shoulder.

Words stuck in my throat as I growled like a beast of old, coveting my treasure. It was not his to claim, I thought, though a small part of me knew this wasn't how I would go about obtaining her offering if she were already marked as my mate.

"Move," Tensel demanded of my sister to step aside for his pound of flesh owed from my actions against him.

I untied the hair ribbon from his severed red locks and tied the offering to my own hair in challenge.

"Mine," I ground out with my fangs on display. All my muscles tensed in preparation for a duel, a sick kind of pleasure in believing the goddess would not deny me this right. That pestering voice in my mind warned me that she had already forsaken me since spawning.

Cracking his neck, General Tensel grunted as he forced his epul to lengthen along his legs. "When I win this duel, General Sou-el, you will submit to me and be restrained, or you will die. Which is it?"

"That isn't necessary," Rokva tried to plead, but when she saw my resolve she questioned, "Right? As your commander, I cannot interfere with a duel that is done with honor..."

"*My* honor," I said, then licked my fang, believing with everything down to my epul that this was my duel to win.

Reluctant to leave us, when Rokva made the decision to step aside, her movement was the flag with which we saw victory. Both Tensel and I launched into battle. The few warriors that were following the commander around during her rounds stayed to the outside. They would watch us closely to avoid our duel, but they would watch. To leave a Rakture once initiated was not our way. This was my chance to prove I was a worthy mate, and I would honor my mate by making sure all knew I was willing to lose my life for her.

As we darted like projectiles through the space, Tensel's fist launched forward, epul sharp and deadly from his knuckles. A game of Hargom's Cliff, who would retreat first as we headed for the edge. Honor or death, we would chant as spawnlings. My sister had taught me to evade strikes without retreating a battle, the wisdom of time to have honor and mitigate risk. I twisted my torso to escape his punch, but I was not fast enough to avoid all damage, as a line of blood was drawn from his smaller epul on his forearm that he had extended out last nanosecond. While he was focused high, I aimed low. Taking the hit was a sacrifice for victory as my boot slid out to catch his ankle. An adept warrior wouldn't fall, merely stumble, and Tensel was skilled. His stumble was exactly what I needed to cut the back of his calves with my own extended epul spikes.

It surprised him more that I focused on attacking the more dangerous areas. This was also a tactic of Commander Rokva, it was rare for anyone to challenge her, so many didn't watch her duel. She'd train me in private for the skills I'd need to survive, and in public with the skills to appear stronger to the tribe. I was not a dedicated warrior with applied experience, but I was a survivor. I risked damaging my own legs to damage his own first. Both of us suffered the consequences of my actions. I grinned at him as he bounded backwards and winced on his landing. He howled in his growing adrenaline rush of a duel. He would need blood to calm himself, and after he would seek out someone to mate with that was not Renee currently trapped in stasis.

Victory came in many forms, I thought ruefully. Winning this duel had nothing to do with destroying General Tensel. He was the superior warrior in every way, and this duel of strength would be his for the taking, as to be expected with a future commander. The duel of mates on the other hand would be mine, because my mate was safe, and a fresh conquest would force him to choose someone else to satiate his needs. Renee had already proven by hiding in the stasis pods that she did not wish to have more than one mate. Nor did she wish to be nothing more than a means to balance our glands.

"You'll regret that, Sou-el!" He charged at me with speed and a mesmerizing grace like battle was a dance that he was the master of.

All the while, my smile stayed plastered to my face like I'd lost my mind to the rut. Perhaps, I had to some degree. I'd never have attempted this kind of recklessness without a bit of crazed motivation. His speed was faster. His maneuvering agile and precise. General Tensel had underestimated me in the beginning, and he wasn't taking the chance that I had extra tricks up my sleeve this time. I was outmatched as he swiftly targeted the weaker areas of my torso to stab into me with his knuckle epul, lifting me up above his shoulder epul.

He hovered there for a moment as I knew the inevitable drop down on his large epul would come. It was an ancient art to skewer our prey on our shoulders so that our food would be carried easily while keeping our hands free to defend ourselves.

I closed my eyes waiting for the pain of having one of my hearts destroyed as my chest slid onto his epul. My sister's screams echoed in the room as General Tensel released his knuckle epul and I slipped down to have gravity lead me to my defeat. My only thought was that if I survived this, I would still have a chance to prove myself to my mate without General Tensel's interference. If my mate was not in stasis, I would be devastated to know that he would have charged straight to her as I was escorted to the medbay. Losing this duel would have meant he had the right to claim her, winning the Rakture duel.

Renee was safe. He would claim his victory with another tonight, foregoing his claim to my mate. A duel of Rakture with a competing mate was clear. We dueled for Renee, and he will choose another. He cannot duel me again for this claim. I grunted as my stomach landed on Tensel's shoulder and I waited for the pain. All I felt was the previous aches of the few cuts I received from earlier across my chest, and along my legs.

It was tortured bliss to lose this duel, because I knew it meant winning for our future. Times such as these made me believe in fate instead of science, because if Renee had not gone into stasis, and I had not dueled and forced the general to choose another mate after a Rakture, he could have challenged my claim and won before I ever had a chance to make her mine.

General Tensel whispered so that only I could hear as his arms wrapped around my torso to keep me positioned on his shoulder like I was a sack of grain, "If you try to move before

I place you in confinement, I will release my epul and you will suffer."

Moments passed in shock at what had happened. He withdrew his epul before I landed on his shoulder, and I was relatively unharmed. With labored breathing, he escorted me to the holding brig, and slammed the button on the restraints that snapped out to lock me into the chair. The compartment in the wall tapped open and he gritted his teeth while blindfolding me with a sensory dampener. Both my hearing and sight were gone. The minutes ticked by in my mind as I felt my blood drip down my fingers, and along my legs.

Worry plagued me as I wondered if his restraint was a sign of me not being able to draw enough of his blood to trigger his instincts to mate. Would he return to his duties without claiming victory? He didn't take my blood, and I couldn't tell if he rushed from the room after the dampener was firmly over my eyes and ears. Did I lose for nothing? The pain of the injuries I did sustain were growing more persistent and my blood loss was more than the cuts General Tensel gave me, but from using my epul so roughly. I was bleeding from the inside, and the dizziness overwhelmed me, until there was nothing but the face of my mate haunting my dreams.

Chapter
Seventeen
Renee

W aking from stasis was better than I thought it would be. I was a bit sore, and groggy, but overall, this was a relief to be awake. It felt like I'd only just entered the stasis pod, and now I was rubbing at my eyes that I discovered had some kind of slime on them, keeping them sealed.

"Ah," a male's voice soothed while gently grabbing my hands and guiding them away, "It will fall off naturally when the nanobots are done. My name is Medic Cenkal. You've been in stasis for the remainder of our travels to Trillume. I have been the one tending to your preacclimation from stasis. The process takes humans around a week of therapy before we wake them fully. For a warrior, less than a day, as our glands are highly efficient at healing ourselves. You've woken slightly earlier than anticipated. My apologies if you are still sore and uncomfortable."

"It isn't so bad," I assured him.

"That is reassuring."

"So, we're on Trillume then?"

"Within the Blue District labs, yes. Your spawnling comes by every day to check on you after her shifts. She's learned quiet a lot and has gained favored honor from the Commander of this Research Center."

I smiled with pride, thinking about how Becky was thriving in her internship.

"That's wonderful. In such a short amount of time, that's amazing."

He cleared his throat. "There was a bit of a situation."

"What kind of a situation?" I sat up straight in the bed, and wished I wasn't blinded so that I could see the expression on the medic's face. It was natural to worry and think the worst. Was Becky okay?

"Sou-el suggested humans were better at receiving information when good news was delivered first then ease into the rest and then let them process the information." The mention of

General Sou-el was a comfort that made me think he had been just fine without me, but along with the comfort that he was okay was also disappointment that I was just a pet to the necia warriors. A vessel to help them balance their body so their hearts didn't explode from adrenaline overdose. But, he had said there was an incident, and I couldn't hear my daughter's voice in the room.

"Out with it!"

"Yes, right. Good news is that your spawnling is doing well."

"Becky," I snapped, "her name is Becky."

"Becky, is doing well."

"You've said that." I was exasperated by this point. What exactly was the issue that he was avoiding? If it wasn't Becky, then what? Why was I so irritable? It felt like my skin was crawling and the very air around me was stifling. I was so thirsty, and I ached all over, but it wasn't pain.

"I am not supposed to be telling you this, but General Sou-el is my brother, and I would happily dishonor myself to help him."

"What are you talking about?" A flash of my alien warrior as he was restrained in that room, blindfolded, as I left the room tore at my mind, wrenching at my heart. That was the last time I spoke to Sou-el. He wasn't at the lounge, and I had no rights to feel anything for him when I clearly couldn't trust my body's response to anything. With my husband, I felt nothing when he touched me, and in the same week I'd been an eager flame to whichever alien touched me. It must have been something about the necia warriors that I responded to, and I couldn't trust it, but that didn't stop me from wanting to know what happened to Sou-el. I leaned in with concern, waiting for the medic to tell me. The look of distress set my nerves on fire, itching to move and make sure Sou-el was okay.

"He has been dishonored, title suspended, and has only been granted access to stay in the Blue District if he works as a participant first to earn the honor of returning as a researcher." Seeing my shock, he continued, "I'm telling you this because he is convinced that you are his mate, and only you can return his lost honor, as he refuses to leave the Blue District without you."

Guilt tore at me about having given the bead of my blood to another warrior. I thought it was him, but that didn't matter, did it? He would find out and I couldn't bear to see that pained look in his eyes as he did when he knocked himself out after I told him I was married. My body would betray me again, and perhaps the aliens were right... humans were nothing more than mammals, pets to protect.

"What do you expect me to do about it?"

"Ah," he hesitated, "He is banned from going near you of his own accord. Commander Tensel has issued a challenge, and all warriors will not act against his orders."

"Get on with it!" I was already standing, with the sheet held up against my chest, ready to storm the station. I'd tie this fabric like a toga if I had to. My feet touched the cold metal of the floor, and normally I'd shriek at the sudden temperature change, but I was burning up, and it took all of my will power to not leave without any direction or plan. I wasn't sure why I was so agitated, but the only thing on my mind was finding Sou-el and seeing him.

What would I say to him when I did see him? I wasn't sure, but I guessed I'd start with trying to explain that I didn't mean to give the offering to someone else? That he should move on, and find another mate that wouldn't betray him? Why was he so set on me being his mate when we hardly knew each other? Every mom instinct in me wanted to protect him and remind him that lust and attraction were not the same thing as love, or forever. I should know. He needed to leave here and regain his honor in his tribe.

"Right, yes. If you were to find him yourself and claim him as your mate, then the tribe would accept that he had every right to defend you by dueling Commander Tensel."

"He dueled?"

"If the commander wasn't merciful, Sou-el would have died in that battle. It was foolish to challenge a warrior far beyond his skill to defeat."

"I don't understand, are you saying he picked a fight and lost? Because of me?"

Tortured between flattered and pissed off, both feelings warred for dominance within me. I'd never had anyone fight for me, but also it was stupid to get hurt for no reason. My fists clenched at my side and I understood the dilemma he must have gone through while faced with Tensel, because in that moment I didn't know whether I wanted to punch him for getting hurt, or yell at him. Use my words, or physically shake sense into him.

"Sou-el will be upset that I have told you, since it is not endearing to a mate to lose a duel, but if you truly are his mate, you will not leave him because of his failure."

"Where is he?" I was done talking to someone else about what was a conversation I needed to have with Sou-el himself.

"That's the issue, really. He is not to interact with anyone associated with you. Not even I know exactly where he is this past week. All I know is he is likely in one of the Blue District observation rooms. Though for him, it is more like a cage, as his only option to leave that room is to leave the planet. I would be informed if he left, as I have followed every mission of his since we were spawn together."

I smiled at that. "You're his best friend."

"His brother," he corrected, but I was beginning to understand that the term was used more as a term of closeness than of biological relation. They looked nothing alike.

"So, you have no idea where he is, and I'm supposed to find him?"

"That is what I am saying," he affirmed.

I lifted a brow and I asked curiously, "You've had a week and haven't found him." I'm assuming as his brother he's been searching for him.

He appeared offended that I even insinuated he might not have. "I do not trust the medic units in his room to keep him safe in my absence."

"Then how am I supposed to do what you haven't?"

"You are his mate," he said like that explained everything.

"Right..." I pressed my lips together to stop myself from arguing with him.

"That is the challenge given to him by Commander Tensel. If you are indeed his mate then you will find him by instinct. I'm to give you his blood if you wish to prove the bond. I have samples that were collected before he was taken away. That is all I have to offer."

"I'm human," I insisted he was mistaken. "What you're asking is ridiculous. We aren't like dogs that can sniff some blood and find something. I could eat a bloody steak and not be able to hunt down the cow that it came from!" My feet were moving to the door before I could think about it. Adjusting the sheet around myself, I rolled it and pulled it under my arms and around my neck like I used to with a sarong at the beach. Where were my clothes? I sighed resting my hand on the wall, and I felt a click. Blinking, I glanced up and spotted that as I removed my hand, a storage pocket was revealed, and it was cold with a bio-controlled lock. Medic Cenkal was behind me and placed his hand on the lock.

It opened, and several vials of blood were stored in there.

He said nothing, but he didn't have to. There was an unsaid understanding that both of us were wondering if I was indeed like a dog, hunting my mate. He took a step back and didn't pick out the one that would be Sou-el's, fully expecting that I could find it myself, even with all the vials labeled in an alien language. My mouth was dry, and my fingers twitched. This was silly, I wasn't going to find his blood this way.

I wasn't his mate, right?

But the longer I stared at only one vial in particular, the more my doubts crumbled into a strange desire for it to be true. I reached for it, holding it in my hands with curiosity. Was this his blood? I didn't know for certain, but what if it was?

Medic Cenkal held out a contraption that looked like a gun with an empty slot for the vial.

"Is this his?" I asked him with wonder. The vial clicked in, and I knew I was supposed to inject it. I'd seen these before when I was being evaluated for the exchange, and again when Cenkal took blood samples for my bathing compatibility.

"I'm not allowed to verify or deny anything, or I risk the results of the experiment. There are multiple warrior samples in that storage unit. One of which, is indeed Sou-el's, but there is also Commander Tensel's sample in there as well. By my honor, and Sou-el's, I cannot say more. It was already a risk to tell you what I have about Sou-el's choice to stay on planet, and his duel for you."

"So, this could just be some random warrior's blood I'm injecting into myself?"

He nodded.

Fuck, I thought. This was very unsanitary, and against everything I was taught about preventing diseases. There were tons of viruses in history born from humans stupidly messing around with bodily fluids of other species. Plague, Ebola, Rabies, Bird Flu, Mad Cow Disease... to only name a few. Should have thought of that before I licked Sou-el's blood from his knuckles and had him lick and plunge those bloody fingers into my traitorous vagina as I came all over his face. I flushed at the thought and pulled the trigger on the injection stinging my forearm.

Guess we were doing this?

"Do you have some clothes?"

He handed me some white flowing dress that was no more than a gauzy see-through drape.

"Uh... what is this?"

"The traditional garb of the final mating duel of Raktu-ran. The whole tribe has been awaiting your consciousness. The facility has cameras everywhere, and many of us have been watching when we are not on duty to celebrate your union or share this experiment's results with other research teams. The only one who knows Sou-el's location is the one running the Blue District labs, and Sou-el himself. Ah, see for yourself," he tapped his implant, and motioned for me to do the same.

Right, I thought, they gave me upgraded eye implants while I was coming out of stasis.

Tapping the back of my ear, a screen appeared in front of my eyes. It was me, and Cenkal. My eyes widened and I turned to stare at him, and the screen moved with me, staying in the same spot within my sight. I could see him like the screen was a phantom overlay over his body and face. No wonder he wouldn't tell me which vial of blood I had, he was being watched. I was being watched, and I couldn't do anything about it. My mind whirred. This was all within the rights of my contract with the Blue District. They weren't forcing me to do anything, but I was being observed regardless.

The screen switched views like I was watching a tv broadcasting of a live-action drama. It was Sou-el! He was strapped to a chair in a room with his eyes covered.

"Why is he bound?" I demanded.

"Sensory deprivation is normal for warriors in rut. It is for his own safety," Cenkal explained and held out the clothes again.

"Those aren't clothes."

He averted his eyes in embarrassment as he tried to explain, "I'm growing more accustomed to humans over the last few months, and I'm aware that humans find displaying themselves to be uncomfortable, but should you successfully find Sou-el, you would be walking into a room with a warrior in rut. He will claim you, and the tribe will watch as he bathes in his victory, and reclaims his mate, title, and honor. There will be no place for your human... uh," he was trying to think of the word to use, "modesty. These robes are traditional of our mating ceremonies, and as you can see, he is not with any himself..."

He was right, now that I passed the shock of seeing him restrained, it was clear he was naked... and ready. I gulped. He was covered last time, and though I saw an outline, I hadn't truly taken in that he was alien in all ways. It was tinted the same coloring as his scales, and there were... nodules pulsing in and out of his shaft. A few of them were protruded more like a tuning fork at his base... where was that going? I licked my lips and tapped the implant to remove the display from my eye. My legs were clenching together, and I was already hot all over. A tingling ran down my legs, and I rubbed my arms just to feel the pressure on my skin.

"You're showing elevated signs of response to the blood. Your eyes are dilating appropriately. If you'll let me approach, I'd like to do a scan to be sure you're not in distress."

I didn't move, or agree, but he placed a finger on my arm and swiped gently. His eyes moved back and forth, reading his screen only he could see in his eye implant.

"Very good," he approved of whatever he saw. "You're responding nicely. Our blood is known to increase mating interest. The increase in temperature your experiencing is a defensive mechanism to prevent infection when you mate with a warrior. Just so that there is no confusion about your consent, please state for the tribe that you are offering your blood to the warrior you find freely. We have laws against influencing and forcing bonds with beings that do not have natural defenses of a warrior's glands or epul."

"I..." What was I doing? Was I doing this? Breathing deeply, my whole body buzzed with heat and an itch I realized could only be scratched by Sou-el. What was the harm in giving him a mate, and returning his honor? I'd still return to Earth and he could return to his life after, right? This was just one night... "I consent." I wanted him, even if it was only one night. What was it like to feel something more than obligation? I needed to experience whatever this was before I returned to my life on Earth.

"Very good. It is an honor to be given the rights to hunt in a Rakture Ceremony. Not even the Queen of Necias Prime was the hunter, though I heard when I arrived on Trillume that she did pounce on the king from a tree after she ran. So, perhaps you are the second human to be the hunter?"

It took a bit to process his words, my thoughts still consumed with the way Sou-el made me feel with his fingers inside me. After a long pause I finally asked, "The queen is human?"

"A great honor," he agreed without fully confirming anything. "Oh, I almost forgot. Your," he caught himself from saying spawnling again and added, "Becky, said it would be important for you to be told that she would not be watching the experiment. Should she not be here to tell you herself, she wished for you to know this, and I had warned her that saying so would be considered a mark of disapproval in our culture, but she assured me that it would make you more comfortable."

I smiled and nodded. "She is giving me privacy, and her approval in our own way. Humans do not want their close family to see such things."

"Strange, but I cannot give you the same assurances. It would be a great dishonor for me to not watch my brother claim a mate. Even Commander Rokva delayed her next mission to be here for him."

No longer looking at Medic Cenkal, I snatched the useless garment from his hands, and couldn't even think about how many people were going to be watching me do this. They were all strangers, I kept repeating to myself. I wouldn't see them again when I left Trillume. I was one of many matings these researchers have seen, easily forgotten among the memories. I could do this.

The door slid open as I approached, and my limbs shook with nerves. The gown draped over my breasts but hid nothing. My sides were open to the curve of my waist with a few flimsy bit of layered flaps at my ass and front. All my flaws were on display for the whole facility, including my stretch marks that Sou-el had licked as he caressed my stomach. He didn't seem to care about any of that while waiting for me to be his mate. He was risking everything for me to find him. He was that certain I was his mate that he gave up everything for me.

I choked on a sob as I stepped out of the room and into the hall. All of my emotions were so raw on the surface. When had someone given up anything for me? My daughters aside, I'd never felt like this, and I hardly knew him...

How could I trust this?

The injection could have been some random warrior's blood into my veins that wasn't his at all. I'd see how I felt when I found him. If I found him. Commander Rokva was waiting for me.

"Renee," she addressed with a bow. A commander bowing to a human... "This way to the Blue District rooms. There are masks and sensory deprivation tools for various species to enter the halls. As you pass the rooms there are filtration vents that allow for the scent in the rooms to permeate the air around them. Human noses are not as sensitive, but with his blood in you, you should be able to find him. I have tried myself, so I could speak with him, but I was told that until you enter the hall his room would not be filtered into the hall. It is traditional for mates to have exchanged offerings, so I will give this to you now."

She took out a bead and leathers similar to the one I made for him, but much more ornate, and done with more skill than I could ever hope to achieve. It was beautiful with ivory-looking carvings dangling from it. Rokva continued, "This was made by our elder for Sou-el. He always knew one day he would have a mate to give it to and asked me to look after it for him.

When Sou-el is clear-headed enough to understand what you're wearing, he will know that he has the honored approval of his elder for the match, as well as his commander and sister."

That was too much, and my lip quivered. "I can't accept this..."

"You can, and you will." She said gruffly while her fingers were gentle and detangled my hair. "I told you, I have the blessing of matchmakers in my veins, and whatever is holding you back in that brain of yours is nothing more than a self-made barrier you must fight through to claim your mate. My own mate has these barriers, and I have given him my patience, but you do not have this luxury. You may spend more time courting after you've mated. For now, you must decide to take his mark or not."

"His mark? What exactly does that entail?"

"He will take your blood, and while his blood is in you, this will activate the bond. You will have his mark on your skin, and he will form yours on his. It is normal to sleep during that final marking process. There are bets among the warriors on if Sou-el will sense you in the room before you remove his sensory dampeners, so when you find him, give them a bit of a show by staying still for a few seconds before approaching."

"But he can't see, hear, or smell?" How was he supposed to know I was there?

She grinned mischievously and nodded. "That's the point. He shouldn't, but he will. Those few seconds won't just be for the tribe watching, but for you to know things are as they should be."

"I don't understand?"

"You will."

Rokva finished braiding my hair back, and in it was the offering Sou-el's elder made for him to give to his future mate. My fingers lifted to touch the carved beads dangling in my hair.

She flicked one of them and smiled. "Each one represents a blessing to your mating. Sou-el can explain them to you later. To your honor and my brother's." Rokva opened the door to another room and turned away. The room was small, like a mudroom in a house it had masks hanging from the wall, and various gloves, strange devices I wasn't sure what their function was, but as the door closed behind me, a blue light scanned me, beeped, and turned yellow. On Earth that would have meant something was wrong, but to aliens... blue was stop, and yellow was good.

"Welcome to the Blue District," my implant spoke. I assumed the facility connected with my implant when it scanned me. "We hold the largest selection of species for your pleasure, company, and research. Please utilize the wall to your right as you wish, masks are most common for sampling different scents with more precision, only filtering through when approaching a room. Any room with a golden glow are open, simply apply your biomarker to enter and it will change the room's glow to blue to signal occupied. There are a few species that prefer to scan your metrics for compatibility before entering, these rooms are identified with a green glow."

I now understood why they called it the blue district beyond the obvious of blue being considered a warning color and representing a more risky district of pleasure. Blue was the color of an occupied room, and the corridors ahead were lit up in mostly blue. A scattering of yellow, golden as they called it, and some green could be seen in blips down the rooms, but the halls were in several shades of blue, both from the glow of lights, and the color of the doors, a blueish metal.

The voice returned to my implant as I stepped out into the hall, "Please enjoy your stay here and follow the laws of the Blue District. Damaging any species while on the premises is strictly forbidden. We understand there are varying degrees of what is considered damaging among species, please refer to the species chart for clarification, access through all implants during your stay. Your implant has been approved for a single room entry, no time limits. Several floors are currently under construction, please remain on floors 6 through 34."

They had several... floors? How was I supposed to find Sou-el with several floors as long as this one?

Chapter Eighteen
Renee

The door slid open, and my implant informed me that my Blue District credit was consumed. Feet unmoving, I stared in shock as a blue glow from the light above the door and from the adjoining hallway filtered through the room.

How was this happening?

Across from me, in the center of the room, sat Sou-el restrained in a metal chair. He was here... I made it. I found him. How was this possible?

Run to him, I thought, but I couldn't move. I gasped, but he wouldn't hear me, given the sensory deprivation of the blindfold, and his implant being turned off.

Warmth pooled in my gut, and I watched in amazement as he lifted his head like he could see me through the blindfold, and I saw the metal strap across his neck. Another across his bare chest, his legs, and I couldn't see his hands as they were behind his back, but they must have been strapped down the same as the rest.

How would I get him out of that chair? Would they unlock it when the door closed behind me?

My hands were covering my mouth in shock, before I rubbed at my heated cheeks in disbelief.

"Pulsunne," he said with a strained grunt.

There was no way he should know I was there, and yet... he did. With no eyes, ears, or scent, he knew. His fangs lengthened as he panted against his bonds. The blood in my veins heated, and as I stared at his lips, my breathing matched his own, like our bodies were syncing. This shouldn't have been happening. He was behind a blue door, next to a room that had a foul scent that overpowered anything around it, and there was no way I should have found him given the circumstances. I wasn't a hound dog, sniffing out my mate. Humans didn't work that way, I insisted internally, still dumbfounded.

My heart thundered faster, and without realizing it, I had stepped forward with the door sliding closed behind me. The pleasant voice in my implant told me to enjoy my stay at the Blue District before I heard the door suction shut. Not wanting to startle him, I went to him and leaned over to touch his cheek from the side. The rest of him was too risky that he might stab me with this epul. His shoulder epul were fully extended, as well as a few that peeked out around his forehead like a crown, those were new.

"I'm here," I said, even though he couldn't hear a word.

His chest rumbled and a low moan escaped his lips at my touch. It was all I could do not to tear at the blindfold and the straps keeping him locked down. I didn't have the strength to remove them like that, and after several strained moments, nor could I find a switch or latch to remove them. Was this another test? First find him then unbind him?

"How do these blasted things work?" I grunted in frustration and actually did yank at them with no progress or give.

He could feel what I was doing, and... did he laugh at me? "Mine," he growled and licked his lips and over his fangs.

Oh right, I thought. I was supposed to offer my blood to him voluntarily. Before, when I had been blindfolded, it was Tensel that had taken my offering. This time I knew, and I slid my palm along his jaw until the pad beneath my thumb was pressed to his fang. I pressed lightly, and a small bead of blood surfaced for him to take. Sou-el leaned into the touch as much as he could and his lips pressed to my pierced skin, then licked my offering.

He groaned, and forced out, "More."

I thought he meant more blood, but movement along his thigh as his cock twitched and his hips strained against the bond along his chest told me otherwise.

"Claim me, Pulsunne," he demanded, and left no doubt of his intentions. I shouldn't have been surprised; Commander Rokva had said as much. He was a warrior in rut, and he needed me, not just to find him, but to show his tribe we were mates and regain his honor. Even if I wasn't sure about the future, I was sure he didn't deserve to lose everything because he fancied me.

"But you're still bound," I said concerned, forgetting he couldn't hear me. I pressed my lips together in uncertainty. My mind was made up before I started searching for him that I would help him regain his honor and be his mate... for now. I couldn't deny that I felt something with him, and I owed it to myself to explore that.

My hesitation prompted him to growl, and any normal person would have jumped back, but I found myself leaning closer like he was drawing me in. My eyes darted down to his cock weeping with precum. Ridges gathered his interest in their grooves, and I wondered if that was their function aside from creating more friction, to help more of their sperm to stay inside their mates. Not that any of that would matter for me. I wouldn't be having any more children at my age. Fingers trailed down his chest, itching to touch him, to grab him and squeeze. I stopped over his hardened torso, at the start of that delicious 'v' that led to his readied cock. He struggled with his bounds, and I doubted I was doing what I should. This felt strange to do this while he was strapped to this chair, unable to see or hear me.

He was restrained, and everything in me said he wanted me to touch him, but I couldn't stop that little voice from reminding me that I wanted him to touch me too. My other hand went to the blind fold, and tugged at it, but though it was wrapped in leather and cushioned for a slight bit of comfort, it was secured in place with a metal plate just like the rest of the restraints. But I remembered what they said when I was blindfolded before, it only takes away the sight, the implant was what blocked his hearing. Quickly, my hands flew up to grab his face, and my fingers probed behind his ears at his implant, waiting for some kind of click or sign that I had found his and activated it.

"Sou-el, Sou-el," I repeated over and over.

"Renee," he finally said, and I tensed, hoping it wasn't a false response.

"Can you hear me?"

"There is no more beautiful sound in this universe," he said and then licked my wrist as I cupped his face. "Show the tribe that you want me, Pulsunne. I've asked that they keep my restraints active until you've claimed me."

"What do you mean? Why? How is this possible?" Questions flurried out of me all at once.

"The song of a warrior's hearts cannot be hidden. It is in our blood. I want no one to doubt that it is you choosing me."

I felt it, as his skin brushed against mine. That heat building within me, begging to be touched. And the only relief was holding him as I stood between his legs. His cock pressed into my stomach, and nodes pulsed out of the sides, soft bones like his epul, but not sharp, thrummed and made my thighs clench together, wishing his cock was lower so I could rub against him.

"Do you want me, Renee?" he rasped.

And I did, I thought breathlessly. Though, the words wouldn't form, I found myself climbing on his lap, wrapping my arms around his neck. The gauzy skirt flaps of the dress easily parted with my movement, baring myself against his engorged cock. I hovered a moment before I made contact, allowing one of my hands to trace down his chest until I could rub my thumb along his shaft. Up over each ridge, around the side to feel the epul pulse out, verifying they felt similar to cartilage and not a weapon ready to skewer me. With every touch, my breathing grew more rapid, and I wrapped my hand around him, squeezing until a new bead of cum surfaced for me wipe up with a finger that I brought to my lips. Tasting him elicited a moan and my hips angled until my clit pressed the underside of his cock as it flexed against his abs. I rocked to gain that friction as I pulled forward with an arm around his neck, my forehead rested against his chin, a low whimper trembling from my lips. I'd never taken what I wanted before. Always giving, I thought, and even though the actions were similar, this felt different, like I was taking him as his cock slid between my wet pussy and those ridges flicked along my clit as I ground into him. Could it be possible to give pleasure while seeking out your own? That it didn't need to be one or the other?

Sou-el groaned as I moved his cock along that little bud of pleasure that had denied me for so many years. "Take what you want, Pulsunne, I am yours," he demanded, but it was the first time someone had demanded I take from them, and not give them something from myself. It was the most precious gift for him to want the focus to be whatever I wanted it to be.

I rocked harder, holding on to him tighter. My pussy slid up and down his cock, using his ridges to stimulate my clit and tease my swollen labia with the pressure of something hard and pulsing. His precum lubricated my movements, but it wasn't necessary as I coated his cock in my arousal. Back and forth, up, up, and slipping down, I use his cock as my personal scratching post to itch that need building at my core. Riding along his length, feeling the tug of his ridges bump as I ground harder until I rocked too far, and his cock got caught at the notch of my entrance. With one swift movement, the head of his cock stretched me. I sat on his tip, stilled as I gasped, and he groaned his own pleasure at feeling me squeeze.

So tight around him, I didn't think it'd be possible to take his girth.

"I belong inside you, Pulsunne," he said in his sultry, deep voice that made me shiver.

I panted, eyes closed, and liquid gushed from me until I spasmed and slammed down, sitting on him. As his head hit deep inside me, and his cock slipped farther and farther as I buried him to the hilt, every part of me throbbed with an intense feeling that I couldn't describe. Pressure built up and I didn't know what I needed to release that ache until a vibration against my clit had me scream out his name. A sudden and shattering pleasure had my muscles tense and release so violently, I practically collapsed against Sou-el's chest.

What was that? I tingled all over, and there was pressure still against my clit. As I calmed down, I rocked up and it vibrated again, sending new thrills down to my toes as they curled. A throaty moan broke free from my lips, and his cock pulsed inside me. Sweat dripped down my thighs, and I panted against him, unsure if I could continue with my limbs trembling.

I was so still, feeling him move within me with every breath.

It happened so fast, and my pussy throbbed as that heat that begged to take from him again built within me.

"It is divine torture not to taste your ello on my tongue, Pulsunne, but that is not nearly enough to quench my thirst for you. Until I am bathed in your ello, mate, and they can hear only my name on your pretty screams, will I mark you," he then growled and demanded of whoever was watching us to release him.

I shivered at his promises, and he moaned as I clenched around him. Those little nodes along his cock pulsed, and I bucked in response, a small whimper cooing from me before I lifted my head to his and tugged at his plump lower lip with my teeth.

"What if I want you to have *my* mark?"

"You've marked me the very moment we touched, Pulsunne. Deep in my hearts, there is no other touch I desire but yours."

I lifted and stroked his cock within me as I sat slowly to feel every ridge and node, torturing us both until those prongs slipped against my clit once more and I silent screamed while spasming against him. Every nerve was sensitive and on fire. My eyes were closed, so I didn't see or notice his restraints being released, but his hands wrapped around me, one grabbing at my ass and pushing down for his cock to hit deeper and give me more pressure against him. I pulled back just enough to lift my head but kept my hips grinding to chase the heat I felt as we moved together. The blindfold was dangling from the chair, and black eyes stared back at me before I caught the flick of his tongue on his lips. Then his mouth was on mine, needy and devouring as we consumed more of each other.

Chapter Nineteen
General Sou-el

M y chair was set up with every intention of being freed as soon as my implant was unmuted. The silence of only hearing my inner thoughts was more maddening than I anticipated. My body worked against me, my health was declining, and I would happily choose this fate again for the chance to have her in my life. To feel this moment of completeness with my mate if only once. All of the restraints were paired up with my access codes and once Renee re-activated my implant with her probing fingers, I had the means to take her. But her voice sweetly calling to me gave me pause. With her blood in my system, a sense of normalcy returned that comforted my raging hearts. As soon as my blood burned for her when she entered the room, I knew she was near, but it wasn't until her blood was on my tongue, did I finally think clearly.

She was here, and she had come for me even with my dishonored state.

She chose me, and that alone had my hearts soaring.

My rut was under more control than I'd observed from other studies of our tribe, but I was not immune, despite my glandular deficiencies. My cock was hard for her, and when she traced her thumb along my ridges and moved along my sensitive epulknot pulsing in and out along my shaft, my reason abandoned me. All there was was my mate, my Pulsunne, and I wanted to be buried inside her. Claiming her with my mark, and my life. It was all hers, if she wanted it.

But I would not unbind myself until she was sure, until she claimed me first. I would not have my tribe dishonor me with doubts about my mate's choices. Commander Tensel could still claim it was my blood in her that made her choose me. But being restrained, it would be her choice to complete the mating. As her soft flesh stroked up and down my shaft, I nearly choked on a moan as my epulknot slipped into her entrance and my precum helped lubricate and relax her muscles to stretch and fill her.

Renee collapsed on my chest moments later as she came on my cock as my epul at my base extended out and I could feel them vibrate and shiver against her hardened bead of pleasure. For a necia female there was usually a few epul that extend out from there for my own to latch onto and secure my cock before the knotting process began, as our epul are sensitive near there, it was pleasurable for them, but the way my mate shuddered against me tore all of my willpower away. I released my bonds, and pulled her hips down to feel more of her as she squeezed around my cock, nearly making me knot inside her.

Not yet, I thought growling with the intensity of her wrapped around me. I wanted no other mate, but her. And out of all the females I'd bathed or mated with, none of them made me want to knot within them. None of them were my Pulsunne, my Renee.

"Sou-el," she panted my name as she rocked her hips.

"If I mark you, Pulsunne, I'm yours, always," I strained to warn her, and it took everything in me to stop myself from coming, knowing she was different and my epul would knot the moment I finished. "Will you have me?"

"Yes," she said softly, then again stronger, "You're mine." Her mouth crashed into mine, and I could not object to her statement. I was hers, forever.

Our lips moved, a dance of tongues that spoke of a desperate need of removing that singularity of separation into one of unity and passion. I didn't want this moment to end, but until it did, we would forever be in want, craving that connection only a first knot could give. Elders spoke of what claiming a mate did for both warriors once their DNA. was shared in knotting, but I had never experienced it myself. Only in observation have I witnessed the expressions and vitals as the mate's pleasure was enhanced, and the wildness of their claim transformed into something closer to unified rhythm of two souls joined as one. I explained this mating with science, probabilities, correlated data points, and now all I could write about this moment would be utter perfection as my epulknot expanded with my mate.

"Pulsunne," I moaned as I pulled her closer, never wanting to let her go. My mate's lips quivered as she bit down, drawing my blood into her mouth. No pain, only pleasure erupted through me as my own fangs grew and I buried them into her neck with a possessive howl. Our hips rocked, tugging at my knot as my cock buried deep within her. Her heart rate slowed and I knew the sedative qualities of my first knotting were working their way through her.

"Don't leave me," she whispered against my chest, and my hearts warmed. Nothing could keep me from her now that we were bonded. I smiled fondly at the tender soreness that laced with pleasure where she bit my lower lip. It was already healed over, and I felt stronger than I had in weeks.

"Wherever your heart desires, Pulsunne, I will go. Rest, I will be here when you wake," I assured her.

"Sou-el," she prompted sleepily, and then yawned. "Is this a dream?"

I chuckled and kissed her forehead. "If it is, let us never wake from it."

Her limbs relaxed more, and I released a few epul on my hips that were only activated by intention for our mates, delicately placing her calves over the blunted curves that would hold her legs in place while I wrapped my arms around her to secure the rest of her as she slumbered. I would not release my knot for some time, and she would not wake until my DNA was accepted within her body. Some of my tribe would wait to congratulate me on my mating until my mark showed on her, while Rokva and Cenkal would have no doubts that we would succeed in completing the bond.

Our bodies hummed together, and I sighed with a contentment I never thought I'd get to experience.

I had a mate, and she had chosen me.

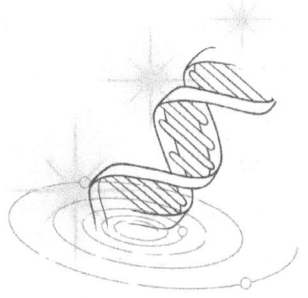

Chapter Twenty
Renee

S tretching my hands over my head, I moaned with how delicious the soft ache between my legs still felt, even after sleeping. It was like my pussy could still sense him near and was eager to be filled by him all over again. My mate, I thought with a lazy smile. I rolled, smacking right into him, my leg and arm flopping over his firm chest and legs. A pleasant chuckle rumbled through his chest, and I could listen to that anytime. I had been afraid before of the whole mate thing, but he was still here even after we slept together. Would it be forever? I didn't know, and I honestly didn't want to worry about it when everything felt so right in the moment.

Maybe he would leave me tomorrow, but I wouldn't change what we shared together for anything. I'd never felt anything like it before, and I'd probably never feel anything like it again.

But I could sure try, I thought deviously as I squeezed my eyes shut to stay in this dream a little longer and trailed my fingers down his torso to a readied cock in my hand. Fuck, I was horny for him and I hadn't even opened my eyes. I felt like the wanton my mother warned me about, and I didn't care that all I wanted to do was wake up to his cock inside me. He moaned as I rubbed my thumb along his ridges and he grew larger until his epul throbbed along his shaft for me.

He wrapped his arms around me and tugged me beneath him as I squealed and finally opened my eyes to take him in. He was... everything. My heart swelled in my chest as I watched the way his amber eyes stared at me with wonder and desire. His cock rubbed against my entrance and with a groan he begged, "Open for me, Pulsunne." I widened my hips and let my knee move to the side, wrapping my heel around his ass. He growled as the head of him sunk in, and I whimpered, arching my back to lift myself up for his cock to fill me deeper.

"There's a good mate," he praised as I took him to the hilt, and his epul shivered inside me while a few longer ones at his base slipped up to stimulate my clit. My hands tangled in my hair and I thrashed, rubbing myself against him. If it were possible, it felt better than it did the first time, all my nerves were on fire, and my skin practically vibrated with need to feel all of him. "Take what you want. I'm yours."

"Fuck, fuck," I panted as I came on his cock, spasming and rubbing my clit against his vibrating epul. He stilled, allowing me to use him for my own pleasure, and as I came down from the high for a moment, he grinned at me. Embarrassed, I tried to turn away, but he cupped my face and leaned over me with strong emotions in his eyes. They weren't black like they were before, he wasn't in rut now, this was all him. His choices, his unfettered desire without the influence of his rut.

"Don't turn from me. I wish to see every expression you make as you take my cock for your pleasure."

His hand cradling my face, he stared at me deeply, as he began to slowly slip out, then back in with tortured rhythm, letting me feel every ridge of him as he moved. Each thrust was faster than the last, until we both grunted as his cock hit so deep with a jerk that I saw stars, my eyes unable to see beyond the otherworldly glow of his eyes. I rocked my hips with him riding that high of every ridge, epul, and thrust sending pleasurable waves through my body until my muscles tensed and coiled, my toes curling as I arched into the shattering of my world as I knew it.

Liquid heat filled me and gushed down my thighs as we moved. His fingers scooped between us and lifted to his lips with a groan. He was tasting me, and as he sucked his fingers, he spasmed inside me, sending new pleasure through to my very bones. My pussy throbbed as he locked inside me, and I cut my lip as I bit down. He smiled and propping himself on his arms, he lowered to lick my blood. What was strange was that I didn't feel the cut of my teeth at all. As I swiped out my tongue to catch his own, I gasped as it slid over a sharp fang. My eyes widened, as they weren't his.

They were... mine.

My hands snapped up and rubbed at my teeth, catching on a sharp fang, but I didn't feel anything but the pleasure of our bodies joining as one. The cut on my lip was gone, and I stared up at him in shock.

"Bite me," he growled out. Sou-el moved his silver hair to the side, over one shoulder, his epul retracted for me to get closer. My stomach grumbled in reply, and at first I kissed his skin gently, before I found myself scraping my canine down his neck. I hadn't noticed it before, but there was a patch of skin thinner than the rest, without any scales, or protection that I could even see his vein pulse just beneath the surface. It was just there that my fangs sunk in, and we both moaned as his blood warmed me from the inside out. I licked where there should be a wound, but there wasn't one, already healing itself as I withdrew.

"You heal so fast," I stated in amazement.

"So do you now," he said as he rubbed my own neck where he had bitten me before. His fingers traced over what felt like bumps on my skin, and when I reached up to grab his hand, my fingers slid over hardened ridges. He explained softly, "I'm pleased to say that my mark has decided to protect you from any other warrior that may think to steal you from me."

"I don't understand..."

He dragged my hand over his chest and down to his scales on his abs, he flexed, and the suede scales hardened similar to how my neck felt. I had scales?

My heart rate picked up with a bit of panic at these changes and the only thing keeping me from jumping out of my own skin was the rush of pleasure still warming me from his blood, and his cock locked inside of me, flexing with every movement we made.

"They are fading the more I touch you," he said soothingly, "It is likely they will only be visible with extended time apart, as a defense mechanism. Before we rutted, they covered more of you." He touched under my breast, down my belly, and they stilled over where my stretchmarks darkened my waist. He stared at them with a kind of yearning, and pride that made my stomach flip inside. Did he wish to have a child himself and be the cause of more stretch marks on my skin? After a few moments, he smiled softly and distracted us both by continuing, "It's possible you may control them with time as I do with mine."

I tried to move away, to find a mirror or something, but I chuckled when he simply came with me, attached by his cock stuck inside me. "When does it release?" I questioned with a wicked smile. It would be good to know what that process was for the future, I thought. The future, I repeated in my mind, I guess I saw more of this for us, and I hoped I wouldn't be disappointed when reality crashed into us, and we left this bubble of ours. We weren't in the office I had come to know as his room on the ship. This was a rather large room for a spaceship, even if he used it as an office as well, it was huge.

He saw me looking around and played with my hair as he explained, "I'll try not to knot within you next time, Pulsunne. It can take quite some time to release, as it is a primitive function to increase the odds of spawnlings. My body doesn't distinguish that we aren't rutting for procreation but for pleasure. If you should have need of something, my body is designed to carry my mate while attached. There are special epul that are used only for unne mates to secure you. This is our room for now, for as long as you want it to be."

"It's so big," I said in awe, ignoring the subject of babies, and the idea that he was willing to carry me around like an odd appendage attached to his cock like that was normal.

"As befitting my title as General of Research on this compound, and second to the lead researcher from AsunGor who, though not part of my tribe is equivalent to a commander in title. Should he step down from his duties I would be promoted to Commander here within the Blue District."

"You regained your honor," I stated with relief that he had his life reinstated, and that we were still close to where my daughter was stationed as an intern.

"Becky tells me that our customs are extreme for humans, but I did not regain my honor. It was you who restored it, I simply benefit for being your mate."

"That doesn't make any sense," I admitted.

He nodded and moved a strand of hair out of my face, and behind my ear with care. "The test wasn't to have my honor returned. It was designed to prove humans are more than mate compatible, but worthy of title and honor themselves within our tribe, and capable of claiming a mate of their choosing. Every warrior is tested before they may officially be part of the tribe. This was your test, not mine. You are part of my tribe by mate bond, but you are part of Commander Tensel's tribe by challenge. You are a human warrior of Necias Prime in two tribes."

I blinked at him and furrowed my brow. "I'm a what?"

"A human warrior of Necias Prime. You proved that humans can indeed track their intended mates through the blood bond. Commander Tensel set up the challenge himself. I was placed behind a door that was labeled as occupied and not available to trick your mind, near another room with a species that has a particularly potent scent that should block your ability to track by smell, and only one chance to open a door so you could not search by elimination. It isn't proof that all humans can do this, but it is evidence that Commander Tensel has reason to believe given the results of your challenge that humans with certain

DNA markers could be descendants of interspecies breeding between ancient necia and humans."

"You're saying that I may have traces of DNA in me from an ancestor that mated with a necia warrior?"

"It's possible," he agreed. Seeing my shock he added, "Your ancestry is irrelevant to my feelings for you."

"And what are those?"

"My feelings?"

"Uh huh," I mumbled nervously.

He wrapped me up in his arms and kissed my forehead. "Holding you brings me more joy than I thought I would ever have for myself. Knowing that I will be by your side no matter if I'm a General, or a warrior with no tribe or title, excites me for our future whatever it may hold. If you wish to return to Earth, I will do what I must to earn clearances. If you wish to visit my home world, then I will take you and build us a fine home and teach warriors the way of the mind. If you wish to stay here, with your daughter, I will help Pryxus of AsunGor and we can make a life here for as long as you wish to stay."

It sounded like he already knew where I would choose to be. Of course, I wanted to stay with Becky, but I also wanted to go back to Earth to make sure Laurel was okay. I still haven't spoken to her since I left, and I didn't get a chance to send a message either. Laurel was always more independent, but that didn't mean she didn't need me. But now that I had Sou-el, I couldn't risk his health with him joining me on Earth.

"I need to think about it," I told him honestly.

"My feelings will not change, no matter your decision. I don't care how it happened, or why, and that is strange for me. Seeking out knowledge and understanding is how I've survived my life to this point. But now that I have you, this unexplainable feeling beats in my hearts that beyond reason knows that if I lose you, I would cease to be. You are part of me, Pulsunne."

My breath caught, and I felt tears well up within my eyes with this fullness of happiness. But I had to know what that word that had no translation meant. "What does that word mean?"

"It has no translation," he admitted, "because the implants have trouble separating words in my home language, Cial. It is two of our words, deconstructed down to their ancient roots, and put together. It is the act of taking every heart from two warriors and syncing together in one rhythm. Which means in my mother tongue, the song of my hearts. Yours is the heart that my hearts sing for, when our hearts sync together, they aren't merely one rhythm, they are music only we can feel."

A tear dripped down my cheek and my lip trembled. "You mean that?"

"I feel that," he took my hand and placed it over his chest, then took my other hand and placed it over mine. "This, between us, is a song any warrior would die for."

"You nearly did," I choked out. I felt as our hearts were beating together, syncing, and I closed my eyes enjoying the warmth that filled my chest as I didn't listen, but felt the pulse of our blood bond together. "It's beautiful."

"It is," he agreed.

We laid there on our new bed, listening to a song only we could hear. No matter what happened next, I believed him, we'd face it together. I was enough. He was more than I could ever hope to have, and he was mine.

I wondered if it was alright if I started calling him my Pulsunne too. It worked both ways didn't it? He was my heart song too. I guess not everything needed an explanation, and if a researcher could care less about understanding it, then so could I. I cared more about enjoying it for as long as our hearts kept singing.

"Pulsunne," I said tenderly back to him, and he smiled so the corners of his amber eyes crinkled, and I pulled him for a kiss.

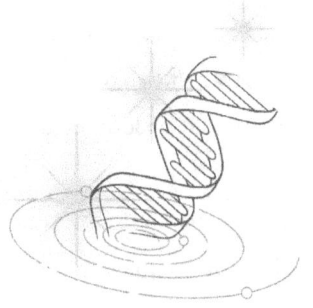

Chapter
Twenty-One
Renee

E ventually, we left our room. Our room, I thought with a smile thinking about how even that small difference of whose room it was made this whole situation even more surreal. Even after twenty years of marriage, I still thought of the house as Tyler's... I simply lived in it. But here, in a place I'd never been in before felt like mine just as much as it was Sou-el's, and it had nothing from either of us to show anyone else that it was ours. It wasn't the space at all, I knew, it was who I was with.

As newly mated, we were given time to stay in our room for as long as we wanted. The room was a lot bigger than the office that doubled as Sou-el's room on the ship, and with a food dispenser and a lavatory, we didn't have much reason to leave. I found his knot could be soothed into releasing me after I stroked his back with my fingers. He'd relax, and we could go for another round... or more. I didn't want to let him go. I liked how connected I felt when we mated, so when exhaustion was close to taking over, I'd rest my head on his chest with his knot throbbing inside me. He'd stay with me until I shoved him off in my sleep, but no matter where I flailed on the bed some part of me had to be touching him, even if it was just a foot next to his knee.

Night after night we fell asleep in each other's arms. After a month of being at the Blue District Labs, Sou-el surprised me with what he called a mating gift. All those times he disappeared with Pryxus, the lead scientist at this facility, he'd been working on finding technology for me to visit Earth.

"So, what is this thing?" I asked as I sat in the cross-universal communicator chair. It wasn't exactly the chair that made the communication across large distances possible, it was just how they stabilized a body for the way the communication took place, I was told.

Medic Cenkal handed a book to me and said, "Hold this, and Chief Olben will make sure you're connected, while I monitor your vitals."

"Is this all really necessary?" I asked, my nerves making me anxious with excitement and worry. It wouldn't be the first time something alien had strange effects on me. Sou-el's blood bonded with me, and I found him when it shouldn't have been possible. When we mated, his DNA merged with mine, and while I was unconscious for a little over a week, I grew fangs, and apparently scales on my neck that blended with my skin color until they hardened and took on a purplish hue and protected me like armor. It still shocked me, even after seeing it for a month now. Becky told me it was incredible and another piece of evidence that supports the theory that the trace DNA marker they found in me could be ancient necians that made their way to Earth long ago.

"Sou-el went through great effort to convince Pryxus of AsunGor to obtain this communication device. With the help of Chief Olben you'll be able to visit your spawnling," Cenkal paused, and rephrased, knowing I didn't like him ignoring our names, "Laurel, on Earth, whenever you wish without having to put your body through unnecessary cycles of stasis, or risk your own health returning to Earth. Your DNA is more susceptible to the toxins of Earth's atmosphere now that you've bonded with Sou-el."

This would normally be the time I'd be heading back to Earth after being awake on Trillume for my contracted amount of time, if I wasn't exempt by Necias' Law, I'd be leaving all of this.

Sou-el sat next to me, and placed his hand over mine as I held the book that acted like some kind of teleportation device for my consciousness. He would join me on my visit to Earth, if this all worked out. If it didn't, I wasn't sure I'd pass whatever exams they did upon returning to Earth to be allowed to return to my old life anyways. I was just as much necia now as I was human.

"This will work, right?" I eyed the actual technology specialist in the room, Chief of Security, Olben. He nodded as he swiped through the air at whatever he was working on within his screen only he could see. This had to work for me to see Laurel again. Becky was here and thriving at the research station, at least there was that I assured myself.

I squeezed Sou-el's hand, and my blood heated with a comfort only he could provide.

"We're connected," Olben announced. "Prepare for transfer."

How was I supposed to prepare for... My vision blurred, and I gasped as it felt like I was going under anesthesia. But when I blinked again, I was standing in the same room during exchange orientation where I got to see a hologram of the world and species I'd see. I touched my arms and they felt real enough, and I moved around the room freely. How was this possible?

"Touch one of the wristbands over here," Sou-el said, and I turned to see him grabbing something off the wall.

"What is that?"

"These are what they give humans who reject implants. It will stabilize our connection here, and allow us to leave this room, or so Chief Olben assured me."

"I've been expecting you two," that cranky voice I'd come to know during my preparation for my exchange, Joel, could be heard from the doorway. "You better hold up your end of the bargain. I'm not risking my job for nothing."

I lifted a brow at Sou-el as if to ask about what bargain was made, but he simply smiled and assured Joel, "Our Security Chief tells me all things are settled for your visit to Trillume using the same technology. Just keep the wristband that you have on for him to contact you."

"Well, it's not like I'm actually breaking any intergalactic laws, considering you aren't actually here, are you?" he grumbled.

"Exactly," Sou-el agreed. "Only holograms here."

Joel chuffed and led us into another room. He worked at this H.E.T. station because he wasn't cleared to travel into space by medical. They deemed him too old to be a good candidate for the advanced medical technology that could prolong his life, and his bone density too weak to travel the universe without medical assistance. It was the same reason Holden couldn't join the attraction study. Well, not the being old thing, just the bone density. For some reason, that was a dealbreaker for receiving the advanced medical technology as the body would be too weak to accept the nanobots from doing their job properly. Joel made a deal with Olben to use this communication technology to travel to Trillume without his body ever leaving Earth.

As the door slid open, I screamed, and rushed inside leaving Sou-el behind. There stood my baby girl, Laurel, and her girlfriend Jennifer. Her eyes widened and she rushed for me too, and our arms wrapped around each other. I thought for sure that my arms would fly right through her, but she was solid in my arms. I felt the pressure of her hold on me, and I could just cry. Who was I kidding, I was crying.

I wasn't sure hologram covered what we were, considering the current definition of a hologram was a 3-D recording of wave lengths that were based on light, and had no "physical" form to touch, but somehow, what we were doing had our consciousness here without the lag of traveling space between planets, and my mind could feel hugging my own daughter, and she could feel me.

"Mom!" she yelled in my ear, through my hair, and I didn't even care that it was much too loud when we were so close. "How is this possible?"

It was Sou-el that answered, "The wristband you are wearing is interacting with the wristband stabilizing the hologram. It will feel as if she is solid for both of you. I don't know the mechanics of it. I'm not that kind of scientist."

"And who is that," Laurel asked in a pretend whisper that everyone in the room could hear, even Sou-el.

I sniffled, though I knew there wasn't any fluid to wipe away, being a hologram and all. Even the tears I knew I would have been shedding right now were just me imagining them there. This was my consciousness, nothing more. With a chuckle, I gave Laurel another squeeze. I pulled away to take a look at her, take in the fact that she was whole and healthy.

Another voice I didn't realize was in the room spoke up, "I'm Laurel's father, and you would be?"

My breath caught and I glanced over to see Tyler was here and I whispered to my daughter urgently, "Laurel?" She had some explaining to do, because the invite didn't extend to my ex-husband, and I wasn't sure I was ready to have that conversation about not returning to Earth with him present. I guessed I owed it to him to say something, but I thought I'd have more time. Perhaps talk with him the next time I used the communicator... Why was he here?

Tyler's hand was extended in greeting to Sou-el, and Sou-el bowed his head in his own greeting.

"General Sou-el," he offered and then assumed correctly, "You must be Tyler, honored guardian of my mate's spawn-lings. I must thank you for your service towards their hap-piness."

I stared between them both, stunned, when Tyler replied with a smile, "It's nice to put a face to the transmission messages."

A what to the what? Were they talking to each other?

Tyler continued, "The request to divorce was granted after the state received your statement of mating, as we discussed."

As they discussed, I thought, not being able to do anything but repeat what they said to each other over in my mind, processing this all in the moment.

"Very good, I'm told this will give you more freedoms to seek out your own mating on your planet. As I have said, Becky is doing well in her studies and would like for you to know that she will arrange a time to visit with you next month at your home as long as you can keep that wristband with you. Our Chief Security Olben has said he is working out the long-distance issues by experimenting with communication using a smaller device. It is why he started by connecting with the H.E.T. main hologram room, but seems confident in refining the connection in the coming rotations."

Tyler smiled and nodded. "I'm looking forward to it." Then he turned to me, still staring at them both, as he said, "I missed you, Renee."

He'd been a part of my life for twenty years, the father of my children, and he was always so good to me, but I didn't know what to say to that. He missed me, but the way I missed him wasn't the same, was it? Of course, I thought about him. How could I not? But, what I missed wasn't us, it was the way we were before we married. My best friend.

I said nothing, and Tyler nodded again in understanding. I couldn't say I missed him, and that broke my heart. I felt awful, but he lifted that burden with his next words, "I knew you'd find someone." He chuckled awkwardly. "Is that weird? I was upset about it when you left. I didn't see you off, but I'm grateful for the life we had together. I'd have kept you for the rest of our lives, and I know that's selfish, but—" He glanced over at Sou-el, who was inching his way closer to me, only for them both to be interrupted by Laurel, who was still holding my hand.

"Dad means to say he loves you but is happy that you've found someone who makes you excited. He supports you." She pointedly eyed Tyler and added, "Right?" She whispered to me next, "I didn't invite him, I was heading out of the house with Jennifer, and he grabbed his coat and said that he was invited to the H.E.T. offices to meet your 'mate'. Are you going to have a wedding? Did you already have one?"

"Right," Tyler said quickly after, while eying Sou-el. "What I meant to say is that, we were... *are* always friends, and I hope that you'll keep me updated about your life, and not simply through our kids... You deserve every happiness, and he seems like a good," he paused unable to say the word 'man' because he wasn't one, so he settled on saying, "mate."

I beamed, looking over at Sou-el, who was practically puffing out his chest, and his shoulder epul were on full display, large and imposing. "He's my heart. I'm pretty lucky."

"Pulsunne," he rumbled low, and I knew he craved to feel that connection between us again. We may have felt things in our holograms, but that tingle and heat in the touches here were different than being in person. Our blood bond was missing in these forms. But I still felt as if my heart was pounding just from the dark look in his eyes as he watched me, a promise of what was to come when we returned.

Someone from the door behind me cleared their throat, and I laughed. It was nice to feel that giddiness like I was a teen again. Age truly was in the mind, and in this case in the heart as well.

"Look what the universe dragged in!" A familiar voice chimed.

"Uncle Holly!" Laurel squealed. "You made it!"

"Wouldn't miss it," he said with a smile on his face as he looked between me and Sou-el. "I believe you've seen the sun, Renee." I lifted a brow, already expecting the joke that would come after, because I was one of the palest people I knew. The sun wouldn't do anything but turn me red. So, either he was commenting about how red I was even in hologram form, for the heated cheeks I probably showed, or... He finished his punch line before I could continue to guess what he was up to, "Clearly, you are not lacking in Vitamin D."

Laurel, Jennifer, and myself filled the room with laughter that the other males in the room didn't seem to catch on as quickly to the joke. It was a case of alien dick that had me seeing stars, and I regretted nothing. Holden grinned at Sou-el and added, "You've stolen the finest treasure from Earth. Our Renee, here, is priceless."

"You will be invited to our Rakture Ceremony on Necias Prime," Sou-el said without realizing that Holden wouldn't be able to travel space to get there.

"I'll be there," Holden agreed, and I stared at them both.

"Am I missing something?" I asked.

"General Sou-el, here, said out of all the humans on Earth, you couldn't live without me, so he pushed for an exemption on my medical as long as it was overseen by Medic Cenkal, and that I was okay with the risks. I'm going to meet you on Necias Prime before you know it, with a regimented dosage of nanobots specific to my needs."

"How many mating gifts are you giving me?" I asked, my lip trembling with emotion I couldn't contain.

Sou-el preened with a devious grin while he replied, "Your happiness is mine, Pulsunne. There is no number to our mating gifts. I give them freely for the rest of our lives."

A pressure built behind my eyes, but I knew no tears would actually fall without reconnecting with my physical body. The ache in my chest settled in deep and I craved his touch to reaffirm the feelings I had for my mate after saying words that were now burned into my soul.

How could I ever begin to give him the same happiness that he gave me every day?

As if he could hear my self doubts he bent over and whispered into my hair, next to my ear, "Nothing I give will ever be enough to express how much being claimed by you resonates in my hearts."

I blushed and realized everyone was watching us, but that didn't bother me anymore. I wanted them to know, the people in my life that meant the most to me, that I was happy. And that happiness wasn't because I had a mate, but because I found someone that didn't think it was any inconvenience to listen to me as I figured out who I was, and who I wanted to be in the future.

Laurel said Becky sent her messages about things, and that she'd use the hologram to come visit after. Her place was on Earth, for now, and she was happy. Holden would be treated by the best medic I knew, Cenkal, and eventually, I'd have my best friend with me again. When we were ready, Sou-el and I would visit Necias Prime for an official Rakture Ceremony among his tribe as witness, and I'd get to meet the Queen of Necias Prime, who was apparently a human!

Whatever the future held, we'd figure it out because I knew we'd listen to each other.

I squeezed his hand as my vision blurred from the connection to Earth ending, and my reconnection with my body on Trillume coming back into place.

"Your happiness is mine too," I used his words, because I couldn't think of a better expression for what he meant to me as well. "Pulsunne," I called him my heart song in his own tongue, just as my body pulsed with heat, reminding me that I was home.

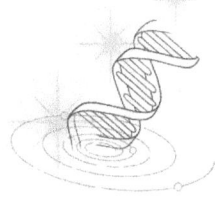

Thank you for reading Her Alien Warrior! If you enjoyed this book, give a heart-filled thank you by taking a moment to rate and review the book on all the places books are shared. It helps indies like me reach new readers and supports more books coming to life! The more people read and share the book the more motivation us indies have to keep providing you new adventures!

Swipe ahead to catch a teaser of what's to come in the next book Her Alien Captor, book three in Necias Alien Warrior Series, and don't forget to join Sky Robert's newsletter to grab your free book Her Alien Exchange and keep up to date on new releases and loads of goodies and behind the scenes! https://books.steviemarie.com/heralienexchange

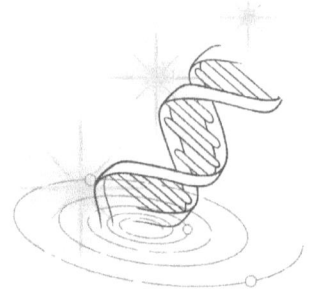

Chapter
Twenty-Two
Commander Tensel

I'd kept my ship at the Trillume Port for longer than was proper, but the results of the study were paramount to our species. When Princess Klemon contacted about the virus Ganpan Fal and her studies about a cure within humans for our fertility crisis, this new information about a potential DNA marker suggesting ancient warriors hiding among Earthlings was pivotal to our survival as a species. I was even willing to mate with one of the humans to give evidence of the claims being true.

The human was capable of a blood bond, how could I deny it?

She found her way to her chosen mate through obstacles that would be tough for even a trained tracker to follow. Were humans capable of a true fated bond? Was such a myth even possible?

I acquiesced to a blood bond and trace markers of necia DNA, but I was skeptical of a goddess given mate even for pure-blood warriors.

We were either compatible or not. Chosen or not.

There was no such thing as finding a mythical Pulsunne. I scoffed at such a notion as our hearts beating to a strange musical enchantment. It was simply a story our elders spoke about to give the gullible something to hope for.

Not being chosen by the human stung. I believed our time together would have been pleasant, I enjoyed the sound of her voice, but she was still a human, and there were plenty of compatible mates if I had a mind to be looking for one. There was plenty of time for such matters after more conclusive data could be gathered on humans with trace necia DNA. Renee was a single human that passed my challenge and now was part of my tribe, regardless of our mating status. It was hardly enough evidence, but it was something. And I had no desire to harm General Sou-el when he was exhibiting signs of rut. I had expected it, even goaded him to duel me. It was part of my plan to force him into challenging the human to prove the blood bond was possible.

My implant connected to the visual of the princess. Wearing the traditional royal robes of Trillume, she was finally taking on some of her responsibilities to her planet it seemed. Her green skin was lighter than her mothers and her eyes didn't hold the same cold detachment I'd seen in intergalactic news vids from the former queen.

"Commander Tensel," she addressed, "Small is her sight when focused on but one instead of many, but from one to all do I strive to serve."

"Princess Klemon," I bowed my head with my pinky finger pressed to my temple, as her own implant would show my form before her, and I wished her respect. "In many we rise," but I hadn't missed how she changed the traditional saying and added my own bit to show my support of change within the trill's customs, "it may take one rock to stir the ocean."

Her hologram image within my viewing implant smiled, but she kept her lips closed as their teeth were designed for shredding meat, and they were a polite sort of species. They liked to hide their predatory nature behind flowing robes, and disarming smiles. I was told by my new king that she was to be trusted, but I was of the solid opinion to trust... but verify.

"Did you give the antidote to the human?" Princess Klemon got straight to the point. I could respect her directness.

"I have selected a human," I replied with no remorse for my small rebellion against following her order exactly. She was not my future queen, she was a future queen of Trillume, and my planet now had our own rights returned to us. I was not her commander.

"I assume you will be keeping which subject was injected a secret until you can verify results personally," she said without any indication of being upset about my decision to comply, but in my own way. She appeared to have expected this turn events or didn't much care which human was injected to verify her theory that this new injection was a cure for the Ganpan Fal. I couldn't risk such a thing without having the specimen examined. According to Medic Valmeh, it was a blood sample. The only unusual thing about it was that it was both necia and human, which by deductive reasoning would mean that Princess Klemon wished for me to inject another human with blood from a human mated to a necia, or a possible rare necia-human hybrid.

What was so special about this blood? I couldn't risk running more tests, there wasn't enough sample to do so and then still have enough to inject another human for any changes to their own DNA. All I had confirmation of was that this human had the same marker present as the other subjects.

I finally answered Princess Klemon, "I'll be in touch with the results." Ending our transmission, I pulled up the file of Becky Grant of Earth. She was who Princess Klemon wished to inject the antidote to, young and at the peak of human breeding, but her mother had two spawnlings without an antidote. Princess Klemon may have developed the Ganpan Fal to begin with, but she was not thinking clearly. This subject would not give us the desired confirmation of an antidotes' effectiveness. It was possible she would breed fine regardless of any efforts.

Jayden of Earth, the one human who signed up for the re-search program and missed her shuttle. All the contracts were secured, and under normal circumstances she was one human among many, and her absence would be discarded, but when I returned to Earth to drop off the finished contracts, I would find her, and she would fulfill her contract even if I had to capture her to do so.

Keep posted on Jayden and Commander Tensel's story, Her Alien Captor, and when it releases by joining the newsletter and grabbing Her Alien Exchange, a fun full-length novel for free when you come aboard! https://books.steviemarie.com/heral ienexchange

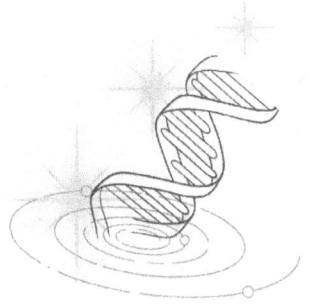

Author Note

T hank you for reading Her Alien Warrior!

I'm just a mom and monster lover standing in front of a reader asking them to eat their veggies. (Insert eggplant) Yes, the kind of veggies you can only get in a spicy alien/monster romance!

This all started off because I was tired of finding so many prison/slave tropes with aliens that were proliferating the genre. I wanted drama, but with adventure and strong warriors that get on their knees for a taste of their human mate! Don't get me wrong, I love a good abduction, and even a spicy dark romance, but I needed a palate cleanser, so to speak. I read the books that I enjoyed so fast that it didn't feel like there would ever be enough in the genre to satiate my thirst. So, I wrote my own and the Trillume Universe was born.

And it warms my heart that readers can retreat to my alien romances and get out of their reading slumps the same way writing them gets me out of my own!

It's a tough market out there for indies to be seen, but the alien romance community has been so welcoming and what started off as a small writing detour turned into a massive interwoven series. Originally, I had thought, well, I've built this universe and I can write in it whenever I need a fun break from my other writing projects. I'll just write one book here, and one book there when I get around to it for funsies. Next thing I knew, I had more fans and readers for my alien romances than I did for my romantasy books... and then I wrote three books within a year for this series! Over the course of three months, I went from having zero people know about this pen name to over 5,000 people reading my newsletter, and so many encouraging words to write the next one, that I write more alien romances than I do my romantasy books!

Your reviews, your ratings, your comments, and excitement for books helps fuel more books! So, thank you, and keep sending the love by leaving your own review/rating, sharing your love of the Trillume Universe to other alien lovers and let me know what you think of Her Alien Warrior!

The next book I'm working on is Ashley and Gaven's Fated Mates story in Her Alien Insurgent? And yes, every book is a standalone and can be read in any order, but I HIGHLY recommend reading Her Alien Prince to prepare for Her Alien Insurgent (as you meet GAVEN in this book before Ashley comes into the picture.) And if you started with this book and haven't read Her Alien Savior yet, then you can back track and read book one to meet a little bit of Ashley! That's the fun about the series is that the universe is interwoven and every book layers and makes the next book you read even more fun!

Then I'll start working on Commander Tensel's story after that, so don't worry, he gets his own book! Are there other characters you want to see more of? Your excitement and suggestions help fuel ideas and nudge me towards writing the next book as fast as my fingers can rub some words onto a page, so keep cheering!

To follow along on what's coming, see teasers, progress, what I'm reading, exclusive goodies, or just say, "hi", join my newsletter and grab Her Alien Exchange for freesies, or join the Sky's Smut Between the Pages on Facebook! I hang out on Instagram more often than Twitter these days, so give me a follow: @authorsteviemarie

Thank you so much for being a fan of my alien romances, it means the world to my squishy heart.

Sky

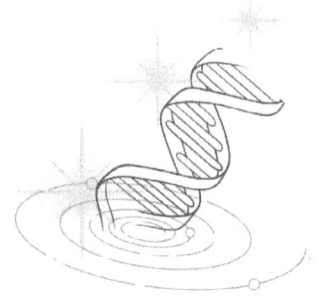

Want More?

For more information about upcoming books in the Treasures of Trillume or Necia Warrior Series (or any other books by Sky Robert) like me on Facebook or subscribe to my newsletter.

Thanks for reading! You are a book hero!
All the squishies,
Sky

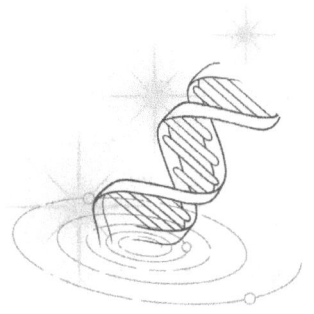

Book Heroes

T his page is dedicated to book heroes that made this book what it is today, from cheerleaders of moral support that helped push through writer's block, to early readers willing to comb through and point out errors, and all the indie fans that helped share the love to new readers!

You, the reader, for taking the time to delve into my world and sharing your love with other readers.

ARC/BETA Readers and social butterflies who caught typos, shared thoughts, and gave words of encouragement. You know who you are! Here are a few that have given me permission to share their names, a special thank you to: Michal and Jamie for being the very first eyeballs to read the book all within 24 hours and catch some typos along the way! Michelle, for always being down to dig in and help catch typos and giving me a smile! LaWanda for being my very first fan and being super supportive! Ketty for being my personal cheerleader and sounding board for all things bookish! And the ever-growing list of supportive book heroes that email me when they catch a typo: Lauren and Nunky, and if you happen to catch a typo, email me and you too can join the list the next time I update the book files! skyrobertromances at gmail dot com!

Special thank you to my street team and all the book heroes who took a chance on me.

Family and Friends:

For supporting the time needed to write, edit, and market my imagination.

About the Author

SKY ROBERT

S.M. McCoy Writing as Sky Robert for Spicier Smuttier Romances

Sky Robert is a mom of two tiny humans in training, narrates audiobooks for fantasy/sci-fi indie authors, and when she isn't writing (which is MOST of the time) you can find her consuming copious amounts of coffee, promoting indie authors, reading alien smut, fantasy, sci-fi and romance books, chowing down on Indian butter chicken, and when she actually hangs out with people in person, in real life, outside of the internet (gasps), she's playing board or card games. All around nerd, lover of the strange, and all things fantastical.

More from the Treasures of Trillume Universe:

- ↴ Jewel of the Alien Bandit
  https://book.steviemarie.com/jotab
- ↴ Her Alien Prince
  https://book.steviemarie.com/heralienprince
- ↴ Her Alien Insurgent: Coming soon!

Necia Alien Warriors: (Part of the Trillume Universe)

- ↴ Her Alien Exchange (Free)
  https://book.steviemarie.com/heralienexchange
- ↴ Her Alien Savior
  https://book.steviemarie.com/heraliensavior
- ↴ Her Alien Warrior
- ↴ https://books.steviemarie.com/heralienwarrior
- ↴ Her Alien Captor (Release TBA)

Also by S.M. McCoy

The slow-burn fantasy romances
https://linktr.ee/authorsteviemarie
www.steviemarie.com

Dark God Rising Series
- ☙ Taking Medusa (2023 N.N. Light Book Award Winner)
  https://book.steviemarie.com/takingmedusa
- ☙ Breaking Fate
  https://book.steviemarie.com/breakingfate
- ☙ Rending Olympus (Title Pending)

Acatalec Series:
- ☙ My Abett Book 0.5: Published 2022
- ☙ Kingdom of Acatalec Book One: Published 2022
- ☙ Available Wide on all Retailers including audiobook
- ☙ Acatalec Chosen Book Two (TBA)
- ☙ Acatalec's Sword Book Three

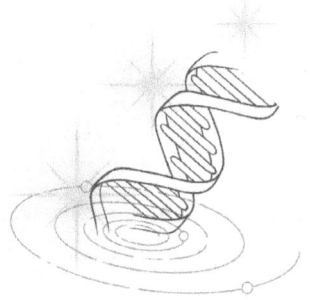

Her Alien Exchange

R ead this book for free and join my author newsletter: https://dl.bookfunnel.com/f2fwrjww4p

She thought joining the alien exchange would only be for a year...

Violet

Human Exchange Trade, H.E.T., was my ticket off Earth. Leaving the planet to get away was probably an over correction and impulsive, but I needed a change. And what bigger change was there than to hop on a shuttle to a large spaceship that would take me to an alien host on the planet ASunGor for a year. I get to learn a new culture, fool around with a few hot aliens, and come back to Earth with a better perspective on my life. At least, that's what I thought, before I rushed the whole thing, and my host wasn't there to pick me up. Another exchange girl named Evie was heading to the planet Necias Prime looking terrified, and I had time to kill, so what harm was there in taking a detour to make sure she was okay? I mean, my reasons had nothing to do with the sexy alien that had come to escort her.

Commander Roe-el

I was reluctant to leave Princess Klemon's protection when she told me to escort a human to my home planet for a mating experiment, but in my haste to return to her side, I left without asking the name of the human. When I got to the station... there were two of them waiting, and one of them was making me regret not having tasted a female in years. Her scent did things to me, and I found myself going into rut when it was my job as commander to protect the humans, not screw them. Humans were much too fragile for a necia warrior, but the fire in her eyes made me question my priorities, and I couldn't say no when she boarded my ship. Everything inside of me needed to claim her, but she needed to say, yes, first.

Dive into a fated mates, spicy monster love romance with instalust, exhibitionism, strong female empowerment, alpha male with consent, and alien extremities. Join the fated mates of the alien warriors of Necias Prime in the Treasures of Trillume Universe. All stand-alone romances, within a fun interwoven plot of the universe.

VIOLET

As soon as the Human Exchange Training was open to the public, I was first in line to join. That might seem reckless, to immediately seek to abandon Earth for a year-long, alien-job training program, but anything was better than what I had going for me now. My ex was psychotic, and he didn't take my whole let's-be-friends conversation as well as I'd hoped. You really don't see all the red flags until the end. Sure, I was feeling uncomfortable with him for a few months now, but all that crazy made for great sex and had my mind all addled over the idea of leaving him simply because he seemed a bit clingy when I wanted to hang out with the girls. I had a decent job as a marketing consultant for what used to be the biggest IT company. But ever since we—meaning humans—were introduced to how big the galaxy was by these aliens called the Trill, well, our IT was way behind the times.

Too many people were more obsessed with the technology the aliens had to offer instead of what mere human mortals were working on. IT took a huge dive, and so did my career. I was a bartender now; that's how I met Mick... and he needed some time to cool off and find a new obsession. Living for a year with aliens while also getting training in a new career sounded like a win-win.

I left the recruitment center more excited than ever after being accepted by an alien host from some planet called ASunGor. It wasn't too far from the planet Trillume, which was where the trill were from. ASunGor was beautiful, with its purples, yellows, and oranges, and red gaseous clouds that, if they didn't tell me otherwise, I might have thought were poisonous. Red was usually associated with warnings, like my ex with all of his red flags. But I was assured the red was merely a reaction to the iron particles in the air hitting the oxygen, and the concentration was mostly in the atmosphere, not on the surface where there was a reasonable amount of breathable air for humans to survive without any harm.

I got a data packet about the aliens that lived there sent to my brain implant, which was updated with an alien language translator, so all that was left was to wait for the transport shuttle to take me to the ship waiting in Earth's orbit. I'd be gone for a year.

Before I could think on it more, I was interrupted by a cringe-worthy voice that was all too sickeningly familiar. Damn it. I had been so careful about getting here without being followed.

"What do you think you're doing, Violet?" he said from behind me, leaning against the brick wall of the recruitment center.

Clearing my throat, I jutted a hip out in defiance while replying, "None of your business, Mick."

He rubbed his gorgeous face with his hands in exasperation. That's what got me the first time around. Mick was too damned pretty, and I let that cloud my judgement for too long. The kind of sweet, chiseled pretty that made you think he was both adoring and capable of sinful things. And he certainly was capable of all sorts of sinful things that I used to look forward to—with relish—but it wasn't worth it.

"I know the IT industry has seen a dive, and you weren't looking to be a bartender your whole life, but offworlding? Come on, Violet, that's low; even for you. There have been plenty of news stories about how most of those aliens want to experiment with us, and a pretty girl like you... Violet, if you need a good fuck, you don't need to jump on a shuttle to find it," Mick said with equal parts disgust and interest. It was amazing how he could twist his words to both insult me and imply that his dick was good enough for the job, all at the same time.

I smiled sweetly at him, but anyone with eyes could see my derision as I retorted, "Oh, honey. I don't have to go anywhere for a good fuck. I've got myself covered just fine." I showed him my two favorite fingers and then lowered one to leave only the middle, silently saying 'Go fuck yourself' and ending with a little wink. It wasn't right to tease him. He liked it when I played hard to get, but I wasn't playing at anything this time. I was more than happy with my own company. Anything was better than the constant, back-handed compliments I received from him regularly. At least my own fingers knew my clit was bigger than just the tip that was visible. It was a whole fucking organ, and he wasn't its musician anymore.

Mick pushed off from the wall, and my whole body froze like a deer caught in headlights. I talked a big game, but the dark look in his eyes was terrifying and crazed. That same determined gaze used to make me smile, knowing we were about to have some great hate sex. But when I wanted it to end, the feelings changed, and he wasn't willing to let me go. I gulped back my fear as he slowly approached, but my feet wouldn't budge. His knuckles brushed against my cheek, and I instinctively pulled my face away before he harshly pinched my chin in his grasp to force me to look at him.

"You know you like it when that foul mouth of yours wraps around my cock before you scream my name. Your fingers can still do whatever they want when I'm fucking the sin from your dirty thoughts," he purred, pushing his mouth on to mine. My hands scrambled to find purchase, to shove him off, but he held me firm, and I struggled to slide my mouth away from his, gasping for air.

"Get off of me," I growled, and he released me at the same time as I shoved, making me stumble backwards and I lost my balance. He let me trip, falling to my ass, and he shook his head at me like I was a piece of trash that he'd have to pick up for the betterment of the world. I wiped his saliva from my cheek and forced myself to spit at his feet, to rid the taste of him from my tongue. "You're disgusting."

It wasn't that I didn't particularly like dirty talk; I did. But the way he said things was anything but endearing. It was possessive in a way that made my skin crawl. Like I needed to burn the clothes I was wearing to get the feeling of his hands groping me seared from my memory.

"No one will touch you the way you want it like I do, Violet. Not even an alien dick, if they even have one, would touch you after they found out what makes you scream," he threatened while licking his lips, trying to get me to think about all the things he wanted to do with his tongue. "Don't make me wait too long; this game of yours is getting old." Mick left me there sitting in what I now realized was a puddle left by the rain from the night before. It certainly wasn't my own juices that had soaked through my pants this time.

"Fucker," I gritted out, getting back to my feet and stomping back to the recruitment center. I opened the door a little more aggressively than I'd intended, but I was amped and pissed. Waiting for the later shuttle to "gather" my shit wasn't an option anymore. I was leaving tonight, even if I had to sign some extra waivers or agree to an extended exchange program. I didn't give a crap. I was leaving now!

Mick was lucky I ever touched his dick, and he was right. The game was getting old, but not the one he thought we were playing. I was sick and tired of him harassing me, and the authorities said there wasn't enough to get a restraining order. Not that it would have stopped him, I thought with disdain.

"Miss Thorn... did you forget something?" my recruiter, Beth, asked with a quirked brow at my now soaked pants and probably reddened face.

"Yes, I need you to get me on the next shuttle."

Beth pursed her lips as if I were insane. "You have no personal items with you. And usually people wish to say goodbye to their friends, family, someone before they go. You should really wait for the next shuttle in a few weeks," she insisted.

"No," I snapped before calming myself to reiterate in a less intimidating tone. "I want to leave on the one I overheard you saying was leaving today." I paused, then added, "Please." I forced a smile to my face and waited for her to deny me because what I was asking for was ridiculous. It was the most insane thing I'd ever asked of someone.

She lowered her voice and wrapped her arm around my shoulder to lead me away from the prying eyes of the other recruits in the lobby, eying me with concern. "Are you in trouble?"

I sighed, not wanting to get into this with practically a stranger, but she seemed so sweet and trustworthy, unlike my usual friends I hung out with. They were more encouraging of my bad choices. This was not a bad choice though, I reassured myself. This was crazy, but it wasn't a bad choice. As far as decisions went, sure, I should probably wait for my scheduled shuttle in a few weeks. But what did I have to lose besides a creepy ex and girlfriends that didn't even know a single thing about me, other than I was fun to have a drink with? Come to think of it, they probably mostly liked the cheap drinks I got for working at the bar... I shook my head. I was over the whole thing.

"I've got an ex stalking me, and a year away will be good for both of us," I admitted, but I didn't let her know that a sick part of me knew that if I didn't get on this shuttle, two weeks was a long time, and I didn't think I had the strength to resist Mick when he reflected on his actions in a day or two. He'd come back, sweeter than ever, and we'd have mind-blowing hate sex, and I'd hate myself even more for letting him get under my skin. I deserved better than what he was offering. I knew that in theory. But in practice... he was right. I was fucked up, and I liked how he made me feel when he wasn't being a petty asshole. He knew how I liked to be touched.

This was for me. I needed to recalibrate my brain and my body.

I didn't need his kind of possessive veneration.

"Yes, but you won't have time to go home and grab personal items. No matter how strong a person is, everyone gets Earth sick and misses the smallest of things that remind them of Earth when they are away." Beth was trying to talk me out of it, and she was doing a shitty job. I didn't give a crap if I missed the dirt or way pizza tasted. Sometimes, cold turkey was the best way to change your bad habits. I'd just keep myself busy to distract myself.

"Beth, I see what you're doing here, and it's sweet, really. But if you don't let me on that shuttle, my life is more screwed than if you let me leave. Trust me." I could see her lips press into a fine line as she led me through the building, probably to a holding cell because I was likely to harm one of us if they didn't board me on the shuttle today. I was that kind of desperate, and pretty much too angry to see reason beyond what I'd set my mind to.

She sighed in what I hoped was resignation, but it easily could have been her annoyance at another crazy she had to deal with in a diplomatic way.

"Violet." She used my first name, which was weird. "You have to be sure about this. The shuttle is boarding now. Once you're on, there is no coming back until your exchange is completed. Do you understand?"

Well, that was unexpected.

"Like, now, now?" My nerves were getting the better of me, and I was just as likely to bolt as I was to follow through with my hare-brained idea of jumping on a shuttle to a different planet.

She laughed, which was refreshing to hear, before she nodded her agreement.

This was happening.

I was leaving.

She was going to let me on the shuttle.

ROE-EL

The Princess of Trillume rolled her eyes at me, and I grumbled. Princess or not, she was asking me to do something that was akin to fucking an animal.

"My Princess, I think I misheard you. I apologize." I tried to show my disinterest without actually outright denying her orders of me. I was a reputable warrior, and I'd never questioned my position to be in her service, but this was too much. She must understand that if any other had asked this of me, I would have considered it an insult that would have been remedied by a duel before I agreed to anything more. Only if I failed would I submit myself to this. My upper lip snarled.

"You didn't mishear," she confirmed with a sly smile. "I need you to train a human in the ways of the Necia and encourage this human to attempt spawning with a Necia warrior. It's important to my research. I'm not asking you to be the warrior that attempts procreation with the human, Commander Roe-el. I'm asking you to escort the human to Necias Prime and train them before they arrive, while encouraging the human to be open-minded about your species."

"You're asking me to have another warrior," I paused to wrinkle my nose at the prospect, "spawn with a human. Do you have any idea what you're asking of any Necia you have do that? Humans are fragile, and deserving of our protection, but they are like pets to us that we've used as entertainment and companionship on long missions across the galaxies. They are NOT mates," I insisted with disgust.

Princess Klemon nodded. "I'm aware. They are not so barbaric to be considered animals, Commander Roe-el. They are just... different, and, according to my research, potentially compatible mates as well. You are assigned to go pick them up right about... well, now. You should head out if you are to get there on time. I know how you like to be punctual."

"Princess, my assignment is to you. Not your project. I would be derelict in my duties to leave—"

"Commander," she stopped me before I could finish. "The project is the reason why you are needed to protect me at all. If it makes you feel any better, I'll be sure to stay hidden in the lab until your return. You're the only one I trust to escort our exchange human to their new host. You won't be gone longer than a few weeks. There and back."

I narrowed my eyes, uncertain if I could trust her to stay within the lab walls while I was away and still grossed out by the idea of mating with a human.

With a huff, she added, "I'll stay put."

"I will not mate with a human," I clarified.

She shook her head in a manner that made me think she thought I was humorous, which made my shoulder epaulets twitch in agitation.

"I'm not asking you to be the one to mate with the human. I already have a willing warrior who is trustworthy and understands my research and what it means to the whole galaxy, not just Necias Prime," Princess Klemon explained, then did that hand motion she used to shoo me away from her research.

"Fine, but if I find that you have left this lab for whatever reason, you will be hard-pressed to have me leave your side in the future. Keep that in mind, should you get the desire to go exploring without protection." It was my job to make sure her family didn't find her and that anyone who knew what she was working on didn't find her. She was right; her research was too important to risk. If she thought I was needed to protect the human, then that is what I would do for her.

Arriving at the waystation, I grumbled, realizing Klemon had tricked me into thinking I was going to be late when I was actually early. Wasting my time waiting grated on my nerves like no other feeling. She was being cheeky when she said I preferred to be punctual, I knew that. I always arrived on time... never early. If I'm to be somewhere at a time, that is the time I arrive. No earlier, no later. On time.

And here I was, waiting like a fool for some human to disembark from their transport to Trillume and then reboard my shuttle to head out to Necias Prime. All the human exchanges came to Trillume first, then to their destinations. Never a direct route, as the humans were strictly monitored and accounted for. Couldn't have secret humans being stowed away and sold off in the markets. We'd never hear the end of it. There would be an open war between species about who had more rights to the humans and to Earth. The only good thing about that was I wouldn't be bored on my glorified babysitter duties of a princess. I might get a few duels in here and there.

The humans left the shuttle and appeared as I expected them to be: like scared animals, shifting uncomfortably around until a new owner came to take them to their temporary homes. One by one, they were being plucked away by ambassadors from various planets claiming their right to have their own human for a while. I realized I hadn't asked which one I should be acquiring for her highness' research. I mean, there wasn't much difference between them all, was there? Did it matter which one I brought with me?

I liked the look of the larger human that appeared to be less likely to be harmed by our Necia females. He would stand a chance of surviving Necias Prime with his muscles, though he still wasn't quite as bulky as I would have preferred to ensure his safety. I cursed under my breath, remembering that Klemon had said there was a warrior who'd agreed to mate with a human, and I hadn't asked if they were female or male. I waited a bit longer to see if another planet was claiming the human male. Shortly, I found out that someone had indeed chosen this male for their own exchange.

There were only two females left after the rush, and I found myself unable to remove my eyes from the one with bright red hair, the color of Necias's oceans. Unlike the other female, who appeared as frightened as I would expect of most who ventured so far from their habitats, this one folded her arms over her chest, highlighting small mounds that had my mouth quirking up in interest. I closed my eyes to rid myself of the thought.

Did humans possess some kind of lure not recorded in their data assessments? Not one warrior had ever spoke of this kind of attraction at the mere sight of the curves of a human's frame. Possibly it was my subconscious playing tricks on me after the discussion I'd had with Klemon. She had planted this idea of fucking with humans, and I had been without a female for some time because of my current assignment. It was difficult to acquire interest, or even spur on a rut, with a protective detail and not many options for duels. There had been no need to prove my strength and encourage my use of bed play.

But there that human was, and, when I opened my eyes, I was still enthralled by her curves and the strong stance of what I could only imagine was her annoyance at waiting there for her host. I blinked, regaining my composure. Waiting for me, I thought, and a sudden surge rippled through my body, sending a jolt to my cock. What on Horv's great vine was happening to me? This couldn't possibly be a rut, could it? Was I so far gone that merely the idea of mating and the mission back to Necias Prime had sent my body into rut? Had I waited so long in a boring assignment that my body found any excuse to claim and conquer even an animal such as this human?

I grimaced, but that didn't stop my eyes from watching as the female adjusted her hips to favor her other leg. Those silvery eyes of hers looked out in search of her alien host, and it was only her and the other female left. What kind of ambassador arrived late to pick up their human? Sure, I was making mine wait, but I was here. Surely the other host would know who they were supposed to pick up.

Wasting time was making my mind wander, and thinking of that human's small, fleshy mounds pressed against me instead of those small arms wasn't doing me any favors in improving my mood. I refused to rut with a human, it was an abuse of my strength to claim such a weak being in such a manner. Humans were helpless creatures that needed protecting, not warriors—or even broodmares—capable of taming a Necia warrior's epulknot in rut. I'm not a monster, I repeated to myself in an attempt to calm the hardening length down my thigh. I had to pick up Klemon's human before I decided to call this whole thing off. I'd just grab the human that didn't make me doubt my sanity and be done with it.

Approaching the females, I tried to move slowly as to not frighten them further, and the dark-haired female flinched and tugged at the other's arm in warning. It was wise for humans to fear a Necia warrior. This female had good instincts for self-preservation. We were predators in this ecosystem. And yet, years of evolution did not stop the other from lifting a brow and smirking at me in challenge.

"It's about time. I was wondering if I had to walk over and get you. Didn't anyone ever teach you that it's rude to keep a lady waiting?" she snapped off in succession. Her words stunned me momentarily as my translator had to catch up with the harsh, yet intriguing, sound of her voice. I towered over her stature and yet there she was, chin held firm as she stared me down. Those silvery eyes had flecks of gold, now that I was close enough to see it, and I could see her beneath me as I tried to count every star in her mesmerizing portals and plunged into her depths. My mouth salivated, and my cock pulsed, seeking a reprieve I could not grant it. This was too far, even for a rut-inflicted mind. I had to control myself.

She was a human.

Not some seductive warrior seeking sport on my epulknot.

Grab Her Alien Exchange for free

Continue reading for freesies: Grab Her Alien Exchange here: https://dl.bookfunnel.com/f2fwrjww4p

www.ingramcontent.com/pod-product-compliance
Lightning Source LLC
Chambersburg PA
CBHW070544260626
47161CB00002B/503